DEADLY CRAVING

A DETECTIVE JANE PHILLIPS NOVEL

OMJ RYAN

INKUBATOR
BOOKS

Published by Inkubator Books
www.inkubatorbooks.com

Copyright © 2022 by OMJ Ryan

OMJ Ryan has asserted his right to be identified as the author
of this work.

ISBN (eBook): 978-1-83756-025-7
ISBN (Paperback): 978-1-83756-026-4

PROLOGUE

Placing his fingers against his victim's carotid, he felt the heart give up as it finally stopped beating. He closed his eyes and offered up a silent prayer of thanks to the gods. They had served him well, guiding him through the months of planning and preparation that had led up to this moment, and he was going to need all their strength to complete the next task.

Staring down at the naked body laid out on the large metal table in front of him, his pulse raced; the journey to immortality had well and truly begun.

After pulling on his latex gloves, he slipped a plastic apron over his head before tying it at the waist, butterflies turning over in his stomach.

'Concentrate,' he whispered to himself as he pulled across the rolling metal table that contained his tools.

'Alexa, play fakanau,' he shouted across the room and a moment later, the sound of women singing filled the air. A wave of calm washed over him as he paused and listened to their soft voices, imagining the women dancing beside him, celebrating his work in honour of the ancient teachings. He smiled, then took a deep breath as he reached for the small circular saw.

'May the gods guide my hand as I release the eternal glory and power locked inside this mortal vessel.'

Flicking the switch, he made the saw burst into life, spinning at a ferocious speed. 'With love and honour, always,' he said, then pushed the blade down onto the dead man's chest, slicing through the muscle like a hot knife through butter. 'Love and honour, always.'

1

MONDAY, 21 FEBRUARY

As Phillips pulled the British Racing Green Mini Cooper left off the main drag, she spotted the flashing lights of the patrol cars up ahead, positioned at various angles on the road outside the old church near Hodge Hill – about fifteen miles south of Manchester city centre. Despite the fact that it was just after 8 a.m., the sky was dark and foreboding, matching her mood. As she came to a stop, her pulse began to quicken in anticipation of what lay ahead.

It had been almost ten months since she took an indefinite leave of absence from her role as detective chief inspector for the Greater Manchester Police's Major Crimes Unit, and for a long time she'd vowed never to return. But as the months and seasons passed, she had begun to feel drawn back to the dark world she had left behind. She still wasn't entirely sure why, but here she was, once again about to step into a crime scene that her newly promoted second in command, Detective Inspector Jones, had described on their call an hour ago as "gruesome".

She climbed out of the small car and the cold morning air

rushed over her face, causing her cheeks to tighten. 'Here we go again,' she whispered, her breath visible in front of her as she closed the car door, then set off walking towards the police cordon up ahead.

As she approached the blue and white police tape, she pulled out her ID, which she presented to the uniformed officer standing guard.

'Ma'am,' he said, then lifted the tape.

She stepped under and continued across the churchyard where she could see the white tent of the CSI team. DI Jones and his sidekick, DC Bovalino, stood at the entrance dressed in white forensic suits. Not for the first time, she marvelled at how different each of them looked in their overalls: Jones's scrawny frame lost in his billowing suit – whereas the man mountain that was Bovalino resembled something akin to a hot-air balloon in full flight.

Just then Jones turned and spotted her, beckoning her over.

'So what have we got?' asked Phillips as she reached them.

'IC3 male, deceased, with his heart cut out of his chest.' Jones's accent was still thick South London despite almost twenty years living in Manchester.

Phillips nodded as she cast her gaze towards the tent.

'Probably not what you were hoping for on your first day back, hey, Guv?' said Bovalino as he handed her a forensic suit. His voice was deep and unmistakably Mancunian.

'Not quite, no.'

'Evans has already started inside.' Andy Evans was the senior crime scene investigator assigned to the majority of MCU's cases.

A few minutes later, suited, booted and gloved-up in line with the strict forensic protocols demanded by modern-day policing, Phillips stepped inside the tent. With

Jones and Bov at her back, she took in the scene while Evans and his team worked methodically, photographing the body. 'Morning, Andy,' she said as cheerfully as she could muster.

Evans turned to face her. 'Ah, Jane. Welcome back. We've missed you.'

'I wish I could say the same.'

Just in front of them, a naked black man – Phillips placed him in his forties – was lying on his back, his genitals and torso wrapped in a large white shawl. Freshly cut white roses surrounded the body and ran in an arc from the left ankle, over the head and back down to the right ankle. 'What's with the shawl and the flowers?' she asked.

Evans shrugged. 'That's your department.'

'Proper creeped me out when I saw it,' Bovalino added. 'Looks like a bloody burial ground.'

Phillips nodded. 'It definitely looks like somebody's gone to a fair bit of effort to make sure the victim was found like this.'

'Looks posed, doesn't it?' said Jones.

'Yeah. Exactly.' Phillips glanced at Evans. 'Any idea what's happened to the heart?'

'No sign of it yet,' he replied, 'but it's been carefully removed with a very sharp blade, most likely a surgical scalpel or something similar.'

'So are we looking for someone with medical knowledge, then?'

'Far too early to draw any conclusions about that, I'm afraid, but whoever it was managed to leave all the organs surrounding the heart pretty much intact.'

'Time of death?' asked Phillips.

'Judging by the state of the rigor and the body temp, I'd say he's been dead somewhere between ten and twelve hours. It looks like he's been out here all night and the temperatures were down as low as minus two, so you'll have to wait for the PM to get the exact time.'

Phillips continued. 'Was he killed here?'

'No. There's no blood surrounding the body, so he was most certainly killed at another location and then moved.'

'Any ID or a phone?'

'Nothing as of yet. We'll be checking the whole church-yard in time, but for the moment he's clean.'

Jones cut in now. 'Bov reckons he recognises the victim, Guv.'

Phillips felt her face twist as she focused on the big Italian. 'What? You *know* him, Bov?'

'Not personally, no, but I know *of* him.' Bovalino pointed at the body. 'That's AJ Lewis.'

Phillips shrugged. 'You say that as if I should know who he is.'

'He was a pretty decent boxer, in his day. British middleweight champion about ten years ago. He was in line for a shot at a world title fight, but he had to retire early due to injury. His last bout was brutal. He actually won the fight but one of his eyes was so badly damaged they revoked his boxing license. Word at the time was he took it badly and hit the bottle. It was a real shame. He was a proper talent.'

Phillips pulled out her phone and leant forward to take a photo of the victim's face. 'I'll ping this over to Whistler. Hopefully he can give us a provisional ID and next of kin.' She turned her attention back to Evans. 'How long before you run the fingerprints?'

'They'll be with the team later this morning.'

'Good,' said Phillips. 'And let me know immediately if you find the heart.'

Evans nodded. 'Naturally.'

Walking out of the tent, Phillips pulled down the hood on her suit. The ground was still solid underfoot from the subzero temperatures overnight. 'So what do we make of that?' she asked as Jones and Bovalino joined her outside.

Jones removed his blue latex gloves and placed them in a clear plastic bag. 'I thought I'd seen it all before now, boss, but this...'

'You must be wishing you'd stayed at home, Guv,' said Bovalino, half smiling.

Phillips said nothing as she turned her gaze back to the tent, before scanning the churchyard around her. 'What kind of church is this?'

Jones shrugged. 'Church of England, I think. Why do you ask?'

'No reason, really. Just trying to figure out why someone would kill a person, remove his heart and then carefully wrap and place his body in this exact location.'

Neither man responded, each deep in thought.

As Phillips removed her forensic suit, Jones and Bovalino followed her lead. With everything bagged in case they'd inadvertently picked up any trace evidence inside the tent, she emailed the picture of the victim through to DC Entwistle – or Whistler as he was known to the team – the other core member of MCU.

'Right,' she said pushing her phone back into her coat pocket. 'While we wait for the ID and next of kin to come through, how about we get out of the cold and I buy you both a hot cup of coffee. You can bring me up to speed on everything that's been going on while I've been away.'

'Sounds good to me.' Jones was hopping from foot to foot to keep warm.

Bovalino raised his eyebrows. 'Don't suppose there's any chance of a bacon roll as well, is there?'

Phillips grinned as she tapped him on his gargantuan upper left arm. 'Good to see some things never change, Bov. Come on, I spotted a cafe about half a mile back down the road. I'm sure they can stuff half a pig into a bread roll for you.'

The big man clapped his hands together. 'And that right there, boss, is one of the many reasons why I'm glad you're back.'

2

An hour later Entwistle called back, confirming the victim was almost certainly Ajani Lewis – or AJ, as he had been more commonly known. He also had an address for his wife and next of kin, Bethany Lewis.

With Bovalino promptly dispatched back to headquarters at Ashton House, Phillips drove the Mini Cooper towards the south Manchester suburb of Parrs Wood with Jones at her side in the passenger seat.

He tapped the dashboard. 'I'm surprised your dad's not asked for this back yet.'

Phillips glanced sideways. 'He's still got another two months without seizures before they'll let him drive again.'

'Epilepsy, wasn't it?'

'Yeah, well, distance epilepsy. It's slightly different to what people usually think happens with epilepsy. There's none of the fitting; instead it's as if he just stops in the moment and then drops to the floor. Came as quite a shock when he had his first attack. My mum thought he was having a stroke.'

'Jesus. Getting old sucks, doesn't it?'

'True, but it beats an untimely death, any day.'

Jones let out a sardonic chuckle. 'Yeah, you've got a point there.'

The car fell silent for a time as they zipped through the morning traffic back towards the city.

Eventually, Phillips broke the silence. 'So how about we address the elephant in the room?'

Jones's brow furrowed. 'I'm not following you, Guv. What do you mean?'

'I mean *me*.'

'What about *you*?'

'Well. How do you feel about me coming back?'

'I'm happy about it.'

Phillips looked left once more. 'Really?'

'Yeah, of course.'

'So you don't mind giving up command of the team?'

Jones shook his head. 'Jesus. No. Look, I only offered to take on the acting DI job when you took your sabbatical to protect the team. The last thing we needed was an over-ambitious wannabe DI coming in and telling us how to do our jobs. I certainly never expected they'd make it permanent.'

'But they *did* and now here I am muscling my way back in.'

'Which is fine by me,' replied Jones. 'The truth is, I'm not cut out for management and police politics. I'm at my best solving crimes. Budget meetings and bollockings from Fox are all yours, boss.'

Phillips let out a sigh of relief. 'Thank God. I was really worried you'd think I was stepping on your toes.'

'Nah. It's actually worked out really well for me, now you're back in charge. I get a DI's salary but less of the bull-shit. Winner, winner, chicken dinner.'

Phillips laughed. 'I hadn't thought of that.'

'And Sarah's happy too, because it'll mean fewer hours and less stress. Honestly, Guv. The last nine months have been a hard slog without you. Not just for me, but the rest of the team too.'

'Come on, I'm sure it hasn't been that bad.'

Jones nodded. 'Believe me. It really has.'

The car fell silent once more as the world around them slipped by, and before long they were turning onto Woodlands Avenue in Parrs Wood, home to Bethany Lewis.

'This looks like the one,' said Phillips as they pulled up outside a smart looking 1920's semi-detached house.

A minute later she pressed the bell on the front door and heard it chime on the other side. A dog began to bark inside the house and a woman's voice could be heard telling it to be quiet. Next, they could hear a door being closed and the dog's protests were silenced.

Eventually the front door opened and an attractive, tall woman with short blond hair peeped out. 'Can I help?'

Phillips flashed her ID badge. 'DCI Phillips and DI Jones from the Major Crimes Unit. Are you Bethany Lewis?'

The woman's eyes narrowed. 'I'm Beth, yes. What's this about?'

'I think it would be better if we talked inside,' said Phillips softly.

A look of concern flashed across Beth's face before she nodded and opened the door wide, then headed into the belly of the house.

Phillips and Jones stepped inside and followed her along the hallway to what looked like a recently modernised open-plan kitchen and dining room that overlooked the narrow, well-maintained garden beyond.

By the time they joined her, Beth had taken up a position standing next to one of the worktops. Phillips and Jones matched her and remained standing.

'Is this about AJ?' Beth's voice was brimming with concern.

Phillips nodded. 'Yes.'

Beth folded her arms defensively across her chest. 'What's he done now?'

Phillips glanced at Jones and then focused on Beth. 'I'm very sorry to tell you this, but a man has been found dead this morning, and we believe it's AJ.'

Beth's eyes widened as the words landed, and she opened her mouth to speak but no words would come out.

'I really am very sorry,' said Phillips.

'B-b-but how?'

Phillips swallowed the lump forming in her throat. 'We believe he was murdered.'

'What? Why?' She reached for the countertop to steady herself.

'Is there somewhere we can sit down?' Phillips asked.

'The front room,' Beth whispered before leading the way out of the kitchen.

In the room next door, Phillips took a seat on an armchair opposite Beth, who had perched on the end of the large brown leather sofa. Jones had remained in the kitchen to make tea.

There were no tears. Instead, Beth appeared to be dazed and confused.

Phillips needed to tread carefully. 'When was the last time you saw your husband?'

'Soon to be ex-husband,' Beth corrected, locking eyes with Phillips. 'We're separated.'

'I see. And how long ago did you split?'

'About six months ago.'

Phillips nodded. 'Do you mind me asking why?'

'The usual,' replied Beth. 'His drinking.'

Just then Jones returned with a tray and three mugs of steaming hot tea, which he passed around before taking a seat on a second armchair. He then pulled out his notepad and pen.

'So, when did you last see AJ?'

Beth stared down at the mug of tea cradled in both hands. 'About a week ago, I guess.'

'And where was that?'

'He came here. Wanted to talk about selling the house. Well, actually, he wanted to talk about me buying him out – said he needed the money.'

Jones scribbled in his pad.

'Do you know why he needed money?' asked Phillips.

'Not specifically but I know he was up to his eyes in debt through the business.'

'And what business was he in?'

'Security. He started it when he packed in the boxing. Did very well to begin with, but then he started drinking and it all went south.'

Phillips placed her mug of tea on the coffee table between them. 'What do you mean, it went south?'

'He started pissing the profits up the wall, and when he wasn't drinking, he was gambling. Made a right mess of everything and ended up borrowing loads of money to try and sort it all out.'

Phillips's interest was piqued. Money was always a great motive for murder. 'Do you know who he borrowed the money from?'

Beth shook her head. 'No. He refused to tell me. Said he didn't want me to worry, but the fact that he wouldn't tell me made me worry even more.'

Jones cut in. 'Did he ever mention how much he borrowed?'

'No. Again, he said he didn't want me worrying.'

Phillips took the lead once more. 'You said you saw him a

week ago, but did you have any other contact with him in the meantime?'

Beth screwed up her face for a second, then pulled her phone from her pocket. 'Oddly enough, he did send me a text message last night, which wasn't like him at all. He hated tech.' She held up the phone for them to see.

Phillips read from the screen. '"The lion now roars for eternity." What do you think he meant by that?'

'I have no idea. I couldn't make head nor tail of it, other than the fact that he has a lion in the company logo. It was the same one he used to wear on his shorts when he was boxing.'

Jones made another note in his pad.

Phillips continued. 'You said he hated tech. What do you mean by that?'

'AJ was old school. He preferred to talk face to face. Refused to get a smart phone. It was all Bernie could do to get him to buy computers for the business.'

Phillips raised an eyebrow. 'Bernie?'

'Bernie Sutton,' replied Beth. 'His best mate and number two at work. They boxed together as kids and have been together ever since.'

'I see,' said Phillips. 'And where can we find Bernie?'

'AJ's gym in Salford. The business's offices are above it.'

'Do you have an address?'

Beth nodded. 'Corporation Row, just behind the railway arches.'

Jones scribbled down the details.

'Did AJ have any enemies?' asked Phillips a moment later.

'Not that I knew of.'

'What about his movements lately? Anything seem unusual to you?'

Beth remained silent and appeared deep in thought. 'Well, there was one thing that was a bit odd.'

'Go on.'

'Even though we were separated, he's always stayed in touch. Called most days just to check in. I think he kind of hoped we'd get back together.'

Phillips nodded.

Beth continued. 'Well, a couple of months back, towards the end of last year, he just disappeared for a week or so. Never said where he was going, and when he came back, he wouldn't say where he'd been either.'

'Do you have any idea where he went?' asked Jones.

'Not a clue. If AJ wanted to keep something a secret, that's exactly what it would stay. It was another reason why he was so hard to live with at times.'

Phillips nodded slowly. 'Beth, I know this is probably the last thing you want to think about, but we need someone to formally identify the body. Is that something you could do for us?'

Tears began to well in Beth's eyes now as she nodded silently.

'A family liaison officer will call today to make the arrangements. They'll also be able to support you through the investigation. In the meantime, is there anyone you can call to come and sit with you?'

A tear streaked down Beth's cheek. 'I'll go to my mum's. She lives just round the corner.'

Phillips passed over her business card. 'If you need anything or you think of anything else that might help us, please call me, day or night.'

Beth clasped the card in her hand.

'We'll need your number to pass onto the family liaison team,' said Jones.

Beth nodded and dictated it.

Jones made a note as she did.

'You've been very helpful, Beth. Thank you.' Phillips stood

and Jones followed suit. 'We'll let ourselves out.' With that, she headed for the front door.

Outside, as they approached the Mini, Phillips turned to face Jones. 'I think we need to get a better understanding of just how much debt AJ was in.'

'Yeah. Money usually means motive,' quipped Jones.

'My thoughts exactly.'

'So where now?'

'Bernie Sutton,' said Phillips as she opened the driver's door. 'If anyone knows what was going on with AJ's finances, it appears it could be him.'

3

The journey from Parrs Wood to Salford took just over thirty minutes, in which time Phillips called Entwistle at Ashton House. She was keen to find out if any large cars or vans had been spotted last night on ANPR cameras in and around the churchyard where AJ's body had been found. And if anyone could find them, it was MCU's tech guru, Whistler. As expected, he'd promised to see what he could dig up as quickly as possible.

As they approached the destination Phillips had keyed into the satnav, the heavens opened and rain began pounding the Mini's tiny windscreen. She flicked on the wipers at full speed, but they offered little resistance to the torrential downpour. A few minutes later, as the road began to narrow, they soon found themselves driving through a labyrinth of Victorian red-brick industrial buildings, many of which had been abandoned or seen better days. Finally, as the road came to an abrupt end, they stopped outside the gym-cum-offices and Phillips switched off the engine.

'Charming spot,' she said sarcastically as she gazed out through the rain at the old building.

The windows on the lower ground floor were fitted with frosted glass and covered in metal mesh, which had become bent and buckled over time and was now covered in graffiti. The main front door was made of solid wood. It had likely been painted black some time ago and was now in need of a fresh coat, as it peeled at the edges. The only clue to the inner workings of the building itself were two low-key signs fixed to the outside wall to the right of the doorframe. The top one said, 'Lewis Security Ltd.', the one below, 'AJ's Boxing Gym.'

A minute later, Phillips and Jones rushed from the car to the front door and stepped out of the rain onto the hard stone floor. The air smelled stale and reminded Phillips of the old colonial school she had attended as a young girl growing up in Hong Kong. A door to the left led into the gym and a sign to the right pointed up a set of stone steps, to the security offices located on the first floor. Phillips led the way upstairs and a moment later pushed open the door to Lewis Security Ltd.

A short but solidly built man who was sitting behind an old wooden desk looked up from his laptop, his brow furrowed. 'Can I help you?'

Phillips presented her badge. 'DCI Phillips and DI Jones. We're working with Major Crimes and looking for Bernie Sutton.'

'And what do you want with Bernie?' the man replied.

'I take it you're Bernie?'

'That depends.'

Phillips was in no mood to play games. 'We're here investigating a murder, so are you or aren't you Bernie Sutton?'

'Murder?' The man's eyes widened. 'I don't know anything about a murder.'

Phillips took a seat opposite him, and Jones sat down on a plastic chair beside her. 'Let's stop pissing about, shall we, Bernie? When was the last time you saw Ajani Lewis?'

Sutton flinched. 'AJ? Why do you ask?'

'I'm sorry to tell you this, Mr Sutton, but a man matching AJ's description was found dead this morning in Hodge Hill.'

'Fuck! *You're joking.*'

'No. I'm afraid not.'

Sutton stared at them open mouthed for a long moment. 'How? What happened?'

'I'm afraid we can't share the details, but we do believe he was murdered,' said Phillips.

Sutton recoiled, shaking his head. 'But that doesn't make sense. Why would anyone want to murder AJ?'

'We were hoping you might be able to tell us,' Jones cut in.

Sutton continued to stare at them, wide eyed. 'I honestly have no idea.'

Phillips scrutinised his face for any tell-tale signs of guilt or shame. Sutton appeared genuinely shocked.

'Jesus. Does Beth know?'

Phillips nodded. 'She's the one who gave us your details. She said you and AJ were close.'

Sutton exhaled loudly. 'Yeah. Since we were kids.'

'When was the last time you saw him?' asked Jones.

'Yesterday. He came into the office early doors to sort some invoices and then he headed out.'

'What time?'

Sutton paused before answering. 'About eleven, I guess.'

'Do you know where he went?'

Sutton shook his head. 'No idea. He didn't say and I didn't ask. To be honest, AJ rarely told me what he was up to these days. Just came and went as it suited him.'

'Beth said he was the face and you were the brains of Lewis Security,' Phillips ventured.

Sutton offered a faint smile. 'A good team.'

'Did he have any enemies that you know of?'

'AJ? No way. Everyone loved him. He was a bit of a legend round here.'

'Dangerous game, security,' Jones interjected. 'Maybe he pissed off the wrong person on one of the doors?'

'I can't believe that. Not AJ. Everyone respected him for what he did in the ring, and despite his ability to fight, in ten years of business, I never once saw him hurt anyone. All he ever had to do was talk to the punters about calming down and people would listen. It was a gift. In fact, I used to call him the "arsehole whisperer".' Sutton smiled again.

Phillips changed tack. 'Beth said he went missing for a week, a few months back. Do you remember that?'

Sutton nodded. 'I'm pretty sure it was October time. I seem to remember him being away around Halloween, which is a busy time for the business.'

'Any ideas where he went?'

'No. Like I say, he rarely told me where he was going or what he was doing outside of work. I just assumed he was on a bender.'

'Drinking?'

'Yeah,' replied Sutton. 'Every now and again when he got stressed out or things got too much for him, he used to get on the piss and he'd disappear for days at a time. I just figured he was at it again.'

'So was he stressed at the time?'

'You could say that, yeah.'

'Why was that?' asked Phillips.

Sutton flinched slightly. 'Things were tough, business-wise.'

'Beth said he'd got himself into quite a lot of debt. Is that true?' said Jones.

Sutton nodded.

Jones continued. 'How much did he owe?'

'Well, he told me he borrowed forty grand.'

Phillips glanced at Jones, then back to Sutton. 'And who did he owe that money to?'

Sutton swallowed hard. 'I really can't say.'

'Can't or *won't*?' asked Jones.

'Look.' Sutton shifted in his seat. 'You've gotta understand, the guys he was involved with don't fuck about.'

'Neither do we.' Phillips stared him dead in the eye. 'Bernie, we're investigating a murder here. If you're with-holding information connected to that murder, that's called perverting the course of justice and could see you locked up.'

Sutton swallowed hard.

Phillips held his gaze. 'So, you can either tell us who he borrowed the money from here and now, or you can come back with us and spend a night in the cells. What's it gonna be?'

Sutton dropped his head into his hands. 'Shit,' he muttered.

Phillips continued. 'Who did AJ owe the money to, Bernie?'

Sutton took a moment before he lifted his head and locked eyes with Phillips again. 'Look. You didn't hear this from me, ok?'

'Go on.'

'AJ got into bed with Seamus Hernon.'

'As in the traveller Seamus Hernon?'

'That's him. Part of a big gypsy family. Claims to run his own groundworks company, but the truth is he makes most of his money from loansharking.'

'So AJ owed him forty thousand?' asked Phillips.

'And the rest,' Sutton scoffed. 'The weekly interest was huge, so it was more like fifty-five at the last count.'

'That's a lot of money,' said Jones.

'Yeah, and business wasn't great, so AJ was struggling to

keep up with the payments, which if you know anything about the Hernons, is not a good place to find yourself.'

'Did Hernon ever threaten AJ?' Phillips asked.

Sutton paused again. 'Look, I know you've got a job to do, and I really want to help, but seriously, I can't say anything else.'

Phillips sat forward now. 'Bernie, we believe somebody murdered your best mate. If you know anything that might help bring his killer to justice, you *have* to tell us.'

Sutton closed his eyes for a long moment, then nodded as he opened them again. 'The night before AJ went AWOL in October, Hernon came to the office with a couple of his brothers. Seriously big lads. I mean, I've fought some nasty buggers in my time, but these boys scared the shit out of me.'

'So what did Hernon want?' said Phillips.

'His money. AJ had missed a couple of payments and he wasn't happy about it. Said it made him look bad; that people would think he was soft. Hernon told AJ that he wanted his money within the next seven days *plus* interest, otherwise he'd end up buried in concrete on the M62.'

'And do you think the threat was real?' asked Jones.

'Well, later that night, AJ's car was set alight, so I'm pretty sure it was legit.'

Jones continued. 'You're saying Hernon set the car on fire?'

'Who else would want to do that?'

'Did anyone actually see him set fire to it?' said Phillips.

'No, but AJ was convinced it was Hernon sending him a message.'

'And is that what you meant when you said he was stressed about the business?' asked Jones.

'Yeah. It proper spooked him, and the next day he took one of the work vans and buggered off.'

'Did AJ replace the car that was burnt out?' Phillips asked.

'No,' replied Sutton. 'He carried on using the work van. Said he couldn't afford another car.'

Phillips nodded. 'Would he have been driving the same van yesterday?'

'Yeah, for sure.'

'Do you know where it is now?'

'No, I don't,' said Sutton.

'So you don't have GPS trackers in them?' asked Jones.

'No. We're old school. AJ preferred it that way.'

Jones frowned. 'Well, can you at least tell us the registration?'

Sutton began typing into the laptop. A second later he found what he was looking for. 'We have three vans and they all use a variation of the same registration. AJ's is, L-three-W-I-S.'

'Lima, three, whiskey, indigo, sierra,' Jones said aloud as he made a note in his pad.

'Yeah, the plates are supposed to look like they spell Lewis.'

'Is there anything else we might need to know about AJ's relationship with Hernon?' asked Phillips.

'No,' Sutton said firmly. 'I've told you everything I know. I swear.'

Phillips stared at him in silence as she scrutinised his face once more. 'Ok, well, I think that's all we need for now.'

Sutton sat forward in his seat. 'Please, you won't say anything to Hernon about me, will you?'

Phillips stood. 'As long as what you're telling us checks out, you've got nothing to worry about. We'll be in touch.' Phillips passed across her business card. 'Call me if you think of anything else.'

Sutton remained silent as Jones led the way out.

As they stepped back out into the rain, Phillips noticed a patch of scorched asphalt to the side of the building. 'Must have been where AJ's car was parked that night,' she shouted as she pointed to the spot.

'Looks like it,' said Jones grabbing greedily at the passenger side door.

Phillips dropped heavily into the driver's seat and slammed the door shut as the rain continued to batter the car. 'Let's get that van registration over to Whistler and Bov.' She glanced at her watch. 'By the time we get back to base, they may have already found it.'

'Will do,' said Jones then pulled his phone from his pocket.

4

Phillips guided the Mini into her allocated parking space at the front of Ashton House, the Greater Manchester Police's purpose-built headquarters, located in Failsworth, just a few miles north of Manchester city centre. As she killed the engine, she stared out at the glass building and exhaled sharply.

'You ok, Guv?' Jones asked from the passenger seat.

Phillips nodded as butterflies turned in her stomach. 'Just been a while since I've been here, that's all.'

'It's bound to feel a bit weird on your first day back after so long away.'

'Yeah, it really does.' She reached for the door handle. 'I'm just hoping it doesn't stay that way.'

The MCU office was located on the third floor and Phillips preferred to take the stairs whenever she could, so it was another five minutes before she and Jones walked through the main doors of Major Crimes.

Bovalino was sitting at his desk, hunched over a desktop computer well past its best.

Jones made his way over to his own desk in the bank of four, removed his coat and hung it over the back of his chair before dropping into his seat next to the big Italian. As ever, the spare desk remained unused, but unusually, Entwistle's chair was also empty. 'Where's Whistler?' Phillips took off her coat.

'Went for a pee a couple of minutes ago,' replied Bovalino. 'Should be back any second.'

Right on cue, the main doors to MCU opened and Entwistle strode in with purpose.

Phillips turned to face him.

'Guv!' he said with a flash of his perfect teeth. 'Good to see you.'

'And you, Whistler,' Phillips replied. 'And you.'

Entwistle was what many of the female officers referred to as the 'Ashton House Hottie'. A tall, muscular man in his late twenties with the chiselled features and dark skin of his West Indian mother and the bright green eyes of his Irish father. He certainly wasn't Phillips's type – and far too young for her even if he was – but she could certainly see why he was rarely without a date.

'I've got a hit on Lewis's van,' he said as he moved past Phillips and took a seat at his desk.

'That was fast,' said Jones.

'You know me, Jonesy,' said Entwistle with a grin. 'Actually, truth is uniform found it this afternoon and called it in, over near Wisterfield.'

'That's not far from where Lewis was found, is it?' said Phillips.

'About a mile,' Entwistle replied. 'Sadly through, it's been burnt out. Forensics are bringing it in to check it over, but by the sounds of what's left of it, I doubt they'll have much luck finding any evidence.'

'Shit,' muttered Phillips.

'I know. Sorry, boss.'

Phillips dropped into the chair at the spare desk.

Entwistle continued. 'I've also compiled a list of large cars, SUVs, vans and lorries spotted on ANPR cameras within a two-mile radius of the church last night. I've passed them on to the support team to start working through their owners' backgrounds. PC Lawford's collating the results.'

'Good work,' said Phillips as she folded up her coat and placed it on the desk.

'The fingerprints have come back from Evans,' added Bovalino. 'The body is definitely AJ.'

'Is he on the system?' asked Jones.

'Yup,' said Bovalino. 'He got into a bit of bother when he was a teenager and did twelve months for GBH. I'd forgotten about it, to be honest, but now I think about it, I do remember him being interviewed on TV, talking about how boxing got him back on the straight and narrow.'

'On that,' Entwistle interjected. 'Family liaison have arranged for Bethany Lewis to make the formal ID tomorrow morning at ten.'

'Right. Once she's done that, we can release it to the media,' said Phillips. 'Given his boxing profile, I suspect there may be a fair bit of interest in the case.'

'I think you're right, boss,' replied Bovalino. 'A lot of people watched his fights.'

For the next ten minutes Phillips and Jones brought Bov and Entwistle up to speed on their earlier conversations with Beth Lewis and Bernie Sutton.

'So what's the priority now?' asked Entwistle.

'We need to find out where AJ's van went between leaving the office yesterday and being found this afternoon. Somewhere on that journey he met his killer, and we need to know where.'

'I'll check ANPR cameras.' Entwistle made a note in his pad.

'And I'll look at CCTV for the two locations, as well as Lewis's phone records,' added Bovalino.

'Great, and first thing tomorrow morning, Jones and I will pay a visit to Seamus Hernon. See what he has to say for himself.'

Jones nodded.

Phillips got up from the spare desk and made her way into her office. Stepping inside, she noted that nothing had changed since she had last been here many months ago. Not a single thing.

'I never bothered moving in.'

Phillips turned to find Jones standing in the doorway.

'It didn't feel right, boss.' He stepped inside. 'And I guess I always hoped you'd be back.'

Phillips wandered over to the window and took in the familiar view of the car park and semi-landscaped gardens of Ashton House. Last time she'd gazed at it, her life had been very different. Her partner, Adam, had been in a critical condition in intensive care and she'd felt like she was losing her mind with worry. Not to mention the fact that she had been trying to solve a series of brutal gang-related murders. She could almost feel the anxiety of that time weighing down on her again.

'Glad to be back?' asked Jones.

She turned back to face him. 'Jury's out on that one, Jonesy.'

Jones nodded. 'I'll let you get settled back in. You know where I am if you need me.'

Phillips offered a faint smile. 'Thanks.'

As Jones made his way back out to the main office, Phillips sat down behind her desk, and took a few deep breaths to settle her nerves. After exhaling loudly, she pulled open the bottom drawer. She soon found what she was looking for, and a few minutes later she began updating her first decision log in nine months. 'Here we go again,' she whispered for the second time that day.

5

P hillips and Adam had recently moved out of her terraced house in Chorlton and into a jointly-owned semi-detached property on the other side of the village. Built around the same time as Bethany Lewis's home, it was almost identical in design and, unlike the house she had left behind, it had a driveway with enough space for two cars. As she arrived home that evening, she parked next to Adam's S Line Audi TT and switched off the engine. The time was approaching 7.30 p.m. and for a moment she sat in silence in the dark as she attempted to process the day behind her.

A few minutes later, she stepped through the front door and was instantly hit by the delicious aromas of Adam's cooking. He'd always known how to cook, but having been off work for the last nine months himself, he'd really expanded his range of recipes. After removing her coat and hanging it up, she wandered down the hall towards the kitchen and wondered what delights awaited her tonight.

Adam, who was standing over the stove, turned to face

her as she walked in and a wide grin spread across his face.
'Hey, babe. So how was your first day back?'

'Put this way, I don't need a drink. I need a bottle.'

She drew him into a hug.

'That bad, huh? What happened?'

Phillips held him tightly for a moment before pulling
back slightly. 'I can't give you the details, but let's just say that
by 8 a.m. I was looking at the body of a man whose heart had
been cut out of his chest.'

Adam grimaced. 'Jesus.'

Phillips stepped away and slipped onto one of the high
stools next to the large cooking island in the centre of the
kitchen.

Adam filled a glass from an already open bottle of pinot
grigio on the countertop and slid it over.

'Thanks, love,' she said, then took a large mouthful of the
ice-cold drink.

'So do you think you've done the right thing going back?'

Phillips blew her lips. 'I honestly don't know. I mean it's so
weird. I've been away for such a long time and then first thing
this morning – without missing so much as a beat – I was
staring at a dead man lying in a churchyard with his heart cut
out, and it felt normal. *Totally* normal. What does that say
about me? About what I've become.'

Adam took a sip of his own wine and held the glass in his
hand. 'That you're bloody good at what you do.'

'Does it? Or does it say I'm a cold-hearted bitch who's
become immune to people's suffering?'

'Not at all. Look. I get it, and I know what it's like. When I
was working in A&E I saw some horrific injuries that would
scare the crap out of most people, but as a doctor, it was my
job to assess the damage and figure out how to fix it as
quickly as possible. I didn't have the luxury of time to really
look at the person underneath. There were plenty of nurses

and support staff to do that. My only thought was on saving lives. The same applies to you.'

Phillips took another mouthful of wine. 'But does it?'

'Of course. Your job is to see the crime scene. To assess the evidence and find the person who committed the crime. If you allow yourself to get sucked into having feelings for the victims, it'll cloud your judgement and make you less effective.'

The wine was starting to do its job and she could feel her shoulders and neck muscles beginning to relax for the first time all day. 'I guess so.'

Just then, Floss, Phillips's white Ragdoll cat snaked around her legs. 'Oh, you've finally decided to come and say hello, have you?' She bent down to pick her up. 'You know, there was a time she'd be waiting at the door for me to come home, but not now.'

'What can I say?' Adam chuckled. 'She's got a new friend to play with.'

Phillips cuddled Floss as she purred loudly.

'Anyway,' said Adam. 'Speaking of work, I've been thinking it might be time for me to go back too.'

Phillips placed Floss back on the floor, then sat upright. 'Are you ready? Your body took a helluva battering.'

'I know, but I really think I am. The physios are happy and to be honest, I'm not sure how long I can sit around doing nothing. I'm a doctor and I want to get back to helping people.'

'If that's what you want, you know I'll support you.'

Adam stared at his glass for a moment. 'The only thing is, I'm not sure if I should try a different field. I've been in A&E for almost fifteen years. Maybe it's time for a change.'

'To what?' Phillips asked.

'I dunno, really. Maybe general medicine.'

'A GP?

'Maybe,' said Adam. 'Regular hours, a shorter commute. Bit less stressful.'

Phillips shook her head. 'I'm not sure general medicine is for you. Do you really want to spend your days with a load of old people moaning about their aches and pains, snotty kids with colds and chickenpox, house calls, mountains of paperwork?'

'But if I go back to A&E it's back to night shifts, weekend work, us hardly ever seeing each other.'

Phillips slipped off the stool and hugged him for a second time. 'All I want is for you to be happy. If that means we see a bit less of each other, then so be it. We'll just have to make the most of the time we *do* have together.'

Adam held her tightly against him and kissed her on the forehead.

Philips pulled her head back. 'Whatever you decide, I'll support one hundred percent. Just make sure you're making the right decision for you, not just for us.'

'I will,' replied Adam.

Phillips nodded in the direction of the stove. 'So what's for dinner?'

'Thai jungle curry with sticky jasmine rice.'

'Sounds delicious.'

Adam nodded. 'Better make the most of it, because if I do go back to A&E again, it'll be microwave meals for one for you.'

Phillips feigned shock. 'I've changed my mind,' she said playfully. 'I think general practice would be *perfect* for you.'

6

The next morning Phillips headed into the office early for a prearranged meeting with her boss, Detective Superintendent Carter.

It was just after 8 a.m. when she strode into the outer office, and his assistant, Diana Cook, was not yet at her desk.

A second later, Carter appeared at the door to his own office. 'Jane. I thought I heard you. Come through.'

Phillips followed him inside.

'Take a seat. Can I get you a coffee?'

'Please.'

'White, no sugar, right? said Carter.

'Well remembered, sir. I'm impressed.'

Carter took a few minutes to prepare the drinks.

As Phillips watched him she noted he appeared to have put on a bit of weight since they last worked together. She'd not noticed it when they'd met a month or so ago to arrange her return to duty, but as he stood in front of her now, the white shirt of his uniform appeared to fit a little more snugly around his middle than before. That said, for a man in his fifties, he still looked athletically built, and his salt and pepper hair gave him an ever so slight resemblance to George Clooney.

'There you go,' he said as he handed Phillips her mug of coffee, then took his seat behind his desk opposite her. 'So how's Adam?'

Phillips sipped her coffee. 'He's great. Thinking of going back to work, actually.'

Carter smiled. 'That's brilliant news. And his injuries, they're all healed?'

'The ones you can see, yes. I do still worry about how it's affected him mentally. I mean, being almost stabbed to death on your own doorstep has to have had an impact on him.'

'Has he shown any signs that he could be struggling mentally?' asked Carter.

'No, but then that's Adam. He never complains, just gets on with things.'

'Sounds like someone else I know,' said Carter stifling a grin.

Phillips chortled. 'Touché.'

'Look, I am really sorry I wasn't around yesterday. Bloody typical of Fox to call a quarterly review on your first day back.'

'How is the chief constable?'

'Her usual supportive, motivating self.' Carter's tone was sarcastic.

'I can imagine.'

'So how was it? Your first day back, I mean.'

'Full-on is probably the best way to describe it, sir.'

'I understand you were called out to a homicide.'

'Yep, my day started in a churchyard in Hodge Hill at 8 a.m.'

'We hardly eased you back in slowly, did we?' Carter took a mouthful of coffee.

'I wouldn't expect anything less with MCU.'

Carter nodded. 'Indeed. So what are we looking at?'

Phillips placed her cup down on the desk. 'Bit of a weird one, to be honest, sir. An IC3 male, naked all but for a white shawl. The victim was also surrounded by white roses, perfectly placed in an arc around the body.'

'Posed.'

'Yeah, and the body was also moved from where the victim was killed; no blood around it at all.'

Carter's brow furrowed.

'But it gets even weirder, sir.'

'In what way?'

'The victim's heart had been cut out,' replied Phillips. 'And as yet, we've not been able to locate it.'

'Bloody hell, I've heard it all now.'

'And there's more, I'm afraid.'

Carter sighed. 'I knew it was going to be one of those days.'

'The victim was a man called Ajani Lewis, or AJ, as most people called him.'

'How do I know that name?'

'He was a professional boxer in the mid-two-thousands,' said Phillips. 'British middleweight champion, according to Bov.'

'*That's it.* I remember him. Quite a fighter, as I recall.'

Phillips nodded. 'And quite a big name in Manchester.'

'Which means the press are going to be all over it.'

'Exactly, sir. Our fingerprint analysis confirmed that Lewis is our victim, and his wife will make the formal ID this morning. Once that's done, the media team will obviously need to release it to the press. It's likely it'll get a lot of attention.'

Carter drained his mug and placed it on the desk. 'Well, I'll need to brief Fox. She won't be happy, of course.'

'Why change the habit of a lifetime, hey?' said Phillips sardonically.

'So do we have any leads, as yet?'

'Nothing concrete, but his business partner, Bernie Sutton, confirmed Lewis was in a lot of debt, namely to Seamus Hernon.'

'Hernon? Is he known to us?'

'Yes,' said Phillips. 'He's the head of a large traveller community now based on a permanent site in Stockport. Officially he runs a groundworks business, but unofficially we believe he's also a loan shark. Apparently, Lewis owed him upwards of fifty grand and Hernon had made threats to Lewis. Said if he didn't pay what he owed he'd end up in a hole on the M62.'

'Can anyone corroborate the threat? asked Carter.

'Bernie Sutton heard him say it, but he's unlikely to go on the record for us. He's terrified of him and reckons Hernon also set fire to Lewis's car as a warning.'

'Any proof of that?'

'No, sir. There were no witnesses and no CCTV, but Sutton's convinced it was Hernon.'

'I take it you'll be paying Mr Hernon a visit today?'

'Yep. Jones and I are heading over there as soon as we're done here.'

'Good. Well, in that case, I won't keep you any longer. You go and do what you do best.'

'Thank you, sir.' Phillips drained her mug and stood. 'And thanks for the coffee.'

'You're very welcome.'

Phillips headed for the door.

'And Jane,' Carter called after her.

She turned.

'Great to have you back.'

'Thank you, sir,' replied Phillips without conviction, then left the room.

7

Seamus Hernon was descended from a long line of Irish travellers with their origins in Connemara, a region on the Atlantic Coast of Western Galway. His father, Jonny, had moved to England in the late 1950's, roaming the country with his wife, Mary, and their five sons for twenty years until finally settling in the north-west. Nowadays the entire extended Hernon family lived on a purpose-built permanent traveller site on the outskirts of Stockport, six miles south of Manchester.

The eldest of the sons, Seamus was the man in charge of the family now, but his four brothers were never far away, and together they had fathered close to thirty children between them.

As Jones pulled the MCU squad car onto the site just after 10 a.m., Phillips stared out at the rows of static caravans arranged neatly on either side of the narrow road. Outside each was either an expensive SUV or a branded transit van with the name 'Hernon Groundworks' emblazoned on the side. Despite the fact that the temperature outside was just above freezing, kids of varying ages swarmed around them in jeans and jumpers, kicking footballs, riding bikes and screaming excitedly.

'Shouldn't this lot be in school by now?' said Jones.

'A lot of travellers home-school,' replied Phillips as the car came to a stop.

Just then a large man well over six feet tall with a barrel chest stepped out of one of the caravans, wearing jeans and trainers, with only a black and white Adidas tracksuit top to protect him from the February wind. His hair was thick and jet black, the cheeks of his round pale face ruddy from the cold.

'That looks like Seamus to me,' said Phillips.

'Put on a bit of weight since his last mug shot was taken,' added Jones.

Phillips climbed out of the car and Jones matched her.

'And what business do the police have here?' said the man, his accent thick, a mixture of rural Ireland and South Manchester.

'Who said we're the police?' asked Jones.

The big man laughed. 'Do me a favour. I can smell it on yer.'

'Seamus Hernon?' asked Phillips.

'Who wants to know?' He folded his thick arms across his equally thick chest as the kids continued running riot around them.

Phillips presented her credentials. 'DCI Phillips and DI Jones. We're from the Major Crimes Unit and we'd like to talk to you about AJ Lewis.'

'I remember that fella,' said Hernon. 'Sure. He was one helluva fighter in his day.'

'What was your relationship with AJ?' asked Phillips.

'Didn't have one. I seen him in the boxing gym from time to time, but that's about it.'

'Really?' Phillips replied. 'Because we understand he borrowed money from you.'

'Me?' Hernon shook his head. 'Don't know anything about that.'

'Word is he was into you for over fifty grand,' said Jones.

'Fifty grand? Now why would a rich boxer type be asking *me,* a road digger, for money?'

'Because you're a loan shark and he was broke and desperate,' said Jones. 'His business was going under.'

'Don't know anything about loan sharks,' Hernon protested.

Phillips was beginning to lose her patience with the game Hernon was playing. 'Look, let's cut the crap, shall we? We know you lent AJ Lewis over forty grand, and with unpaid interest on top, the total amount was close to fifty. We also know you threatened to stick him in a hole in the M62 if he didn't pay what he owed. And on top of that, we have good reason to believe you and your brothers set fire to his car a few months back.'

Hernon smirked. 'And do you have any proof of all this, Officer?'

Phillips ignored the question. 'Where were you on Monday night?'

'Why do you want to know?'

'Because AJ Lewis was murdered that night.'

Hernon's eyes widened. 'Murdered?'

'That's right,' replied Phillips.

'And what? You think I did it?'

Phillips locked eyes with him. 'Did you?'

'Give over, will ya? I'll admit I'm fond of a good fight, settling things the traveller way, but I'm not a killer.'

'He owed you a lot of money, Seamus.'

'So *you* say.'

'Money's often involved in murder,' added Jones.

Hernon's face twisted. 'You see, that doesn't make sense to me. If a man owed me money, why would I want him dead?'

'To send a message, maybe,' Phillips cut in. 'To make sure everyone *else* pays what they owe on time.'

'I don't know where you get your information from, but like I said, my business is roads.' Hernon thumbed over his shoulder towards the nearest transit van. 'Digging them up and putting them back down. I don't know anything about lending money to strangers.'

Phillips scrutinised his face for signs he was lying but the reality was she couldn't tell. 'So where *were* you on Monday night, Seamus?'

'Working.'

'Where exactly?' asked Phillips.

'Simister, Junction eighteen of the M60. Where it joins the sixty-two. We had a big resurfacing job on.'

Phillips nodded. 'Can anyone vouch for that?'

'I was working with two of my brothers and three other lads from ten o'clock through to five in the morning. And you can check with the Highways Agency if you don't believe me.'

'Don't worry, we will,' Jones shot back.

'You do that.' Hernon glared at Jones before turning his gaze to Phillips. 'Now, is there anything else you need? Or can I get back to my breakfast?'

Phillips held his gaze for a moment. 'That's it for now.'

'Good.' Hernon flashed a sardonic smile. 'A *working* man needs a good feed first thing.'

With that, Phillips turned away and headed back to the car with Jones in tow.

'Well, he's a smug bastard,' said Jones as he closed the driver's door a minute later.

'Yeah, isn't he just.' Phillips stared out of the windscreen as Hernon walked back to the caravan, his mobile phone to his ear. 'I want his phone records checked, plus all ANPR cameras around Simister Island and any CCTV the Highways Agency can send our way.'

'I'll get the team straight onto it.'

'He's clearly lying about lending Lewis the money, so let's go through AJ's finances. See if we can find any trace of it.'

Jones nodded as he fired the engine.

'We'll see how smug he is when we come back with a warrant.'

'Too right,' said Jones as he turned the car around.

Phillips checked her watch. 'Lewis's PM is scheduled in the next hour. Let's head over there and see if Tan can shed any light on what really happened on Sunday night.'

8

Chief Forensic Pathologist Doctor Tanvi Chakrabortty smiled warmly as Phillips stepped into the morgue with Jones behind her. 'Well, look who's back. Good to see you, Jane.'

Phillips returned her smile. 'And you, Tan. How've you been?'

'Busier than ever, I'm sad to say.' Chakrabortty pulled her plastic surgical apron over her immaculately pressed blue scrubs. She was a tall, elegant woman in her late thirties with jet black hair pulled back into a ponytail, flawless dark skin, and soft features. 'Shall we go in?'

Phillips and Jones both nodded as Chakrabortty passed them the prerequisite aprons and latex gloves.

Once inside the examination room, the smell of disinfectant and embalming fluid was almost too much for Phillips to bear and she found herself covering her nose and mouth with her gloved hand. After so many months away from this place, her senses were now on high alert.

Chakrabortty had obviously noticed. 'Don't worry, you'll soon get used to it again.'

Phillips offered a weak smile and nodded.

Lewis's body was laid out on a large stainless steel examination table in the middle of the room. A crisp green sheet covered him from the waist down, his torso and head exposed to the bright lights overhead. Phillips and Jones stood together on one side of the table with Chakrabortty opposite them.

'Everybody ready?' asked Chakrabortty as she picked up a large scalpel.

'As I'll ever be.' Phillips was suddenly filled with the same nervous energy she had felt at her very first post mortem, almost twenty years ago.

'Right, then. Let's see what killed Mr Lewis, shall we.'

Chakrabortty was well known for the diligent way she worked with the bodies in her care. She was careful and respectful, yet efficient and incredibly thorough. For the next ninety minutes she examined every part of Lewis's body, removing the organs for closer inspection as well as taking tissue samples for later use if required. As she placed his lungs on the weighing-scales she stared down at them for a time. 'I have to say, whoever removed the heart did a good job of it.'

'In what way?' asked Phillips.

'They managed to take it out without any damage to the surrounding organs. There's not a single mark on the lungs.'

'Evans suggested they may have used a surgical scalpel,' said Jones.

'I'd have to agree with that. The incisions look clean, which rules out a serrated blade, and if they used anything bigger than a scalpel they'd most certainly have impacted the lungs and potentially the top of the liver.'

Phillips felt her brow furrow. 'So do you think we could be looking for a doctor or a surgeon here?'

'The organ was *carefully* extracted – as opposed to the

precision you'd expect from a surgeon. That said, based on the handiwork, I certainly wouldn't rule out the killer having some level of medical knowledge.'

'Jesus. That's all we need. A modern-day Jack the Ripper,' Phillips replied.

When Chakrabortty had completed her examination of the organs located within the torso, she made a large incision across the back of the head with a handheld circular saw and removed the skull in order to examine the brain. It was at that point that Phillips noticed the colour drain from Jones's face as beads of sweat appeared on his forehead. He had never liked post-mortems and was especially uncomfortable when it came to cutting open the head.

Thirty minutes later and the examination was finally complete. After removing their aprons and gloves, they retreated to Chakrabortty's office, which brought some of the colour back to Jones's skin.

Chakrabortty took a seat behind her desk, with Phillips and Jones sitting opposite.

Jones pulled out his notepad and pen.

'So,' said Chakrabortty. 'Mr Lewis has a large quantity of rohypnol in his system.'

'Enough to kill him?' asked Phillips.

'No. Death was most certainly due to him being given a massive dose of the chemical compound progesterone.'

'Which is what?'

'A synthetic pregnane-steroid often found in anaesthetic—'

'Which backs up our doctor theory,' Phillips cut her off.

Chakrabortty shook her head. 'Not entirely. You see, progesterone is most commonly used in veterinarian surgeries, usually under the brand name alfaxalone.'

'Oh great. We've got a killer vet on the loose,' quipped Jones. 'Fox is gonna love that, no pun intended.'

Phillips glanced at Jones then back at Chakrabortty. 'He's got a point, Tan. I mean, who else besides a vet would have access to alfaxalone?'

Chakrabortty shrugged her shoulders. 'Your guess is as good as mine, but don't forget about the dark web. You can get pretty much anything from there if you know where to look.'

Phillips took moment to digest the information.

'There's a large puncture wound on his neck just under the left ear where the progesterone was injected,' added Chakrabortty. 'And mercifully for Mr Lewis, the heart was removed post-mortem. There was very little blood loss from the body, and by my reckoning, it would have been done pretty quickly after death.'

'How quickly?' asked Phillips.

'An hour. Maybe two.'

'What about time of death?' Jones said.

'It's very difficult to be one hundred percent certain because the body was left out for so long in freezing temperatures, but I'm pretty confident it would have been ten to twelve hours before he was found.'

'Which means it was somewhere between 8 and 10 p.m. Sunday,' said Phillips.

Chakrabortty nodded. 'There was some historical damage to the liver and kidneys, most likely due to alcohol consumption.'

'Makes sense,' said Jones. 'His wife said he had issues with the drink.'

'Other than that, the lungs, stomach, intestines and brain were all in pretty good shape. He wasn't the healthiest man on the planet, but neither was he likely to die of natural causes any time soon.'

Phillips focused on Jones now. 'First things first. We need

to find out if any vets in the area are missing any...' she glanced at Chakrabortty. '...what was the brand name?'

'Alfaxalone.'

Jones scribbled in his pad.

Phillips continued. 'That's as good a place as any to start.'

'I'll get right on it,' replied Jones.

'Thanks, Tan. As ever, you've been a huge help.'

'My pleasure, Jane,' said Chakrabortty. 'Oh, I forgot to ask. How's Adam?'

'He's great. Doing really well, even thinking about going back to work soon.'

Chakrabortty's warm smile returned. 'Good. I am pleased.'

Just then Phillips's phone began to vibrate in her pocket. Fishing it out, she could see it was the journalist Don Townsend. 'Sorry, Tan. I'd better take this.'

'Of course,' replied Chakrabortty.

Getting up from the chair, Phillips pressed the answer icon on the screen as she headed for the door and stepped out into the corridor. 'Don. To what do I owe the pleasure?'

'Hi, Jane. I heard a rumour you were back on the job.'

'Yeah. Started Monday.'

'Well, that is good news. Whilst you've been away, it's become apparent that DI Jones doesn't seem to like me.'

'How perceptive of you,' said Phillips sardonically. 'So what are you after?'

'Do I have to be after something?' Townsend's tone was playful. *'Couldn't I just be calling to say hello and wish you well back at work?'*

'No, Don. You only ever call when you want something. So what is it this time?'

'Well, as you asked, I understand the body you found on Monday morning in Hodge Hill was that of AJ Lewis, the former middleweight boxer. And word is, it's suspicious.'

Jesus, thought Phillips. The last thing she wanted was a hack like Townsend trampling all over the case. She needed to choose her words carefully or risk having them splashed all over that afternoon's edition of the Manchester Evening News. 'Look, Don. The formal identification of the victim hasn't taken place yet, so I can't confirm or deny anything at the moment.'

'So it is him?' pushed Townsend.

'You know I can't say.' Phillips had learnt the hard way over the years that it was better to keep Townsend onside than let him run free on his own. You could at least help steer the narrative that way. 'Look. As soon as the ID is confirmed, you'll be the first to know. Ok?'

'And when will that be?'

'Sometime today, all being well.'

'In that case, I'll wait to hear from you.'

'You do that, Don,' said Phillips, then ended the call.

At that moment Jones approached. 'Everything all right, Guv?'

'Yeah. Just Don Townsend.'

Jones rolled his eyes. 'What does that snake want?'

'He's heard about AJ's murder.'

'What? How?'

'God knows,' said Phillips. 'He's got sources everywhere.'

'Well, it wouldn't have come from anyone in our team.'

'That goes without saying, but there were an awful lot of people at the crime scene yesterday from different departments and organisations. Any one of them could be on his payroll.'

'So what did you tell him?' asked Jones.

'Just that we were waiting on the official ID and until we had that, there was nothing to report.'

'And did he go for that?'

'For now, at least,' said Phillips. 'But I'll need to give him something in the next twenty-four hours or he'll just start making shit up, which is the last thing we need on a case as high profile as this.'

'Too right,' replied Jones. 'Fox will go mental.'

'Exactly, so come on, let's get back to the office and find out what we've got so far.'

9

A n hour later, the team debriefed in Phillips's office, each taking up their now habitual positions: Jones and Bovalino sat opposite Phillips, with Entwistle perched against a small filing cabinet to her left. For the next ten minutes she filled them in on the findings of the post-mortem.

'That's some weird shit, Guv,' said Bovalino when she'd finished.

'Yeah, it is. So one of our main priorities right now is to find out if any veterinary practices in the city have been burgled recently. If we come up blank on that, Chakrabortty suggested checking out the dark web.'

'I can look into the vets, Guv,' said Entwistle.

'And I want AJ's finances checked to see if we can find any evidence Hernon did actually lend him the money, as Bernie Sutton claims.'

'I'll take those,' said Bov.

Phillips continued. 'Look. I'm sure I don't need to tell you this, guys, but we need to tread very carefully on this one. I've already had a call from Don Townsend this lunchtime sniffing around for a story. We stay tight lipped on this, ok? Not even your other-halves can know the details at the moment.'

Each of the men nodded.

'So any luck with the ANPR or CCTV searches?'

'Yes, Guv.' Entwistle picked up his notepad. 'I got a hit on Lewis's van the night he was killed. Spotted on one of the cameras about a mile from Hodge Hill, just before 8 p.m.'

Phillips took a moment. 'Which fits with the time of death. He must have been killed not long after that.'

'Looks like it,' said Entwistle. 'Going further back, I also got a number of hits on various cameras in and around that area in late October.'

'Around Halloween?'

Entwistle nodded.

'Whereabouts?' asked Phillips.

Entwistle began reading from the pad. 'Couple of times on the A34 near Hodge Hill, once in Marton, twice in Henbury and three times in and around Monk's Heath.'

'What times of day was it captured?' asked Phillips.

'A mixture, really; Hodge Hill were both early evening, Marton was at lunchtime, as was Henbury, and Monk's Heath was early morning and late afternoon.'

'Any CCTV near those ANPR cameras?' asked Jones.

'I'll be looking at that next.'

'Keep us posted.'

Entwistle nodded. 'Of course, Guv.'

'And what about Lewis's phone records?' asked Phillips.

'Should be with me this afternoon.'

'Great.'

It was Bovalino's turn for an update now. 'So, I've been in touch with the Highways Agency, who confirmed Hernon Groundworks *were* contracted to work on the M60 at Simister and they were on site from 10 p.m. Sunday to 5 a.m. Monday, just like Hernon said.'

'Doesn't mean he was there with them, though, does it?' said Jones.

'No, it doesn't,' Phillips added.

'Which is why I've asked them for all the CCTV footage within a mile of that junction during that time. I've no idea how good the quality will be, but we might get lucky and be able to see who was actually on site during that period.'

Phillips said nothing for a moment, then sat forward in her chair. 'We also need to know if Hernon – or anyone within his family – has any medical knowledge. Chakrabortty said the killer had a high degree of skill when it came to removing the organs.'

Jones's face twisted. 'From what we saw of him this morning, that doesn't really fit, does it?'

'No,' replied Phillips. 'But we've seen crazier things in our time, haven't we? Right, we've got plenty to be going on with, so let's crack on.'

A chorus of 'Yes, Guv's' filled the room before each of them filed back to their desks.

Phillips checked her watch. It was approaching 3 p.m. She picked up the phone and dialled Carter's office.

As ever, Diana Cook answered promptly. *'Detective Chief Superintendent Carter's office.'*

'Di, it's Jane. Is he in?'

'He is. Would you like me to put you through?'

'No. I'll come up if that's ok. I've got some updates he needs to be across.'

'Sure. He has another appointment at 3.30 but he's all yours 'til then.'

'Great. I'm on my way up,' said Phillips then ended the call.

A couple of minutes later, she strode out of MCU and headed for the fifth floor.

THE UPDATE with Carter had taken no time at all and he had appeared grateful for the heads-up on the interest shown by Don Townsend, stressing that the last thing MCU needed was sensational headlines flying round on social media. As ever, Phillips had promised to keep him in the loop with each development as they came in, then set off back to the third floor.

As she walked into Major Crimes, Jones looked up from his desk. 'How's Carter?'

'Like the rest of us, sickened by the results of the PM and glad for the heads-up on Townsend. He's going to update Fox after his next meeting.'

'I don't envy him,' Jones scoffed. 'She'll blow a bloody gasket. She hates Townsend. Mind you, can't say I blame her.'

'He's actually not as bad as people make out,' said Phillips.

Over the years, she'd developed a surprising, strong relationship with Townsend. Their paths had crossed on several high-profile cases, and although they weren't what she'd call close, there was certainly an element of mutual respect between them.

'Well,' Jones hit back. 'After the way he snuck around behind my back when I was acting DI, he can go fuck himself, as far as I'm concerned. His click-baiting headlines caused me no end of trouble with Carter and Fox.'

Phillips chortled. 'You've just got to know how to manage him, Jonesy.'

'Or just have nothing to do with him,' he replied. 'Anyway, you've got a visitor, Guv.' Jones nodded behind her.

Phillips spun in the direction of her office.

'Andy Evans. Arrived about ten minutes ago.'

'Well, I'm honoured,' said Phillips. 'It's not often forensics come over to Ashton House, is it?'

Jones chuckled. 'I almost didn't recognise him without his white suit on.'

Phillips found herself grinning as she made her way into her office where Evans was standing by the window, looking out. 'Andy. To what do I owe the pleasure?'

Evans turned to face her, a soft smile spreading across his heavily bearded face. 'I've got something I thought you might be interested in.'

Jones had a point. Evans looked very different in his black police t-shirt and trousers. She normally only ever saw him covered from head to toe in white forensic overalls and rarely saw his face without a mask. 'Great.' Phillips dropped down behind her desk. 'Please, have a seat.'

Evans pulled his chair close to Phillips and sat down. 'We've been through the victim's van, but as expected it was too badly burnt to offer up anything useful.'

'Well, you didn't come all this way to tell me that, did you?'

'No,' replied Evans as he pushed a brown manilla envelope across the desk.

Phillips opened it and inspected the contents. 'What am I looking at?'

'Photographs of oil samples.'

Phillips felt her brow furrow. 'Soil samples. From what?'

'The victim's feet,' said Evans.

'He was found in a churchyard without any clothing. That's to be expected, isn't it?'

'It is, but these samples bear no resemblance to the soil in the church. They come from ground that is very different.'

'Which means it could have come from where he was

killed?' Phillips felt her pulse quicken. This could be the break they were looking for.

'Or at least where he was moved from before being dumped,' said Evans. 'These samples were taken from both his heels. We also found traces of chloroxylenol on the body, which is an active ingredient in antiseptic disinfectant.'

'So the killer cleaned him up before leaving him at the church?'

'Exactly, but they left tiny fragments of this soil in the cracks of the heels. Based on how deeply embedded it was, I'd guess that whoever killed him dragged the feet along the ground when they were moving him.'

'Do we have any idea where this soil has come from?' asked Phillips.

'Not specifically, but my top-line analysis shows high traces of arsenic and chromium, which would suggest industrial land of some kind. In order to get a more accurate location, I've sent samples over to the specialist Pedology team. They're going to try and identify it and any potential areas it could have come from.'

'How long will that take?'

Evans shrugged. 'Your guess is as good as mine. Thanks to the chief constable's budget cuts last year, the team's been sliced in half and they've got quite a backlog.'

Phillips sat forward now. 'Well, as a murder case, this has to be a priority, Andy. Can you stress that to them?'

'I'll do my best,' said Evans.

Phillips stared down at the enlarged photographs of the microscopic samples and felt a surge of nervous energy rush through her body. If they could locate the origins of the soil, there was a good chance it would take them one step closer to finding the killer. She looked up at Evans again. 'This is first-rate work, Andy. It really is.'

He appeared to blush slightly. 'Thanks, Jane.'

'Was there anything else we needed to discuss?'

'No, that's us for the moment.' He stepped up from the chair. 'We're still working on everything from the churchyard.'

'You'll update me as soon as you find anything, won't you?'

'Of course.' He nodded. 'You'll be the first to know.'

'And don't forget to give Pedology a nudge, will you?'

'I'll call them now,' said Evans, then turned and headed for the door.

'One more thing, Andy.'

He turned back. 'Yes?'

'Anyone in your team ever have anything to do with Don Townsend?'

Evans's eyebrows squished together. 'Who's he?'

'A reporter. Works for the MEN.'

'Can't say that they do, but I can ask if you'd like?'

'No. No. It's ok,' said Phillips. 'It's not important right now.'

He nodded, then turned and left the room.

Phillips cast her gaze back to the images of the soil samples again.

As expected, Jones appeared at her door a minute later. 'So what was so important it brought CSI over?'

Phillips tapped the file on her desk. 'I don't want to get my hopes up too soon, but I've got a feeling Evans has just played a blinder for us. Come, take a look.'

10

The next day, with the time approaching II a.m., Phillips looked up from her decision logs and cast her gaze out into the main office. Each of the team had arrived early that morning and had been glued to their desks ever since as they worked through their allocated tasks. She needed a break from the mountain of paperwork that accompanied any homicide investigation, so headed out.

'How you getting on?' she asked as she dropped into the chair at the spare desk.

'I've been working through the Highways Agency motorway camera footage,' said Bov. 'But it's not great, I'm afraid. Grainy and pixelated, and it doesn't help that it was all shot at night, either.'

'Any sign of Hernon?'

'No sign of anyone specific, Guv. Just bodies moving around in low light. It's pretty useless either way, to be honest.'

Phillips pursed her lips. 'I guess it was always going to be a long shot.'

Entwistle cut in now. 'I've checked the incident logs and

found two vets that reported break-ins in the last month or so.'

'Really? Whereabouts?' asked Jones.

'One called The City Vet Practice in Longsight was burgled on the 25th of January and another, Fisher Veterinary Practice, in Monk's Heath shopping precinct, was broken into on the 28th.'

Phillips tapped her index finger against her lips. 'Monk's Heath. Wasn't that one of the ANPR locations where Lewis's van popped up?'

Entwistle checked his pad for a second, then nodded. 'Yeah, you're right. Spotted three times there during the week he went missing.'

'Well, that can't be a coincidence, can it?' said Jones.

'No such thing in homicide, is there?' Phillips shot back.

Jones grinned. 'I win!' he chuckled as he clapped his hands together.

Both Entwistle and Bovalino sighed, then reached into their pockets and pulled out their wallets.

Phillips eyed them with suspicion. 'What's going on?'

Entwistle passed a crisp ten-pound note to Jones. 'We had a sweepstake on how long it would take you to tell us coincidences don't exist.'

'I had Wednesday,' grinned Jones. 'I knew it wouldn't take long.'

'I was Friday,' said Bov.

'And I was Thursday,' added Entwistle.

Phillips said nothing for a moment as she eyed them all in turn, her expression stern. 'I see.'

Silence descended and slowly the mood changed as each of the team began to appear somewhat sheepish.

'Look, Guv. We didn't mean to offend you,' said Jones.

Phillips remained silent for a few seconds longer until she

felt the discomfort in the room peak. 'Jesus!' she cackled, pointing. 'You should see your faces.'

Each of the guys exhaled loudly, their relief clearly palpable.

'Bloody hell, Guv. You had us going there,' said Bovalino.

Phillips continued laughing. 'Serves you right, you cheeky buggers!'

Bovalino handed over his ten-pound note to Jones.

'Right. If you're quite finished taking the piss out of your boss, we need to check out these vets.' Phillips stood. 'Jones, you and I'll take Monk's Heath. Bov, Whistler, you take Longsight.'

Each of the men nodded and stood up from their desks.

Phillips turned to Jones now. 'And *you,* my friend, are buying me lunch with your winnings.'

Jones grinned and raised his hands in mock surrender. 'Whatever you say, Guv. Whatever you say.'

FISHER VETERINARY PRACTICE was located in a small shopping complex in Monk's Heath and was sandwiched between a chemist and a dry cleaner.

Phillips and Jones arrived just after 12.30 p.m. to find the parking lot outside filled with the type of high-end cars and SUVs the people of Cheshire had become synonymous with. The 'Cheshire Set', as they were often referred to across Manchester, were well known for their high standard of living.

After eventually finding a parking space for the squad car, Phillips and Jones walked side by side towards Fisher's. The rain had stayed away all morning but the air was still cold, their breath visible in front of them. Stepping through the large smoked-glass front door, they found themselves in what smelled like a freshly decorated reception area with an empty waiting room to the left.

Ahead of them, a young woman with multi-coloured dyed hair pulled back in a ponytail was sitting behind the reception desk in a green uniform that loosely resembled surgical scrubs. The left side of her neck appeared to be extensively tattooed. She smiled as they approached. 'Can I help you?'

Phillips noted the name tag on her chest. 'Hi, Sarah.' She produced her ID. 'We'd like to speak to the manager.'

'Can I ask what it's regarding?'

'The break-in on the 28th of January.'

'Really?' Sarah raised her pierced eyebrows. 'The police have already been to see us about that.'

Phillips offered a thin smile. 'We're from a different department.'

Sarah nodded as she picked up the handset on the switchboard and a moment later relayed the request to the person on the other end. After a short pause, she replaced the receiver. 'Dr Fisher will be with you in a moment. Would you like to take a seat in the waiting area?'

'Sure,' said Phillips.

Five minutes passed before a short, diminutive woman dressed in real surgical scrubs and wearing white Crocs on her feet stepped into the waiting room. Her dark hair was cut short and smart; tidy as opposed to stylish. 'DCI Phillips?'

Phillips stood and offered her hand. 'Doctor Fisher?'

'Yes. How can I help?'

'Is there somewhere private we can talk?' asked Phillips.

Fisher's faced creased. 'I'm afraid not; we're having the staff areas decorated at the moment. As you can probably tell, we've just finished this area.'

Phillips scanned the empty space.

'We've got ten minutes until our next appointment is due in, Inspector,' offered Sarah helpfully.

Phillips nodded and turned her focus back to Dr Fisher.

'We understand you were burgled a couple of weeks ago,' said Phillips.

Fisher frowned. 'I've already spoken to the police about this.'

'I told them that,' added Sarah, sounding slightly smug.

Phillips didn't react. 'Could you tell us if any alfaxalone was stolen?'

Fisher recoiled slightly. 'Er, yes. Ten vials of it, actually. Why do you ask?'

'Are the supplies normally locked away?' said Jones.

'Yes, absolutely.'

Jones nodded. 'And who has access to the keys?'

'Er, well, me, of course, my associate, Dr Wilder, and each of our veterinary nurses.'

'Anyone else?' Phillips cut in.

Fisher's brow furrowed. 'I'm sorry, I'm a little confused. Why are you asking all these questions about alfaxalone?'

Phillips glanced at Jones, then back at Fisher. 'We believe it may have been used in another crime we're investigating.'

'Really? How?'

'I'm afraid we can't say at the moment. I'm sure you understand.' Phillips pursed her lips. 'Anyway, we're going to need the names and addresses of Dr Wilder and each of your nurses.'

Fisher's eyes widened, a look of concern flashing across her face.

'Purely for elimination purposes,' said Phillips. 'Oh, and do you have CCTV at all?'

'Yes, we do.'

'Could we get a copy of the night you were burgled?'

'That shouldn't be an issue,' Fisher replied. 'Although, I

doubt it's much use. The other officers looked at it and said the guy who broke in wore a ski mask over his head.'

'Well, we'll take a copy anyway if that's ok?' said Phillips.

Fisher turned to Sarah. 'Could you organize that?'

Sarah nodded as she stepped away from the reception desk, then disappeared through a door at the back of the space.

'The machine's in the back,' said Fisher by way of explanation. 'In amongst all the dust sheets.'

'Thank you,' said Phillips absentmindedly. 'Have you noticed anyone behaving strangely around the place lately? Or anything unusual?'

Fisher ran her hand through her short hair. 'Can't say I have, no.'

'Anyone hanging around?' asked Jones. 'Maybe visiting more regularly?'

'Not that I can think of.'

Jones continued to probe. 'Any customers asking more questions than usual? Odd questions?'

Fisher opened her mouth to speak but appeared to think better of it.

Phillips had spotted it. 'No matter how minor it may have seemed, it might help.'

'Well,' said Fisher. 'There is one old guy who's a bit odd.'

'In what way?' asked Jones.

'He comes in with his dog *a lot*. An old border collie on its last legs. He absolutely dotes on that dog. Then the other week, he started asking questions about what type of anaesthetic we use when we put animals to sleep.'

'And that's unusual, is it?' said Phillips.

'In the main, yeah. For most people, even just thinking of putting their pets down is incredibly upsetting, but this guy was fixated by how we do it.'

Phillips continued. 'You mentioned he's an older man. How old would you say?'

Fisher took a moment to think. 'I dunno, maybe in his late sixties, seventies even.'

Just then Sarah returned, smiling again as she placed a pen-drive on the counter and retook her seat.

Fisher turned towards her. 'How old would you say Mr Olson is?'

Sarah's brow wrinkled. 'Old Henrik? Mid-seventies, I reckon. Why do you ask?'

'I was just explaining that he was in recently asking a lot of questions about how we use anaesthetic to put the animals to sleep.'

'Only because he loves Laddy so much,' replied Sarah.

'Who's Laddy?' Phillips asked.

'His border collie. Loves that old boy.'

'You seem to know a lot about him,' said Jones.

Sarah shrugged. 'He comes in most weeks to buy dry food or pick up Laddy's meds; we usually have a little chat. He's sweet.'

'Do you have an address for him?' said Phillips.

'Sure.' Sarah tapped into her computer, her head tilting to one side as she did.

Phillips couldn't help but stare at the intricate tattoo on her neck: a large heart that surrounded a host of animals including a monkey, a beagle and a rabbit. It was a unique design the like of which Phillips had never seen before.

A moment later Sarah scribbled with her pen before passing over a yellow Post-it Note. 'There you go. He's just around the corner.'

Phillips inspected the note in her hand. 'Well, thank you both very much for your time.'

Fisher shrugged. 'I'm not sure we've been much help.'

'If anything else comes back to you about the break-in,'

Phillips handed her card over, 'or if you can think of anyone else we should talk to, please call me. My mobile's on the bottom.'

Fisher glanced down at the card and nodded. 'I will.'

A couple of minutes later, as Phillips and Jones made their way back across the parking lot, her phone began to ring in her pocket. Pulling it out she could see it was Bov. She flicked it to speaker so Jones could hear. 'How'd you get on?'

'We checked out the Longsight break-in and they do use alfax-alone but none of that was taken. Just steroids and a load of syringes. My guess is they'll have quickly found their way into the local gyms. Probably stolen to order for juicers looking to bulk up.'

'You're probably right,' replied Phillips.

'How about you guys? Find anything?'

'Maybe. A load of alfaxalone was taken when this place was turned over. Apparently, an old boy has been asking a lot of questions, so we'll check it out, but given his age, I'm not sure he'll be capable of overpowering a championship boxer.'

'You never know,' chuckled Bovalino. *'I reckon my nonno could still give me a run for my money – and he's nearly eighty.'*

Phillips smiled. 'Yeah, well, he's just around the corner, so we're going to call in on him now.'

'Ok, Guv. Whistler and I thought we'd best head back and get stuck into the phone records and finances.'

'Good idea. We'll see you back at base this afternoon.' Phillips ended the call and turned to Jones. 'Right. Let's go and see what our poison-obsessed pensioner has to say, shall we?'

11

In a sea of well-presented, gentrified properties, Olson's 1950's detached house appeared to be the odd one out on the salubrious street: dilapidated and in need of major repairs. The metal frames of the single-glazed windows were covered in flaking paint, yellowed by the sun, the front garden overgrown with knee-high grass. Enormous sprawling shrubs blocked half of the lounge window and tall weeds burst from the multitude of cracks that ran the length of the concrete drive.

Phillips stood on the pavement to the front of the house as she took in the scene.

'Charming little place,' said Jones standing next to her, his tone sarcastic.

'Yeah. I bet his neighbours just *love* living next door to him,' she said, then headed for the front door.

A rusted old bell was positioned on the wall next to the door. Evidently it was no longer working, and after a few failed attempts to get a tune out of it, Jones rapped his knuckles on the frosted glass.

After a long pause, someone could be seen moving

towards them on the other side of the door, followed by the sound of a number of locks being released. The door was opened a fraction and an elderly gentleman peered out. 'Can I help you?' His accent was European.

'Mr Olson?' asked Jones.

The man nodded. 'What's this about?'

Jones held his ID in front of the man's face. 'We're from the Major Crimes Unit. Could we have a word?'

Olson stared out at them for a moment without replying. His face was long, with deep wrinkles around the eyes and across his forehead, his greying hair lank and greasy.

'It won't take long,' said Phillips with a soft smile. 'We could just do with your help on something. If you don't mind?'

Finally, Olson relented and opened the door. 'Wipe your feet,' he said, then headed back down the hallway.

Phillips glanced at Jones.

A look of disbelief flashed across his face. 'Wouldn't want to make a mess now, would we?' he muttered as he led them in after Olson.

A minute later, with Olson taking his seat in a battered old armchair next to the fire, Phillips dropped carefully into the only other seat in the room, a black uPVC-covered armchair with a blood-orange coloured nylon cushion. Judging by its styling and overall condition, it was probably close to fifty years old and had likely been the height of fashion in the sixties and seventies. As Jones headed into the kitchen in search of something to sit on, Phillips cast her gaze around the room. Located to the rear of the property, it was evident that this room was where Olson spent much of his time. Old newspapers, books and magazines were piled high on the filthy grey carpet, plates and cups littered every surface, and his old border collie dog lay curled up asleep in a basket next to his feet. The heat from the raging gas fire was stifling in the cramped room.

Just then Jones returned carrying what appeared to be a farmhouse kitchen chair that had seen better days. Plonking it down next to Phillips, he took a seat and, with considerable care, attempted to get comfortable.

'We really appreciate you giving us some of your time, Mr Olson,' said Jones.

'People call me Henrik,' he replied coolly.

Phillips sat forward and smiled as she looked down at the dog. 'And what's his name?' she asked, already knowing the answer.

'Laddy,' said Olson, his accent sharp and angular, which matched his dour demeanour.

'He's a beauty,' replied Phillips. 'How old is he?'

'Fourteen.'

Phillips moved her gaze to Olson. 'That's a good age.'

But Olson appeared in no mood for a chat. 'You said you needed my help. What with?'

'Can you tell us anything about the recent burglary at the Fisher's Veterinary Practice?' asked Phillips.

'Me?' His eyes narrowed. 'Why would I know anything about that?'

'We spoke to Dr Fisher and the receptionist, who told us you're a regular,' said Phillips. 'In buying food and collecting meds.'

'That's correct.'

'Well, we wondered if you'd seen anything strange, or perhaps anyone hanging about around the time of the burglary.'

'It happened on the 28th of January,' Jones added.

'I know when it happened,' Olson spat back. 'It was in the local paper.'

Phillips continued. 'Did you happen to see anything out of place around that time?'

Olson shook his head. 'No. I didn't see anything.'

'Were you aware of what was taken that night?'

Olson shrugged. 'None of my business.'

'Have you ever heard of a drug called alfaxalone?'asked Phillips.

'No.'

'Really?' said Jones. 'Because Dr Fisher said you'd asked a lot of questions about animal anaesthetic recently, and alfaxalone is one of the most common brands used by vets, including Fisher's.'

'Maybe they do, but I don't know anything about it.'

Jones probed further. 'So why were you so interested in animal anaesthetic?'

'That's my business,' replied Olson defiantly.

'That's just it, Henrik,' said Jones. 'It's now become *our* business. A matter for Major Crimes.'

Olson glared at Jones, his jaw clenched, but remained silent.

Jones wasn't letting up. 'So why were you asking so many questions about anaesthetic?'

A snarl flashed onto Olson's top lip. 'None of your business.'

'You must understand how this looks to us, Henrik,' Phillips cut in. 'We hear you've been showing an unusual interest in your vets practice as well as animal anaesthetics, and a few days later, someone breaks into the very same vets and clears them out of alfaxalone. Where were you on the night of the burglary?'

Olson recoiled slightly. 'Me? Why do you need to know where *I* was? I'm not a criminal.'

'In which case you won't mind telling us where you were the night Fisher's vets was burgled,' Jones cut back in.

Olson was incredulous. 'I'm seventy-three years-old! I have never once been in trouble with the police in all my life. Not once. And now you're accusing me of being a thief. In my own home too!'

Phillips raised her hands slightly. 'Look, that's not what we're saying, but we do need to understand why you've been so interested in animal anaesthetics of late.'

Olson took a moment, swallowing hard before he answered. There was genuine sadness in his eyes. 'It was for Laddy. He has an inoperable tumour on his liver.' He leant forward and patted the old dog – who remained sleeping – on the head. 'I wanted to know, when the time comes to say goodbye, how it will be done.'

'I'm sorry to hear that,' said Phillips softly. 'That can't be easy.'

Olson continued. 'I don't want to think of life without Laddy, but I cannot bear to see him suffer either.'

Phillips's mind wandered to her own pet, Floss. 'I have a cat who's been with me for ten years now, through thick and thin. I can understand how hard that must be.'

Olson turned his gaze towards the fire.

Phillips glanced at Jones. Olson was an old man who appeared to be telling the truth. They needed to tread gently. 'Henrik, we're not saying you took the alfaxalone, but we do need to know where you were on the 28th of January. Purely so we can eliminate you from our enquiries and leave you in peace.'

Olson continued to stare into the fire in silence, before eventually turning to look at Phillips. 'I was here. Where I always am.'

'And can anyone vouch for that?'

'No. It was just me and Laddy. Watching TV.'

'Do you remember what you watched?' asked Phillips.

'No. Each night blurs into the next at my age.'

Phillips scrutinised Olsen's face for any movement that might indicate he was lying but he remained unflinching. 'Well, in that case, I think we've taken up enough of your time.' She stepped up from the chair.

Jones took his cue, then carried his chair back into the kitchen.

'Goodbye, Henrik.' Phillips bent down to pat Laddy's head. 'And you look after yourself, sunshine.'

At that moment, Jones returned.

Phillips straightened, then followed Jones towards the front door.

Outside they walked in silence until they reached the car.

'What do you think?' asked Phillips.

Jones glanced in the direction of the house, then pulled his phone from his pocket. After taking a moment to locate what he was looking for, he handed it across. 'Take a look at this.'

Phillips found herself staring at what looked like a photo of an old postcard or small piece of art.

'Recognise that?'

Phillips's eyes narrowed as she focused intently on the screen. 'That's what the receptionist had tattooed on her neck, isn't it?'

Jones nodded.

'Where'd you take this?'

'Olson's kitchen. It's an old flyer that was in a frame on the wall. If you zoom out, you'll see the whole thing.'

Phillips followed the instruction, before taking in the larger image. 'An animal rights protest flyer from 1981?'

'When I saw that tattoo on the girl's neck earlier, I knew I'd seen it before. And as soon as I spotted that on the wall in the kitchen, it all came flooding back.' Jones tapped the image. 'This heart shape here – filled with animals used in lab tests – was on a poster on the wall of a girl I was dating back when I first joined the police. It's the logo of an animal rights group – quite heavy-duty as I recall. She did tell me exactly what it meant – many, many times in fact – but I wasn't really interested so can't remember anymore.'

Phillips raised her eyebrows. 'So what? The old boy was an activist back in the day?'

'May well have been, or at least a sympathizer,' replied Jones. 'Looking at him in there, this may seem like a daft question, but could he be our killer?'

'I wouldn't think he was physically capable.' Phillips turned back to look at the house and noticed the net curtain in the front room move. Olson was obviously watching them. 'That said, if he *was* an activist or sympathiser back in the day, then he may know more about the break-in at the vets than he's letting on. Run a background check on him and see what comes up. Seems as though there's more to this Olson fella than we thought.'

'Sure thing.' Jones deactivated the central locking. 'I'll get Bov onto it as soon as we get back.'

12

H
e found his usual seat at the back of the lecture theatre and dropped into it just in time for the house lights to fade and leave the audience in darkness. Standing under the spotlights on the stage below was the woman he'd come to know very well over the last six months, Dr Juliet Dobson. She was tall and elegant, with pale skin, wavy auburn hair and thick-rimmed spectacles. As the graphic on the large screen behind her stated, she was a practicing psychologist as well as a professor at the University of Manchester – the host for tonight's lecture.

'Good evening, ladies and gentlemen, and thank you for taking the time to join me here.'

He never tired of hearing her speak. Her voice was soft, yet assured, and her elfin face radiated warmth and compassion. He knew from personal experience she was a kind woman devoted to the service and support of others, in particular people suffering with serious mental health issues.

'Tonight, I'd like to give you a glimpse of my ongoing study into the patterns of behaviour displayed by sociopathic prisoners at Manchester's Hawk Green maximum security prison.'

The subject of her lecture was yet another reason why he admired her so much. Stepping into a hell-hole like Hawk Green to sit face to face with some of the country's most evil killers, rapists and paedophiles would be a terrifying prospect – even for the most physically adept men. For a beautiful woman such as her to place herself in that position for the good of the scientific community, it demonstrated the sheer level of courage and strength she possessed.

Dobson continued as the image on the screen behind her changed to an aerial shot of the prison. 'Over the last eighteen months, I have interviewed over thirty Category A inmates at Hawk Green. Each of them has been certified as being either sociopathic or as having sociopathic tendencies. The purpose of the study is to try and determine common patterns of adult behaviour in relation to each individual's childhood experiences, as well as exploring genetic make-up and familial mental health history.'

He was in awe watching her assured delivery on stage. Yet in spite of her effervescent demeanour this evening, *he* knew she was hiding a painful truth from the audience; a secret known only to a select few. Something that would soon see her life change forever.

'For the purpose of the study,' Dobson's voice boomed out from the speakers fixed to the walls of the lecture theatre, 'we split the subjects into three categories: violent offenders, those whose crimes were sexually motivated and those with a history of psychosis...'

As she continued, he relaxed into the chair, closed his eyes and ran the plan over in his mind one last time. He'd been preparing for tonight for many months and now, finally, he was ready to set Juliet free.

An hour later, as the lecture ended, he slipped out of his

seat and headed for the door before the house lights came back on, then made his way across the quadrant and out onto the main road where his car was parked. There was a slight drizzle of rain in the air and a cold wind blowing into his face.

A few minutes later he took shelter in the driver's seat and waited.

Thankfully Juliet Dobson was a creature of habit: parking her car in the same spot each time she delivered one of her evening lectures. She was also very efficient. Tonight was no different and she reached her Toyota Prius within ten minutes of finishing on stage. He watched the indicators flash as the central locking disengaged. A second later, she slipped into the driver's seat and closed the door.

His pulse quickened as he turned on the ignition and waited.

A moment later, as Dobson pulled the car away from the kerb and slipped out into the evening traffic, he followed suit.

Having surveilled her many times over the last few months, he knew her route home to the leafy suburb of Sale well. Again, he was thankful she was a creature of habit. In all the times he'd followed her, she'd never once deviated from this same route.

She was a conscientious driver and could be relied on to always stick to the speed limits, which would make his job a lot easier tonight.

The six-mile journey south from Manchester University to her home in Sale always took between twenty and twenty-six minutes, traffic dependent. Tonight, the roads were relatively clear despite the rain, and they were making good time. As they passed under the M60 motorway, he knew he had only a few minutes remaining before he would need to make his move. His stomach jumped with excitement of what lay ahead.

Like clockwork, as Dobson passed Sale United Football club, she began to slow before turning left onto Dane Road. He copied her and remained at a distance. Not long after, she took another left into Cranfield industrial estate – a shortcut she used each night that took her down what seemed to be a permanently empty road. He matched her speed and found himself directly behind her now – the only two cars in either direction, surrounded by large industrial units long since abandoned for the night.

Up ahead, he could see the traffic lights on red. As a quiet, cut-through road, he knew they would remain that way until a vehicle stopped on the sensors buried in the ground; a fact he was relying on tonight.

Dobson came to a stop about a hundred metres ahead of him and his pulse quickened. For all his planning up to this point, he was relying on the fact that his vehicle was so much bigger than hers, it would still be drivable after impact.

It was now or never.

Pressing his foot to the floor, he began to pick up speed. His heart pounded as he raced towards her. With less than twenty metres between them, he slammed on the brakes, but as planned, it was too little too late. A split-second later he ploughed straight into the back of the Toyota with an almighty crash. Airbags exploded around him as he lurched forwards against the seatbelt before being thrown backwards into the seat as the vehicle came to a shuddering stop. With his ears ringing and the smell of burnt rubber in the air, he took a moment to orientate himself before unclipping the seatbelt and opening the driver's door. As he stepped down, he could see Dobson ahead of him, slumped over the steering wheel of the Toyota, eyes closed, her face resting on the now deflated airbag. He held his breath for a moment fearing the impact had killed her. *Shit shit shit shit shit.* Tentatively he stepped towards her and as he reached the driver's door, yanked it open fearing the worst. But then Dobson opened her eyes and weakly lifted her head from the steering wheel. Her nose was bloodied and split across the bridge and she appeared dazed and confused.

'Oh my God. Are you ok?' he said.

Dobson sat back in the seat and brought her hand to her nose. 'What happened?'

'I'm so sorry. My brakes failed. I couldn't stop.'

She turned to face him now, both lenses of her glasses cracked.

'Jesus! Juliet, I had no idea it was you,' he lied.

Dobson blinked heavily as she tried to focus before a look of recognition flashed across her face. 'I almost didn't recognize you.'

'I'm so sorry, Juliet.'

'What are you doing here?' she asked.

'Don't worry about that. Are you hurt?'

Dobson touched her bloody nose. 'Is it broken?'

'I'm not sure.' Leaning in, he put his arm around her. 'Let's get you into my car and I'll call an ambulance, just to be on the safe side.'

Dobson acquiesced and allowed him to help her out.

'Come on. I've got a handkerchief in the car. We can clean you up a bit.' He guided her slowly towards the passenger side of his car, then opened the door and supported her as she carefully climbed up into the seat.

Dobson winced in pain.

'Wait there,' he said, then headed for the boot. He returned a moment later, a white handkerchief in hand.

'I should call Lee,' said Dobson as she patted her coat in search of her phone.

'Don't worry about that, Juliet,' he said with a smile. 'I'll message him later.'

'No, no. I need to call him.'

'It's fine, Juliet. Trust me. It's all going to be ok from now on.' Grabbing the back of her head with his right hand, he forced the handkerchief over her nose and mouth with his left.

Dobson's muffled screams filled the air as she attempted to fight him off.

'It's time to set you free, my love. A whole new dimension awaits you.'

She continued to struggle.

'No pain. No suffering. Just pure joy.'

As he continued to hold the handkerchief over her mouth, she finally stopped moving and slumped back into the seat. Pulling his hand away, he checked she was still breathing before closing the passenger door and moving quickly round to the driver's side. Scanning his surroundings one last time, he was relieved to see there was no one nearby as he slipped back behind the wheel. Firing the engine, he tentatively reversed away from the battered Prius. His vehicle was still drivable. *Thank God.* Glancing left at Dobson, he allowed himself a smile of satisfaction. All the months of planning had paid off and it had worked. Now it was time for phase two.

13

The freezing February rain was coming in sideways as Phillips stepped out of the Mini. She checked her watch; it was just after 9.45 a.m. Up ahead she could see blue and white police tape covering the entrance to the cemetery, a uniformed officer, as ever, taking on responsibility for standing guard. Pulling up her collar against the weather, she set off towards the crime scene and a moment later spotted Jones walking towards her wearing a full forensic suit. He waved briefly and waited by the tape, before lifting it high enough for her to walk under when she reached it.

'You're going to need to prepare yourself for this one, Guv.' Jones's thin, angular face appeared ashen. 'I'm not ashamed to say I threw up when I saw it.'

Phillips did a double take. 'You mentioned on the phone it's the head this time.'

Jones nodded. 'Come on. I'll take you through.'

Phillips tucked in behind her second in command as he led the way through the myriad ancient headstones that littered the cemetery, some so old they had toppled sideways onto the soft ground.

'Two grave diggers found her at approximately 7 a.m. and called it in,' Jones said over his shoulder. 'Paramedics confirmed life extinct at 8.30, and Evans and his team arrived half an hour ago. They've just started.'

As they turned down the side of the old funeral chapel, Phillips spotted the large white CSI tent about twenty feet away. 'So what's got you so spooked?' she asked as they reached it.

Jones stopped in his tracks and turned to face her. His expression was grave as he handed across her forensic suit. 'Best you see for yourself, boss.'

A couple of minutes later, now dressed in the full CSI garb, Phillips stepped tentatively inside, her phone in hand. For a moment she felt as if she was back at the Ajani Lewis crime scene: pretty much everything looked identical. Evans and his team were hard at work examining the body of a woman laid out on the ground. Like Ajani, she was naked but for a white shawl wrapped around her waist and torso, a ring of white roses arced around her body.

'Take a look at the top of the head, Guv,' said Jones from over her shoulder.

From where she stood, the body seemed to be intact, but when she took a few steps forwards she spotted what Jones was referring to. Suddenly she had to fight her own urge to vomit. 'Jesus!' She winced, turning her head away.

'Brutal, isn't it?'

She took some time to compose herself, then slowly turned back to take another look. Standing over the head now, she could see the top of the skull had been removed and a large cavity indicated where the brain had once been. 'Brutal doesn't even come close.'

'He took her brain. Her brain, Guv!' Jones was clearly struggling to process what had happened.

Evans turned towards them now, his face obscured with a hood and forensic mask. 'It's still early days, Jane, but the similarities to the Lewis murder are incredible. Aside from the mutilation to a different area of the body and the bruising to the face, pretty much everything else is identical. The shawl, the flowers, the staging. And so far, no sign of the brain.'

'Was she moved here like Lewis?'

Evans nodded. 'Yes. No blood around the body and a strong smell of detergent. She was killed elsewhere, cleaned and then placed here, likely about twelve hours ago.'

'Just like Lewis,' said Jones.

Evans continued. 'It was minus five last night, so she's frozen stiff at the moment.'

Phillips squatted and took a couple of pictures of the woman's face on her phone. 'What do you think caused the bruising to the nose?'

'Well, there's bruising to the chest as well. Could indicate an RTA of some kind.'

Phillips stood upright. 'How long before we get the finger-prints, Andy?'

'I'll make it a priority, so the lab will have them on email within the hour.'

'Thanks,' said Phillips. 'And I'm guessing there's no ID or belongings with the body?'

'Nope,' replied Evans. 'Same as last time. Nothing at all, aside from the shawl and flowers.'

Phillips exhaled sharply. 'This is seriously messed up, Jonesy.'

'Totally,' he muttered.

It was Evans's turn to squat now as he pointed to the hem

of the shawl. 'I can't be sure until I get back to the lab but see these discolorations here.'

Phillips followed his pointing finger.

'This looks like the soil we found on Lewis's feet. I'll get it tested as a matter of urgency.'

'Let me know the moment you get the results,' Phillips said.

Evans stood. 'Of course.'

Phillips took a moment to process the scene, then turned to Jones. 'I know I'm stating the obvious, but we seriously need to find this guy before he does it again.'

Outside, the rain had stopped but the temperatures showed no sign of rising. After removing and bagging her SOCO suit, Phillips called the office.

Entwistle was first to pick up. *'MCU, DC Entwistle speaking.'*

'Whistler, it's me.'

'Hey, boss. How's it looking over there?'

'Horrific.'

'Really? Why?'

'Carbon copy of the Ajani Lewis murder, complete with flowers and a shawl, only this time the killer cut off the top of her head and removed her brain.'

'Oh my God,' said Entwistle.

'Yeah. It's not pretty, that's for sure.'

'So, are we looking at a serial killer?'

'Strictly speaking we need *three* bodies to classify it as a serial killer,' said Phillips. 'But there's no doubt in my mind these two murders were committed by the same person, and I have a horrible feeling in my gut this is just the beginning as opposed to the end.'

'So, what do you need us to do?' asked Entwistle.

'Get onto MisPers and see if any women fitting the

description of the body were reported missing in the last week. I'll send a couple of photos of her face.'

'I'm not sure I want to see those, Guv.'

'Just take a deep breath before you open them. And tell Bov to get onto the council and explain the cemetery will be shut for a few days. I know there's a funeral supposed to be happening here this afternoon, but that, and any others lined up, will have to be postponed.'

'We'll sort it,' said Entwistle.

'Thanks. We'll be back in the office in about an hour. We can fully debrief then.'

'Sure thing.'

Phillips ended the call, then turned back to the face the tent, which was now billowing in the wind.

'Still glad to be back?' asked Jones.

Phillips continued to stare at the tent, then shook her head in disbelief. 'This is some weird shit, Jonesy.'

'Twenty-five years I've been doing this, Guv, and I've never seen anything like that.'

'Well, prepare yourself, 'cos I have a feeling this is gonna get a lot worse before it gets better.'

An hour later the team debriefed at their desks.

'I've spoken to the council, boss,' said Bovalino. 'The cemetery is now officially shut, and all funerals are being rearranged or moved as we speak.'

'Thanks, Bov. I know it'll be hard for the families, but we can't have anyone trampling all over the crime scene.'

Entwistle grabbed his pad. 'I checked the MisPers database. A woman who matches the description of the victim was reported missing last night. Juliet Dobson. I checked her out on Facebook and based on the photos you sent over earlier, it's her.'

'Who called it in?' asked Jones.

'Her husband.' Entwistle glanced at his notes. 'Lee Dobson. I also googled her, and it turns out she's a big deal in the world of psychology in the city. She teaches at Manchester University, as well as working with the inmates at Hawk Green.'

'Hawk Green?'

Entwistle nodded.

Phillips took a moment. 'Remind me, did Lewis have any connection to Hawk Green?'

'He did do a bit of time for GBH, but it was a long time ago – probably thirty years or so,' replied Entwistle.

Jones tapped his pen on the desk absentmindedly. 'I wonder if *that's* why the killer took the brain.'

Phillips's eyes narrowed. 'If what is?'

'The fact that Dobson's a psychologist.'

'Go on.'

'Well,' said Jones. 'They call them 'shrinks' in the US, don't they?'

'I never understood that,' added Bovalino.

Jones continued. 'It's because they're *head shrinkers*. Dobson had her head cut open and the brain removed. Could be a connection.'

'Yeah, I guess, potentially, it could,' said Phillips. 'But the real question is, *why* did the killer want her brain?'

Jones shrugged. 'Beats me, I'm afraid. I'm still getting my head round the fact it was missing in the first place.'

Bovalino nodded. 'I must admit. The crime scene looked pretty grisly on the photos.'

'It was, mate,' replied Jones. 'Worse than that in fact. It was bloody horrific.'

Phillips turned to Entwistle. 'Do we have an address for the husband?'

He checked his notes again. 'Eighty-two Roselands Road, Sale.'

'Ok.' Phillips glanced at Jones. 'You and I should head over and break the news.'

He sighed loudly. 'We get all the best jobs.'

'By the way, Guv,' Entwistle cut back in. 'I've been through Lewis's accounts and there's no transactions that specifically link him to Seamus Hernon. That said, AJ did make four cash deposits into his own account of nine-and-half grand each, about six months back. Could that be the forty grand Bernie Sutton claimed AJ borrowed off Hernon?'

'It would certainly fit the timeline,' Phillips replied.

'So why not just pay it all in at once?' asked Bovalino.

'Because you don't have to declare single payments that are under ten thousand pounds,' replied Entwistle. 'Keeps the taxman at bay.'

Phillips sat forward, her elbows resting on the desk. 'We need to see if Hernon was in any way connected to Juliet Dobson.'

Jones's face twisted. 'I can't imagine how she would be. A university lecturer and a loan shark?'

'I'm thinking more about her connections to Hawk Green. Hernon has more than a few associates locked up in that hellhole.'

Entwistle scribbled on his pad. 'I'll do some digging.'

'By the way, Guv,' said Bovalino. 'I looked into your man, Henrik Olson.'

'Anything?' asked Phillips.

'Pretty much as you described him: single, retired and a squeaky-clean record.'

'I thought as much.'

'But I did find one thing of note,' said Bovalino.

'Really? What?'

'Turns out he was a bit of player in the world of animal rights back in the seventies and eighties. One of the top men in an organization called The Blessed Beasts.' He handed over a computer printout. 'This is their official badge.'

Phillips stared down at the image, then held it up so Jones could see it. 'Look familiar?'

He nodded. 'Same as the flyer at Olson's house, as well as the receptionist's tattoo.'

'Ah yes, Sarah Norman,' said Bovalino. 'The rest of Fisher's staff came up clean, but I think it's fair to say Ms Norman has what might be best described as a colourful background.'

'In what way?' asked Phillips.

'Another animal rights activist and also a fully paid-up member of The Blessed Beasts.' Bovalino handed over a second printout, which contained Sarah Norman's police mugshot. 'Has a record for assault on a police officer at an animal rights rally, as well as causing unlawful damage to a lab that tests cosmetics. Both times she was fined and given community hours.'

Phillips stared down at the picture. 'No wonder she was such a fan of Olson.' She looked up again. 'Anything else, guys?'

'Nothing from me,' Entwistle replied.

Bovalino shook his head.

'Right, in that case, Jonesy, let's go see the husband.'

Jones nodded as he stood up and grabbed his coat.

'Remember, this is another murder that has real potential to blow up in the press.' Phillips cast her gaze between each of the team. 'So we need to be careful. Not a word of this leaves MCU for the time being. Ok?'

Each of the men nodded.

'And if anyone starts asking questions, just send them to me.' Phillips stood and pulled on her coat as Jones grabbed his car keys.

15

'Have you found her?' blurted Lee Dobson as he opened the door to Phillips and Jones.

'It's probably better if we talk inside, Mr Dobson,' said Phillips softly.

Dobson's unshaven face was gaunt and ashen with worry, his eyes framed with dark shadows, most likely from lack of sleep. He swallowed hard then stepped back inside the house.

A few minutes later, in an all too familiar scene, Phillips took a seat in the lounge with Jones at her side.

Dobson was in the armchair opposite them. He was unusually skinny, with long limbs and wispy dark hair.

'We understand you reported your wife missing last night,' said Phillips.

Dobson nodded. 'She was due home at about nine, but never came back.'

Phillips shifted in her seat. She hated this part. 'I'm sorry to tell you this, but we found a woman's body this morning and we believe it to be that of your wife.'

Dobson said nothing for a long moment, then closed his

eyes and dropped his head into his hands as he began to wail like a small child.

Phillips exchanged an awkward glance with Jones before placing her hand on Dobson's knee. 'I'm so sorry.'

Dobson was inconsolable and for the next few minutes cried uncontrollably.

Jones headed into the kitchen and returned a few moments later with a box of tissues.

Eventually Dobson's tears subsided. After wiping his eyes and blowing his nose, he sat quietly in the chair, shock etched across his face. 'How did she die?' he asked weakly.

'At this stage we can't say for certain, but we believe she could have been murdered,' said Phillips.

'Murdered?' Dobson placed his fingers against his open mouth. 'Why would anyone want to kill Jules?'

'We don't know, but we intend to find out.'

'I can't believe this is happening,' Dobson muttered.

Phillips changed tack. 'When did you last see your wife?'

'Yesterday morning.'

'You said she was due home at nine last night,' said Phillips. 'Where had she been?'

'She was giving an open lecture at the university. She did one every month as part of her professorship.'

'Had you tried calling her when she didn't come home?' asked Jones.

'Yes, but it went straight to voicemail, which wasn't like her. At first, I figured she may have gone for a drink after the lecture, so I called some of her friends from work, but they said she left straight after she'd finished the talk, which started me panicking. I tried a few more of her friends to see if she'd called in to see them on the way home, but there was no sign of her. When she wasn't back by midnight, I called you lot, but they said she needed to be missing for twenty-four hours before they could send anyone out.'

'Standard procedure, I'm afraid,' said Jones.

'I was beside myself with worry. I just didn't know what else to do. And then around 2 a.m. she sent me a text, which was a huge relief. But then when I tried calling her, it went straight to voicemail again.'

'Text?' Phillips glanced at Jones. 'What did it say?'

Dobson pulled his phone from his pocket and took a moment to locate the message, which he then read aloud. '"My wonderful Lee. Take comfort from the fact that my knowledge is a gift from God that needs to be shared before it's too late".'

Phillips pursed her lips. 'Do you know what she meant by that?'

'No. It made no sense, and I really couldn't understand why she wasn't answering. I just wanted to talk to her. I did wonder if she was having a bit of a moment after everything that's happened lately, maybe taking some time out to think and clear her mind a bit. God knows I wouldn't have blamed her if she did.'

'Clear her mind of what exactly?' asked Jones.

Dobson exhaled sharply. 'Jules had recently been diagnosed with breast cancer.'

'That must have come as a shock to you both.'

'It did. Especially as her mum died of the same thing about ten years ago. Jules knew how she could potentially end up. She was terrified.'

'You said you thought she might have taken some time to clear her head. Had she done that before?' asked Jones.

'Once or twice, not long after the initial diagnosis, but she always let me know where she was and what she was doing.'

Phillips scrutinised his face for a long moment before changing tack again. 'Did your wife have anything to do with a man called Seamus Hernon?'

Dobson took a moment before answering. 'Not that I know of. I certainly don't recognise the name.'

'We understand that Juliet also worked with the inmates at Hawk Green,' said Jones.

'That's right, yes. She was there every Tuesday.'

Jones continued. 'Did she ever mention any of the inmates to you? Anyone maybe she was worried about?'

'No. Not at all.'

'So, nobody ever made threats against her?' Phillips cut back in.

Dobson shook his head. 'Not that she said, but she rarely talked about her work at the prison. As much as she saw the value in studying the inmates, I wouldn't say she really enjoyed it. It was more of a necessity to further her work at the university.'

'Yeah,' said Phillips. 'I'm not sure I'd want to spend too much time with the guys in Hawk Green either.'

'It did worry me, so I tried not to think about it, to be honest.'

'How was your wife getting back from the lecture?' Phillips asked.

'Driving.'

'What type of car did she have?'

'A Toyota Prius,' replied Dobson. 'Was it not with her when you found her?'

'No. I'm afraid it wasn't,' said Phillips.

'Do you know the registration?' Jones asked.

'Sure. It's K-L-nineteen-O-V-T.'

Jones made a note in his pad. 'And what colour was it?'

'Silver.'

Jones continued scribbling.

'I'm sorry to have to ask this, Mr Dobson,' said Phillips.

'Please, call me Lee.'

Phillips nodded. 'Lee. Like I say, I'm sorry to ask this but I'm afraid we must. Where were *you* last night?'

'Me?' Dobson recoiled. 'You don't think I had anything to do with it, do you?'

'It's purely routine,' Phillips replied.

'Er, well, I was here, working.'

'Can anyone vouch for that?'

'I don't think so. I was here on my own putting the finishing touches to a set of plans for my firm's latest project.'

'And what do you do for a living?' asked Jones.

'I'm a civil engineer with GLC Construction. We've just won the contract to extend the width of Regent Road in Salford.'

'Really?' Phillips's interest was piqued. 'That sounds like a big job.'

'Yeah, and a logistical nightmare trying to keep the traffic moving while the work is happening.'

'Do you know who's managing the groundworks on that?' said Phillips.

'Not yet. It's out to tender currently.'

'I see. Would Hernon Groundworks have put in for the job?'

Dobson took a moment to think before replying. 'Doesn't ring any bells, but then I don't manage the tenders; the contracts manager does that. It's possible they may have been added this week while I've been at home. Why do you ask?'

'Just a thought, really,' said Phillips. 'Out of interest, who's the contracts manager at GLC?'

'Kim Blackwood. She's only just joined the firm in the last couple of months. Came to us from McAlpine's.'

Jones made another note.

Phillips smiled softly. 'Again, I'm sorry to ask, Lee, but we're going to need someone to formally identify Juliet. Is that something you feel up to doing in the next day or so?'

Dobson remained silent for a few seconds, then nodded.

'We'll organise a family liaison officer for you. They'll help make the arrangements and support you over the course of the investigation.'

Dobson stared at the floor. 'I just can't believe she's gone.'

Phillips reached across and placed her hand on his wrist. 'Is there anyone you can call to come over?'

'My brother. He lives about ten minutes away and works from home.'

'Would you like us to wait with you until he gets here?'

Dobson wiped his nose with a fresh tissue. 'No. I'll be fine.'

'Ok. Well, in that case, we'll leave you to it.' Phillips handed over her card and stood up from the sofa. 'Call me if anything comes back to you about last night, or you think of anything that might be of use.'

Dobson nodded but remained seated as they headed for the front door.

Outside, the winter weather continued as the rain poured down.

'Let's get out of this stuff,' said Phillips as she pulled up her collar and rushed towards the squad car. A few moments later they dropped simultaneously into their seats and slammed the doors shut behind them.

'God, I love the weather in Manchester,' said Jones sarcastically. 'So, what do you think, boss?'

Phillips exhaled sharply. 'The text messages to the victims' partners are a puzzle. Based on the provisional time of death, Juliet was long dead by the time Lee received her message, so it must have come from the killer. And if that *is* the case, it's highly likely the message sent to Lewis's wife was from them as well.'

'Which is pretty bloody sick when you think about it – I

mean, sending messages from the dead.' Jones fired the ignition. 'Who *does* that?'

'The same kind of sick individual who cuts off the top of a woman's skull and steals her brain.' Phillips pulled out her phone and clicked on the number in her favourites.

The call connected through the dashboard and a moment later Entwistle's voice boomed out through the car's speakers. *'Guv. How did it go?'*

'As well as can be expected, I guess. Listen, we need to find the victim's car. It's likely she was driving it home when she went missing. You're looking for a silver Toyota Prius.'

'What's the reg?'

Jones pulled out his notepad and flicked to the relevant page. 'Kilo-lima-one-nine-oscar-victor-tango.'

They could hear Entwistle typing into his laptop at the other end. *'I'll get it circulated as a matter of urgency.'*

'Thanks,' said Phillips. 'Any updates on whether Dobson was connected to Hernon?'

'Nothing so far, but I've still got a few more avenues to try.'

'Ok, keep us posted.'

'Will do, boss.'

Phillips ended the call.

'So, where to now?' asked Jones as he put the car in gear.

'Back to base, I guess. I need to update Carter. He's going to be over the moon when he finds out we've got a serial killer on the loose who's stealing body parts.'

As Jones pulled the car away from the kerb, he glanced at Phillips. 'Which is yet another reason why I'm sooo glad you're back, Guv. *Rather you than me.*'

16

As expected during their debrief, Chief Superintendent Carter had been more than a little concerned about the discovery of a second body that morning. However, unlike his predecessor, Fox – who was now chief constable – he had immediately offered his full support to Phillips and the rest of the MCU team. It made all the difference having a boss she could trust to have her back no matter how bad things got. Her job was hard enough on an hourly basis without having to deal with the petty politics rife amongst the GMP's senior management.

Now back at her desk, she began the arduous task of updating the decision logs on Juliet Dobson's case.

An hour later, her mobile began to vibrate on the desk. Checking the screen, she could see Don Townsend was calling. Her heart sank. He never called without good reason. 'Don,' she answered.

'Hi, Jane. Any updates on the cause of death for AJ Lewis?'

'Get straight to the point, why don't you?' she replied sarcastically.

'Sorry, it's just I'm chasing a deadline.'

'You always are.'

'So, have you got anything you can tell me? Or am I going to have to make something up?'

Phillips let out a silent breath and reclined in the chair. 'If I tell you, can you promise me you'll treat the information responsibly?'

Townsend chuckled. *'I'm a reporter, Jane. I never make promises, but I'll do my best to be fair and balanced.'*

Phillips remained silent for a moment as she considered the options: tell him the truth and hope he delivered a measured piece or leave him in the dark and wait for the inevitable sensational headlines to land. Reluctantly, she decided to let him in on what she knew. 'Where are you now?'

'In the office.'

She checked her watch. It was approaching 3 p.m. If she could stall him a few hours longer, she could potentially buy herself another day until the story hit the newsstands. There was nothing she could do to stop it going digital before then, of course, but anything that reduced the overall impact had to be a good thing. It also gave her time to let Carter know it was coming.

'Fancy a drink after work?'

'Only if it's served with a large measure of information on our dead boxer.'

'It could be, but it has to be face to face,' said Phillips.

'Really? Sounds juicy.'

'That's the last thing I need it to be, Don.'

'So where do you want to meet and when?'

'How about Dukes 92 at six?'

'That works. I'll see you then. Looking forward to it.'

Phillips ended the call and placed her phone gently back on the desk. Her stomach was turning now in anticipation of the meeting. She really didn't want Townsend crawling all over the case, but she knew she had no choice. Onside, he could be a powerful ally; offside, he would make her job twice as hard. She picked up the landline and dialled Carter's office.

'*Chief superintendent Carter's office,*' said Cook.

'Hi, Di. It's Jane. Is he free at all?'

'*Back so soon?*'

'Yeah. Something's come up he needs to know about.'

'*He's in a meeting at the moment but it's scheduled to finish at five. Would you like me to book you in after that?*'

'Yeah, that'd be great.'

'*No problem.*'

'Thanks, Di.'

Phillips replaced the receiver and stared down at the decision logs on her desk. She still had an awful lot of information to record, but at that moment, little motivation to do it. Stepping up from the chair, she walked over to the window and took in the view. The sun was already starting to fade, and it looked set to be another miserable February night. As the trees bowed in the wind, her mind was drawn to images of Lewis's and Dobson's bodies. Each of them so carefully posed, wrapped in white shawls, and surrounded by roses. What did it all mean and why had the killer removed their organs? The frustrating truth was she really had no idea. Whichever way she looked at it, it made no sense at all. She also had a nagging feeling in her gut that the killer was a long way from finished – a thought that terrified her.

'CAN YOU TRUST HIM?' asked Carter, his face etched with concern.

Phillips shrugged. 'I don't really think I have a choice, sir. Once Townsend gets wind of a story such as this, he's like a dog with a bone, plus he has sources everywhere. In my experience it's much better to keep him close where I can at least try to influence what he writes, as opposed to letting his imagination run free. And besides, after what happened to Victoria Carpenter, he owes me, so I think I can manage him.'

'Carpenter was his girlfriend, wasn't she?'

'Yeah. Murdered and made to look like a suicide. Before your time.'

Carter ran his fingers through his thick salt and pepper hair. 'What a city we live in, hey?'

Phillips nodded. 'So, are you happy for me to give him what we have so far, sir?'

'Like you say, I'm not sure we have much choice. If he's as tenacious and connected as you say he is, he'll get the story one way or the other. We might as well try and at least control the narrative.'

'And what about Fox?'

'Well, she'll need to be briefed and I'm sure she won't like it, but that's nothing new.' Carter exhaled sharply. 'Anyway, that's my problem, not yours.'

'Thank you, sir,' Phillips replied. 'And how do you want me to play it if he asks about Dobson?'

Carter frowned. 'That case isn't public knowledge yet, it is?'

'No, but like I say, Townsend has sources everywhere. I wouldn't be surprised if he already knows about it.'

'Has the husband ID'ed the body yet?'

'No, sir, that's tomorrow morning.'

'Well, in that case, there's nothing to tell him.'

'Understood,' said Phillips.

'So what time are you due to meet him?'

'Six.' Phillips glanced at her watch. It was 5.15 p.m. 'So I'd better get going. I don't want to be late.'

'Of course,' said Carter. 'You get yourself away.'

Phillips stood up from the chair.

'You'll let me know how it goes, won't you?'

'Of course, sir.'

'Right, then.' Carter rolled his chair back and stood. 'I'll follow you out. I really should update Fox about your meeting with Townsend, just in case he sticks anything online tonight.'

Phillips smiled softly. 'She's not going to like it, is she?'

'I very much doubt it.'

'Sorry, sir.'

Carter chuckled as he walked around the desk. 'Sometimes I just *love* my job.'

'I can imagine,' said Phillips then led the way out.

———

If ever there was an example of someone who looked like he spent his days snooping into other peoples' lives, it was Don Townsend: dark hair slicked back against his head, and tanned face thick with wrinkles thanks to his forty-a-day habit.

As Phillips approached the booth he was sitting in, he looked up and cracked a wicked grin. 'Here she is.'

'Don.' Phillips slid into the seat opposite him. 'I see you've started without me.'

Townsend drained the glass in his hand before placing it on the table. 'It's on expenses, so why not?'

'Can I get you another one?'

Townsend nodded. 'Single-malt, straight up.'

'Double, I take it?'

Townsend's grin returned, exposing his yellowing teeth. 'You know me too well, Jane.'

Phillips made her way to the bar, which was unusually

quiet for the time of day, returning a few minutes later with a whisky for Townsend and a white wine spritzer for her.

'So, what's so juicy I have to hear it face to face?' asked Townsend before taking a swig.

'I thought you'd already know, to be honest. What with your spies everywhere.'

'*You* call them spies. I call them *eyes*,' replied Townsend.

'Where do you get your information from, Don?'

Townsend smiled as he shook his head. 'Come on, Jane. You know I can't reveal my sources.'

Phillips eyed him for a long moment. 'Well, you didn't hear it from any of my guys, so it has to have come from either uniform on the scene, the paramedics who attended or someone in the forensic team.'

'For the sake of journalistic integrity, my lips are sealed.'

'Well, whoever it is, you can tell them from *me*, when I catch them, I'm gonna have their job.'

Townsend took another drink. 'I'm guessing you didn't ask me here just to make threats. So, what do you have for me on Lewis?'

Phillips sipped her spritzer as she glanced left and right to ensure no one was listening. 'I'm trusting you to be sensible with this information, Don.'

'Always,' said Townsend.

'Yeah?' scoffed Phillips. 'If only that were true.'

'So come on, stop teasing. What happened to him?'

Phillips placed her drink on the table. 'You were right when you said it was suspicious.'

Townsend's eyes lit up. 'Murder?'

Phillips exhaled sharply. 'Yes.'

'How?'

'I can't say.'

'Can't or won't?'

'Look, Don. You know as well as I do that this information is incredibly sensitive not only from a legal standpoint, but also for the families involved. You of all people should understand that.'

A fleeting sadness flashed in Townsend's eyes.

Phillips decided to take full advantage of it. 'Remember how *you* felt when the nationals reported Vicky's murder?'

Townsend took a slug of his whisky.

'That's why I'm asking you to act responsibly on this one, Don.'

He remained silent for a long moment and appeared deep in thought. 'I know and appreciate what you did for Vicky, but I can't live in the past forever, Jane. It's time to move on. Time to get back to the old me.'

'And what does the *old you* look like, exactly? Doorstepping bereaved families just to get the scoop?'

Townsend shrugged. 'If needs be, yeah.'

Phillips shook her head.

'Look, the reality is, this story will write itself.' Townsend sculled his remaining whisky. 'Former champion boxer is found murdered in a churchyard. This is huge, it's fucking *dynamite.*'

Phillips dropped her chin to her chest. She knew he was right, but she wished to God he wasn't.

'Look,' said Townsend softly. 'I'll do you a deal. You make sure I hear any developments before anyone else in the press, and I'll report *only* the facts. No spin or hyperbole, just the truth.'

Phillips lifted her head and locked eyes with him. It was the best she was going to get out of him right now. 'Ok.'

A broad smile spread across Townsend's face as he picked up his empty glass. 'Can I get you a refill?'

Phillips glanced at her drink. She'd hardly made a dent in it. 'No, thanks. In fact, I really should be going.'

'Suit yourself.' Townsend shuffled sideways as he made his way out of the booth.

'One more thing.'

'Yeah. What's that?'

'When are you going to publish this?' asked Phillips. 'I need to make sure my boss knows when it's coming.'

'Tomorrow first edition, after lunch,' replied Townsend.

'Nothing digital before then?'

Townsend shook his head. 'Not a chance. My editor will want this to land across all platforms at the same time, and for good reason. With Lewis's profile in boxing, it'll be in the nationals the next day. You know that, right?'

'I figured as much,' said Phillips.

Townsend looked like the cat that got the cream.

'Look, Don, I should get home. It's been a long day.'

'You sure I can't tempt you to another?'

'No,' said Phillips as she slipped out of the booth.

Townsend clapped his hands together. 'I can see the headlines now...'

Phillips placed her hand on his wrist. 'Please, Don. Try and manage how this rolls out. For me? Remember, we go back a long way.'

'I'll do my best, Jane,' replied Townsend. 'But like I say, the facts alone are dynamite.'

Phillips eyed him for a moment. 'Enjoy your expenses.'

Townsend toasted her with his empty glass, then headed for the bar, an obvious spring in his step.

Phillips turned away. If she'd been worried about the potential for the story to make headlines *before* meeting with Townsend, now she was absolutely terrified.

17

He opened the freezer door and carefully removed the two plastic containers from the otherwise empty shelves, before carefully carrying them across the room to the large, polished metal table where he placed them side by side. His pulse quickened as he pulled off the lid of the first container and stared down at the frozen heart stored within. It was truly magnificent, and a stark reminder of the abject beauty hidden within the human body – something most people were completely unaware of, but not him. He could not have appreciated it more. Reaching inside with his latex-gloved hand, he lifted out the heart and allowed it to rest upon the palms of both hands as he closed his eyes and quietened his mind. It felt cold against his gloves, but he could almost feel the life that had coursed through its ventricles and atria, the courage it had once contained in life. Courage that now would never end and instead live on to eternity. His chest swelled as he imagined the strength he himself would soon possess. It was the kind of strength and courage he had never known before but was now relying on to fulfil his destiny in the dark days ahead.

Feeling deeply that emotion for the next few minutes, he eventually opened his eyes and cast his gaze upon the frozen heart still balanced across his palms. He smiled before carefully returning it to the container and replacing the lid.

Next, he opened the second box, which contained the frozen brain of Dr Juliet Dobson. Following the same ritual, he gently removed it from the container and once again allowed it to sit across his gloved palms. In its current icy form, it felt almost twice as heavy as when he had removed it from her skull late last night. To him Juliet's brain represented the unparalleled perfection of nature: the gracious curves, crevices and folds that combined to create the most powerful organ of the human anatomy. He closed his eyes for a second time as images of the beautiful doctor flashed across his mind's eye – an amazing woman who had sacrificed so much for the good of others. Soon her ultimate sacrifice would carry her into the next realm, all-seeing, all-knowing and *all-powerful*. Suddenly the palms of his hands began to feel warm, as if Juliet's brain was returning to life and somehow connected to his soul. It was a tantalising thought, but one that would have to wait.

Reluctantly, he placed the brain back in its container and, along with the heart, returned it to the freezer. Taking one last wistful glance at his treasures, he closed the door and removed his gloves, which he tossed in the pedal bin before wandering over to the window.

Outside, the night sky was black and the crescent moon appeared to glow in the darkness. Suddenly he felt a sense of impatience gnawing at his gut, a primal desire to take his next step on the journey to a new form and a new beginning. Keeping his eyes locked on the ruffled surface of the moon, he was reminded of his place in this wondrous process. His duty was to follow the ancient teaching, not to circumnavigate it based on his own flawed human desires. His time would come, he told himself, but for now there was more work to be done and not long left in which to do it.

18

A t 8 a.m. Friday, Phillips and the team gathered in her office for their early morning briefing. Bovalino had provided hot drinks and each of them nursed their steaming cups as Phillips opened the case files on her desk.

'Right, where are we at?'

Entwistle was first up. 'Dobson's car was logged on the system late last night. Apparently, it was reported abandoned on Cranfield industrial estate in Sale around mid-morning yesterday.'

'So how come it took so long to show up on the database? She was killed on Wednesday.' Jones said.

'The uniform team who reported it were behind on their paperwork, or so I'm told,' replied Entwistle.

'Doesn't surprise me,' said Bovalino. 'Thanks to Fox's budget cuts, there's too many incidents and not enough coppers to deal with them.'

'Was it burnt out like Lewis's van?' asked Phillips.

Entwistle shook his head. 'Thankfully, no, but it *had* been in an accident; rear ended by the sounds of it. It's a modern car so the crumple zones had done their job, meaning the back end was almost half the normal size.'

Phillips nodded. 'So where's the car now?'

'On its way to Forensics for analysis.'

'Good,' replied Phillips. 'We might finally get some trace evidence we can work with. Tell Evans I want any updates the moment he has them.'

'Will do, Guv.'

Phillips turned her attention to Bovalino now. 'The way the bodies were posed is very particular and potentially ritualistic. We need to know if there's ever been anything like them before, either in Manchester or the rest of the UK.'

'I'll get onto the NCD as soon as we've finished up here,' replied the big man, referring to the National Crime Database.

'And if that doesn't come up with anything, get online and see if this sort of thing might have happened anywhere else in the world. Thanks to the internet, today's psychos can take their inspiration from the four corners of the globe.'

'Will do, boss.'

'Who do we know at Hawk Green?'

'Tracy O'Connor,' said Jones. 'She was a DS in Serious Crimes until she retired last year. Moved over to the prison service not long after.'

'Great. Find out if she had any dealings with Dobson. See if there are any prisoners we should be taking a closer look at. Just 'cos they're locked up in there, it doesn't mean they can't order a hit out here.'

'Will do, Guv.'

Phillips turned her attention back to the whole team. 'Also, just so you're aware, I met with Don Townsend from the MEN last night.'

'How did that go?' asked Jones.

Phillips reclined in her seat and folded her arms across her chest. 'As well as can be expected, I guess. He promised to behave himself and only write the facts, but you never know with Townsend. He does love to spin a yarn.'

Entwistle frowned. 'You met with him *last night?*'

'Yeah. Why, what's up?'

'I have the MEN app on my phone and haven't seen anything this morning. Certainly nothing in the notifications.'

'And you won't. Not until this afternoon. Townsend claimed the story will land in the first edition after lunch. According to him, the fact that AJ Lewis has been murdered is such a big story they'll push it out across all channels at the same time. He also thinks the nationals will be on it too, so we can expect calls from all sorts of media outlets today.'

'Great. That's all we need,' said Jones.

Phillips waved him away. 'Don't get involved. Just refer them to Rupert Dudley in the press team. That's his job.'

Each of the men nodded.

'But one thing we can't ignore is Fox,' said Phillips. 'We all know how much she hates negative press, so we can expect the pressure to find the killer to kick up a notch as soon as the story lands. No doubt *yours truly* will be hauled over the coals for speaking to Townsend in the first place.'

Entwistle shifted his position. 'I did wonder about that, Guv.'

'Wonder about what?'

'Why you shared the case with him. I mean, he's not exactly a friend of the force, is he?'

'No, he's not, but he *is* the type of journalist who likes to feel important. By giving him the story first, he gets to play the big man over at the MEN. That gives me some bargaining power over what he prints. If he'd found out through the press wires, his nose would have been well out of joint. And – as Jones has experienced in the last nine months – he'd have made sure we paid the price for it in whatever piece he ended up writing.'

Entwistle nodded. 'Enemies close and all that.'

'Exactly. Plus, I gave him nothing more than the fact that Lewis was murdered. None of the details.' Phillips clapped her hands. 'Right, if there's nothing else, let's get to it.'

As the team filed out of her office, Phillips took a sip of coffee and gazed at the images laid out on her desk, of Lewis's and Dobson's mutilated bodies. Who on earth would want to do something like this and *why*? For what possible reason had the killer removed their organs? Placing her cup down, she opened her laptop and pulled up the decision logs for each case, both of which needed updating. With a somewhat heavy heart, she began typing.

It was approaching midday by the time she finally finished her paperwork. It really was the curse of any detective. In many ways she wished she could just crack on and find the killer without having to report what she was doing at every step, but the reality was the decision logs were a valuable evidential tool and had saved her arse – and her career for that matter – on more than one occasion.

Feeling the strain of typing for so long across her shoulders, she pushed back her chair and stood, before wandering over to the window. The day outside was typical of February in Manchester. Dark grey skies threatened rain, and a swirling wind dragged leaves and litter across the car park below. 'What are you not seeing, Jane?' she whispered to herself.

She continued to stare at the parked cars below for the next few minutes as her mind replayed the events of the case so far. The last potentially ritualistic case like this she'd investigated had been the serial killer copycat murders a couple of years ago. Back then, she thought she'd never see anything so depraved again. Clearly, she had been wrong. Suddenly she had an idea. Walking back to her desk, she picked up her phone and scrolled through her contacts until she found what she was looking for. She pressed dial and waited.

A few rings later, it was answered. *'Jane. Well, this is nice surprise.'* The woman at the other end had a soft voice, her accent posh north-east. *'Harry told me you were back on the job. How's it going?'*

'First week back and already up against it.'

'The life of a homicide detective, hey?'

'Yeah. Look, Siobhan, I hope you don't mind but I could really do with your help on something.'

Dr Siobhan Harris, the criminal psychologist and profiler who had helped MCU catch the copycat killer a few years back, was based in Newcastle but had been seconded to support the team, having previously worked with Chief Superintendent Carter during his time in the north-east.

'If I can, I will. What do you need?'

'I'm working on a very strange case I've not seen before.'

'Strange? In what way?'

'Two victims – one IC3 male, the other IC1 female. So far as we can see, they're unconnected to each other but both were murdered in exactly the same way, having been given a large dose of animal anaesthetic.'

'That is strange,' said Harris.

'It gets worse. The male had his heart removed post-mortem, and the killer cut out the female's brain. Not only that, but he also took the organs with him.'

'Wow.'

'Plus, each of the victims was found lying in a churchyard and cemetery respectively. Both naked but for a white shawl wrapped around their torsos and genitals. They were also surrounded by rings of white roses.'

'*Sounds ritualistic the way you describe it.*'

'That's what I'm thinking,' said Phillips. 'Have you ever come across anything like this before?'

Harris exhaled sharply. '*No, I can't say I have.*'

Suddenly Phillips could hear seagulls cawing in the background. 'I'm sorry, Siobhan. Have I called you at a bad time? You sound like you're at the beach.'

Harris chuckled. '*Not at all. I'm working from home today and my balcony door is open. I live by the river, in the centre of the city.*'

'Ah right.'

'*Well, I have to say, I'm intrigued, Jane.*'

'I'm at a total loss as to motive on this one,' replied Phillips.

'*Are you asking for my help in an official capacity or is this off the books?*'

'Off the books for now, but if this guy strikes again, I may need you back here full time for a while.'

'*Ok,*' said Harris. '*Send me through everything you have so far and I'll take a look at them over the weekend. See what jumps out.*'

Phillips felt a massive sense of relief. 'You're a life saver.'

'*I can't promise anything, but I'll see what I can do.*'

'Thanks, Siobhan. I'll send them through now.'

'*No worries,*' replied Harris. '*Look, I'd better go. I have another call coming in.*'

Ending the call, Phillips dropped into her chair, and for the next few minutes pulled together all the case files and photos they had gathered to date into one folder, which she emailed over to Harris.

Just then, Carter stepped into her office, his expression grave. 'Have you seen the lunchtime edition of the MEN?'

'No, sir. I've had my head in paperwork all morning.'

'Same here, but Fox has, and she wants to see *you and me* next.'

'Oh shit.' Phillips's heart sank.

'Come on. Let's get it over with,' said Carter before turning and walking out.

19

T he door to Chief Constable Fox's office was already open when Carter led the way past her assistant, Ms Blair, a middle-aged woman who seemed to be constantly sneering and permanently pissed off.

Fox was seated at her desk, head down, reading the paper laid out on it. Her hair had been recently dyed blond and her skin appeared overtly tanned, as usual. As Carter and Phillips filed in and took their seats opposite her, she didn't look up and instead continued to stare at the paper in front of her. The room fell silent for at least a minute – it was an old-school management technique Fox regularly adopted to make people feel as uncomfortable as possible. It was working to great effect this afternoon, Phillips thought.

Finally, Fox looked up from the paper and stared at Phillips through the half-rimmed glasses perched on the end of her nose. 'Have you seen this *garbage*?'

'No, ma'am, I haven't.'

Fox lifted up the paper in both hands so the front page was facing Phillips and Carter. She narrated the headline. '"Ring o' ring o' roses, a churchyard full of death!"'

Phillips did a double take. *What the hell?*

'How does Don Townsend know the inner details of the case?' demanded Fox.

'He doesn't...' Phillips glanced at Carter. '...I mean he shouldn't.'

'Is this why we went to all the trouble of bringing you back, Jane? It's not even been a week and you're already causing me major problems with the top brass.'

'I understand your frustration, but I didn't give him that information, ma'am.'

'Really? Didn't you meet with him last night to brief him on the case?'

'Well, yes, but all I told him was that Lewis was murdered.'

Fox threw the newspaper onto the desk. 'So how the hell's he got this? The hashtag *boxing ring of death* is trending on Twitter as we speak!'

Phillips shook her head. 'He must have someone on the inside, ma'am.'

'What? You mean a mole? In MCU?'

'No, absolutely not. But it *was* a busy crime scene. There were a lot of different agencies on site that morning. He could be getting his information from any one of them.'

A snarl appeared on Fox's top lip. 'Well, now you've got two people to track down, haven't you? The killer...' she tapped the newspaper with her index finger. '...and whoever is sharing this tripe!'

Phillips's anger at Townsend was boiling on the inside. 'Yes, ma'am.'

'The police and crime commissioner has already been on the phone asking me what the fuck is going on. If he ever finds out someone on the inside is responsible for this, heads will roll. I can promise you that.'

Despite an overwhelming urge to defend herself and her

team, Phillips decided the best option right now was to say nothing.

Fox continued. 'As of now, all MCU leave is cancelled, and that includes *this weekend*. We need to be seen to be doing everything we can to catch this guy.'

Phillips and Carter exchanged a fleeting glance.

'Do I make myself clear?' Fox rasped.

Phillips nodded. 'Crystal, ma'am.'

'Absolutely,' said Carter.

'You'll need to do a piece to camera for the press, Harry,' said Fox.

Carter cleared his throat. 'Of course.'

'Sooner the better. We need to get out in front of this. See if we can wrestle back some control.'

'I'll speak to Rupert Dudley as soon as we're finished here,' said Carter.

Fox nodded and handed her copy of the newspaper to Phillips. 'You can keep this, as a reminder of the stakes involved.'

Phillips accepted it without reply.

'Right. Well, you've a lot of ground to make up, so you'd better get to work, hadn't you?'

'Yes, ma'am,' said Phillips as she stood.

Carter followed her lead and they headed for the door.

'One more thing, Jane,' said Fox.

Phillips stopped in her tracks and turned to face the chief constable.

'Stay the hell away from Don Townsend from now on. Ok?'

'Of course, ma'am,' replied Phillips, then walked out of the room.

BACK DOWNSTAIRS, Phillips took a seat at the spare desk and broke the news to the team that they would now be working the weekend.

'I knew this was going to happen.' Bovalino dropped his pen heavily on his pad and folded his arms. 'I was supposed to be doing the Cumbrian Rally tomorrow. I've been preparing for it for months. Fabio will be well pissed off.'

Phillips understood how much the weekend rallying meets meant to Bov and his co-driver cousin, which only made her feel even more anger towards Townsend.

'Sarah wanted us to take the girls to the cinema tomorrow afternoon,' said Jones.

Phillips turned to face him. 'Do you want me to speak to her and explain?'

He waved her away. 'Don't be daft. She can go on her own. It's not a big deal.'

'So, what plans did you have this weekend, Whistler?' asked Phillips.

Entwistle sighed and linked his fingers round the back of his head. 'I had a lunch date tomorrow with the new girl that's started in the press team.'

'The tall blond one?' asked Bovalino.

'That's the one.'

'God, you don't mess about, do you?' replied the big Italian. 'She only started on Monday.'

A wide grin spread across Entwistle's face. 'What can I say? I like to do things quickly.'

'I hope you don't do *everything* quickly,' Jones shot back drawing laughter from the room.

Phillips got up from the chair. 'Right, well, I am sorry your weekends have been cancelled, and I will make it up to you at some point, I promise. If it's any consolation, Adam and I had plans too. Speaking of which, I'd better go and break the news to him.'

Dropping into her office chair, Phillips placed Fox's copy of the MEN on the desk and selected Adam's number from her favourites. It connected a few moments later.

'Hey, Janey,' said Adam.

'Hi, love. How's your day been so far?'

'*Oh, you know, same as usual; nothing much to report. How about yours?*'

Phillips exhaled loudly.

'*That doesn't sound good.*'

'It's not. Fox is making the team work the weekend.'

'*She can't do that.*'

'She can and she is.'

'*But we're supposed to be going for brunch with Michael and Denise tomorrow.*'

'I know, Adam, and I'm sorry.'

'*I was really looking forward to it, as well.*'

'I know, so was I, but with two almost identical homicides in such a short space of time, it's all hands to the pump.'

Adam exhaled loudly.

'I genuinely am sorry, but there's nothing I can do. Look, I've gotta go. I'll call you later, ok?'

'*Yeah, sure,*' said Adam before he ended the call.

Phillips stared at the handset for a long moment as an uneasy feeling clawed at her gut. She hated letting Adam down, but the truth was the job sometimes had to come first. It was one of the reasons she'd contemplated leaving last year when Adam had almost been killed. Casting her gaze out to the office, she could see Jones, Entwistle and Bov making similar calls to cancel their plans. Glancing down at the headline on the front page of the MEN, she was reminded why Fox had reacted in the way she did. Digging into her contacts once more, she found Don Townsend's number and pressed dial.

He answered promptly. '*Jane. How did you like the story?*'

'I didn't. Where the fuck did you get that information from?'

'Come on, Jane. You know I can't reveal a source.'

'So much for being sensitive to the victim's family.

'Look, I know the headline was a bit out there–'

'Oh, you think?'

'But have you actually read the piece yet?'

'No, I haven't, but I *have* had my arse chewed out by Fox for supposedly giving you inside knowledge of the case. She's livid. Apparently, the hashtag *boxing ring of death* is trending on twitter, for Christ's sake.'

'Yeah, I saw that.' Townsend sounded almost smug. *'Look, as brilliant as the headline may have been, it was my editor Gordon's idea, not mine. I did warn you, Jane. We live in a world dominated by click-bait, and he wanted to make a splash. Read the story. You'll see I just reported the facts. Not a word extra.'*

'Well, that's as maybe, but you reported information that was not for public consumption. Nobody outside of that crime scene knew about the ring of roses. So I need to know which snake has broken ranks.'

'Never gonna happen, Jane. Sorry.'

Phillips took a long breath as she attempted to control her anger. 'Did you know about the roses when we met last night?'

'Does it matter if I did?'

'Yes, it does, actually, because I thought we could trust each other.'

'Look, I'm sorry if you feel let down, but my job is to report what I know, wherever the information comes from.'

She knew how it worked but it didn't make it any easier to swallow, especially given what she'd done for Townsend in the past. 'Just give me a warning next time, will you? You owe me that much at least.'

'Of course, Jane. You have my word on that.'

'Well, that's reassuring.' Phillips's tone was sarcastic as she cut him off before slamming her phone onto the desk. 'Bloody prick!'

She took a moment to gather her thoughts, then once again stared down at the front page of the MEN. Shaking her head, she pulled it across the desk and began reading the article.

20

As the time approached ten-thirty, Phillips parked the Mini on the drive next to Adam's Audi. Getting out of the car, she felt the cold wind against her face as she rushed across the gravel to the front door, which was already locked. After fumbling with her keys for a moment, she opened it and stepped into the warmth of the hallway. As the house around her was totally silent, she suspected Adam had already gone to bed. Wandering into the kitchen she was greeted by Floss, who as usual snaked around her legs, purring loudly. Sitting on the worktop she spied a bowl of pasta with a note next to it that simply said:

In case you're hungry. Gone to bed. A x

Placing the bowl in the microwave, she set the timer for a couple of minutes then poured herself a large glass of ice-cold Pinot Grigio from the fridge and waited for her food. As soon as the microwave pinged, she removed the bowl and carried it along with her wine through to the lounge. After dropping down onto the sofa, she began to eat, suddenly realising how hungry she was. As usual, Adam's cooking was delicious and before she knew it, she'd emptied her bowl.

With Floss now laid out on her lap, purring even louder than before, she reclined into the sofa. Gulping down a couple of large mouthfuls of the wine, she began to relax for the first time all week. The TV was on, but she wasn't really watching it; instead, she cast her eyes around the room at the large collection of framed photos of her and Adam hung on each of the walls, their smiling faces reminding her of their happiest moments together. A wave of guilt crashed over her as she replayed their conversation earlier today when she'd cancelled their plans, and she began to wonder was she in danger of letting the job take over her life once more? She was also reminded of the promise she had made at his bedside in the ICU all those months ago, that she would never again let her work get in the way of their happiness. Had she done the right thing in going back? Or was she kidding herself that she could find a better balance between work and home life? Suddenly feeling very tired, she placed her glass on the small table next to the sofa and closed her eyes. A few moments later she fell fast asleep.

———

THE NEXT MORNING, Phillips awoke on the sofa, still dressed in yesterday's clothes. The rich aroma of fresh coffee filled the air, and she could hear music coming from what sounded like the radio in the kitchen. She checked her watch; it was just before 8 a.m. Getting to her feet, she wandered through to find Adam filling two mugs from the cafetiere.

He looked up as she walked in. 'Morning,' he said.

'Morning.' Phillips rubbed her eyes. 'I must have crashed out last night after the pasta and wine.'

'Carbs and alcohol will do that to you.' He passed her a

mug of coffee. 'What time did you get back? I never heard you come in.'

'About half-ten, I think.' Phillips took a tentative sip from the steaming mug. 'I hadn't actually intended on staying that late, but I got stuck into some paperwork and before I knew it, it was almost ten o'clock.'

Adam took a drink before placing it down on the counter-top. 'Look, I wasn't very understanding when you called yesterday. You're a murder detective. I can't expect life to be nine to five.'

Phillips shook her head. 'Don't beat yourself up. My job does get in the way sometimes. I've only been back a week and I'm already starting to wonder if I've made the right decision myself.'

'You have. The job's in your blood, and as great as it's been to have you at home all these months, it was obvious something was missing for you. You need it and the job needs you.'

Phillips smiled softly as she took another drink.

'Look. I did some thinking yesterday and I feel like it *is* time for me to go back to work. And you were right, A&E is what I'm best at. Being a GP would drive me mad.'

'That's great,' said Phillips. 'So, are you going to speak to Raj?'

'Already have. Messaged him last night, and as luck would have it, he's free for lunch today. We're going to catch up and see how we can make it work.'

Phillips placed her mug down and drew Adam into a hug. 'I'm so pleased for you, babe.'

'Me too.'

'And I will make more of an effort.' Phillips pulled back to look him in the eye. 'I won't let it go back to the way it was. *I promise.*'

Adam grinned then leaned in and kissed her on the fore-head. 'Do you want some breakfast?'

Phillips glanced at the clock on the wall. 'I haven't really got time. Jonesy's picking me up in half an hour. I need to get showered.'

Adam tilted his head to one side and raised an eyebrow. 'And who said the job wasn't going to take over her life?'

Phillips felt herself blush. 'I've already broken that promise, haven't I?'

Adam grinned. 'Why don't you get ready, and I'll rustle up a bacon roll. You can take it with you.'

'Have I ever told you you're the best boyfriend ever?'

'Not enough.'

'Well, you are!' Phillips reached up and kissed him on the lips, before turning and heading upstairs.

21

J ones was his usual punctual self, arriving as planned at 8.45 a.m. sharp. Armed with her bacon roll, Phillips kissed Adam goodbye and headed out to join her 2-I-C in the squad car. A moment later they set off towards Sale and their second visit to Juliet Dobson's husband, Lee, which Phillips had booked the previous evening. Now he had had time to process what had happened, she hoped he might be able to share more details around Juliet's life, which so far, they knew very little about.

'Did you see Carter on the news this morning?'

Phillips shook her head. 'He must have recorded it yesterday afternoon. How did he do?'

'Really well actually. Managed to keep it factual and looked like he knew what he was talking about.'

'I'm just glad he didn't ask me to do it with him. I hate talking to the camera.'

Jones nodded as he gunned the accelerator and moved into the outside lane. 'I can't imagine anything worse.'

They travelled in silence for a few minutes, both evidently deep in thought.

Phillips was the first to speak. 'Did you manage to catch up with Tracy O'Connor at Hawk Green?'

'I did. Spoke to her last night, actually.'

'Any inmates we should be talking to about Dobson?'

Jones shook his head. 'Doesn't look like it. Apparently, she was well liked by all the guys she worked with. Never had any bother by all accounts.'

Phillips exhaled loudly. 'Just for once, I'd like a straightforward investigation.'

Jones produced a lopsided grin. 'Straightforward? In MCU. Now where would be the fun in that?'

Phillips smiled, then turned her gaze out of the window as the world rushed by.

Half an hour later, as they arrived at the Dobson home, the family liaison officer, Sergeant Pam Clement, answered the door and guided them through to the lounge where they found Lee sitting in an armchair watching a Saturday morning news show. He turned to face them as they walked in, his features still gaunt and haunted, his eyes red and swollen, with dark shadows hanging underneath.

'I'll make some drinks,' said Clement.

'I'll give you a hand,' replied Phillips, leaving Jones to make small talk with Dobson for a few minutes.

Clement was one of the FLOs attached to MCU and Phillips rated her as first-class. Her ability to support a victim whilst staying close to the investigation was second to none.

'Tea or coffee, ma'am?' asked Clement.

'Coffee for me, please, Pam.'

'And what about DI Jones?'

'Anything herbal if you have it.' Phillips thumbed towards the lounge. 'So how's he been?'

Clement filled the kettle at the sink before switching it on. 'Up and down, as you'd expect. To be honest, I'm not sure it's actually sunk in yet.'

'Has he said anything about their relationship at all? You know, were they having any issues or problems?'

'Nothing,' said Clement. 'He hasn't really said much at all but based on the few bits he has told me, I think she was the love of his life and vice versa.'

As soon as the kettle boiled, Clement made the drinks.

'Has he had any visitors that you know of?'

'A few friends and his brother have been to see him most days from what I can tell. I usually make myself scarce when anyone's here. Give them some space to talk.'

Phillips nodded. 'Fair enough.'

'Is there anything else you need to know, ma'am?'

'No, I think that's it for it now. I can get the rest from him.'

With a drink in each hand, Clement led the way back to the lounge, with Phillips carrying Jones's chamomile tea as well as her own coffee.

Her second in command was perched awkwardly on the sofa opposite Dobson and his eyes lit up when they appeared. He was clearly relieved to see them; small talk had never been Jones's strong point.

Phillips took a seat next to him, and Clement pulled up a large ottoman close to the fireplace.

'How are you feeling, Lee?' asked Phillips softly.

'Like my world has ended.' His voice was weak.

'I can only imagine what you're going through,' added Phillips.

Dobson's chin dropped to his chest, but he remained silent.

Jones pulled out his notepad.

Phillips placed her mug down on a coaster on the coffee table positioned between her and Dobson. 'We know this isn't easy for you, but it would be really helpful if you could tell us a little bit more about Juliet – to help us better understand who she was as a person.'

Dobson looked up, his eyes glistening, tears not far away. 'What do you want to know?'

Phillips sat forward. 'Well, firstly, did she have any enemies that you know of?'

Dobson recoiled slightly. 'Are you kidding? Everybody loved Jules. I never heard anyone say a bad word about her.'

'I see,' said Phillips. 'When we spoke the other day, you said you couldn't think of anyone specific at Hawk Green who may have threatened her. Have you had any more thoughts on that?'

Dobson shrugged. 'No. Like I said, she didn't really talk about her work at the prison, and I preferred not to ask.'

'And was she happy in her other job?' asked Jones.

'Which one?' said Dobson.

Phillips glanced at Jones, who appeared as confused as she felt. 'Sorry, Lee. Are you saying Juliet had another job in addition to the lecturing at the university?'

Dobson nodded as he took a sip from his steaming mug. 'Yeah, she did some support work at the Mindset Mastery over in Monk's Heath.'

Monk's Heath – where AJ Lewis's van had been spotted on the night he died. 'Mindset Mastery? What's that?' asked Phillips.

'It's a well-being clinic that specialises in supporting people with addictions. She helped with the addiction retreats there a couple of times a month.'

Jones scribbled in his pad.

'Do you know if Juliet had any connection to a man called AJ Lewis?' asked Phillips.

Dobson frowned. '*The boxer?*'

'That's him.'

'Not that I know of. She wasn't big on sports, to be honest. *I* only remember him because my grandma was a boxing fan.

She used to make me watch his fights when she babysat for us as kids. He was on his way up back then.'

'So, Juliet never mentioned him?' said Phillips.

Dobson shook his head. 'He was the one that was murdered and found in the churchyard, wasn't he? I saw it in the papers.'

'Yes, he was.' Phillips changed tack now as she attempted to avoid getting drawn into the details of that case and its connection to Juliet's murder. 'By the way, we found Juliet's car. It appears she was involved in an accident the night she died.'

Dobson's brow furrowed and he appeared confused. 'I thought you said she was murdered.'

'We think the accident happened before she was taken. You may have noticed her eyes and nose were bruised when you identified her.'

Dobson closed his eyes and once again dropped his chin to his chest.

The room fell silent for a long moment and Phillips glanced towards Jones and Clement. Dobson's pain was like a living thing that filled the room around them.

'Was Jules attacked by the same man that murdered AJ Lewis?' Dobson opened his eyes and lifted his face up. 'Is that why you're asking about him?'

In that moment Phillips knew she had a choice to make – tell him the truth and risk inflicting more pain on an already heart-broken husband, or lie and potentially lose his trust when the story eventually filtered out. 'We can't say for certain, but we believe the deaths are connected, yes.'

Dobson swallowed hard, then nodded. 'You never told me where she was found. Where was it?'

'Warford cemetery,' replied Phillips.

'The papers said Lewis was naked when they found his body. Was that the same with Jules?'

'More or less, yes. She was wrapped in a sheet, but naked apart from that.'

In an instant Dobson shot up from the chair and rushed out of the room, and a few seconds later vomited in the downstairs toilet.

'I'll go,' said Clement, stepping up from the ottoman.

'So will we,' replied Phillips. 'I think he's had enough of us for one day.'

Clement smiled softly, then left the room.

Back outside the house Phillips and Jones took a moment to debrief.

'Never gets any easier, does it?' said Jones. 'Seeing the impact on the families.'

Phillips shook her head. 'No. It bloody doesn't.'

'So, what now?'

Phillips opened the car door. 'Let's see what Entwistle can dig up on this Mindset Mastery place before we take a look at it ourselves.'

Jones nodded, then jumped in the driver's seat.

A minute later, Phillips dialled Entwistle's direct line through the central console.

His voice soon boomed through the speakers. *'Happy Saturday, Guv. What can I do for you?'*

'I need you to check out a company called Mindset Mastery in Monk's Heath.'

'Wasn't Monk's Heath one of the locations where Lewis's van was spotted on ANPR?'

'Yeah, it was, and it turns out Juliet Dobson worked for this Mindset place a couple of times a month. Jones and I were going to head over there next. Before we do, see what you can find, will you? And call me back ASAP.'

'Won't be long.'

'Thanks.' Phillips ended the call and turned her attention back to Jones.

He was typing into Google maps on his phone. 'Here it is. Mindset Mastery, Monk's Heath. Says we'll be there in about forty-five minutes.'

'Great,' said Phillips. 'Hopefully that'll be enough time for Whistler to tell us what goes on over there.'

22

Exactly forty-five minutes later, Jones turned left off the main drag and steered the squad car through the impressive stone gateposts at the entrance to Mindset Mastery. A large blue and gold sign confirmed they were in the right place almost immediately, and as they continued along the wide tree-lined drive through manicured gardens, Phillips was struck by the sheer size of the place. Far in the distance the house came into view, and on first impressions, she guessed it had once been a stately home or similar. Currently it had the look of a luxury hotel and spa. All that was missing was the golf course, she thought. The house itself was such a distance from the road it took them almost three minutes to reach the car park, which today was filled to the brim with Range Rovers, Porches, BMWs and many more luxury vehicles.

'This place stinks of money,' said Jones as he guided the car into the only remaining visitors' space located to the left of the front entrance.

'You can say that again.' Phillips scanned the cars around her.

'Look at the size of that one,' said Jones.

Phillips followed his gaze and stared out at an enormous blue 4x4 parked in a spot apparently reserved for the CEO.

'The brand-new Land Rover Defender,' Jones explained. 'I'd bloody love one of those; if I had ninety grand to spare, that is.'

Phillips laughed. 'One day, Jonesy.'

Just then Entwistle's number flashed up on the central console. Phillips accepted the call. 'Whistler. Did you find anything?'

'Just top line at the moment, Guv.'

'Go on.'

'According to their own website, Mindset Mastery bills itself as – and I quote – "the perfect place to reclaim your inner self, overcome your addictions and discover the new you".'

'Sounds like a load of bollocks to me,' sniffed Jones.

Phillips ignored him. 'Anything else?'

'Yeah. It was set up by an American called Lyndon Garcia three years ago. He's still the man in charge, and according to Companies' House, they have cash at bank of a half a million quid, and their total assets less current liabilities is almost five million.'

'So they're doing well, then?'

'Judging by their accounts, it certainly looks that way, Guv.'

'It *looks* that way from here too,' said Jones, gazing at the gigantic Defender once again.

'Nice gaff, is it?'

'Let's just say it wouldn't look out of place on Downton Abbey,' replied Phillips.

'That's all I've got for now, but I'm sure I'll be able to get more by the time you get back to the office.'

'Well, at least we know who to ask for now. We'll speak to you later.' Phillips ended the call and turned towards Jones. 'Fancy a bit of rehab?'

'Don't mind if I do.' Jones grinned.

A minute later they found themselves in the gargantuan entrance hall of the old building, which was resplendently decked out with polished marble pillars, gilt-framed canvases and thick carpet underfoot. To one side sat a surprisingly modern reception desk, which ordinarily should have looked out of place against the classic architecture but in this instance somehow matched the decor perfectly. Jones was right; this place really did stink of money.

'Can I help you?' asked the male receptionist from behind the desk. He was dressed smartly in a white shirt open at the neck that accentuated his dark complexion and bright, warm smile. Phillips placed him in his mid-twenties as she stepped up to the desk and noted his name badge simply said *Henry*. 'We'd like to speak with Mr Garcia, please.' She presented her ID.

Henry's smile never faltered. 'I'm afraid Mr Garcia is delivering a retreat today and cannot be disturbed.'

Phillips couldn't place his accent and wasn't sure if it had its origins in the States or Australia maybe, or even somewhere a little more exotic. She forced a smile. 'I think he'd prefer to break off from that and speak to us now – as opposed to later today, when we come back with a warrant and a bunch of uniformed officers trudging about the place.'

Henry's smile finally disappeared. 'Can I ask what it's about?'

'The death of Juliet Dobson.'

Henry's eyes widened as he took a moment, then stepped up from the desk. 'I'll be right back,' he said, then left through a door directly behind reception.

'*Now he moves,*' chuckled Jones.

Phillips grinned. 'Yeah, I thought he might.'

A few minutes later, Henry returned and gestured with his left arm. 'If you'd like to follow me, Mr Garcia will be with you shortly.'

Phillips and Jones acquiesced and soon found themselves in a large conference room that adjoined the entrance hall. Just like the rest of the building they'd seen so far, it had been lavishly decorated, and a long mahogany desk surrounded by six matching chairs took centre stage in the middle of the room.'

'Can I get either of you a drink?' asked Henry. 'Some iced tea perhaps?'

'Not for me,' replied Phillips.

Jones shook his head. 'I'm fine, thank you.'

Henry made his excuses and left.

As they waited for Garcia, Phillips moved across to the double-height window and cast her gaze to the gardens outside. Everything appeared to be immaculately maintained: the lawns perfectly manicured, the winter shrubs and hedges without a leaf out of place. 'This place is insane,' she muttered.

Just then, the door opened behind them.

Phillips spun on her heels and came face to face with a dark-haired mountain of a man, casually dressed in a white linen shirt, navy shorts and boating shoes on otherwise bare feet, despite the fact that it was the middle of February. His skin was tanned. 'Detective Phillips?' he asked in a lazy US drawl.

'Detective *Chief Inspector,* actually.'

He raised his arms in defeat as he stepped inside the room and allowed the door to close behind him. 'Sorry. In my country, we just have detectives.'

Phillips ignored the comment. 'I'm guessing you're Mr Garcia?'

'Guilty as charged, but please, call me Lyndon.' He flashed a smile of perfect white teeth as he pulled out one of the chairs. 'Shall we sit?'

Phillips nodded and together she and Jones took seats opposite him.

Garcia sat forward and clasped his hands together on the desk, the smile gone, his eyes steely now. 'So, Henry tells me you want to talk about poor Juliet?'

'We understand she worked for you here,' said Phillips.

Jones pulled out his note pad.

'That's right. A wonderful woman who made a huge difference to so many of our clients. I still can't believe she's gone. It was such a shock when Lee called to tell me the awful news yesterday.'

'Can you tell us what Juliet did for you here?'

'Of course,' replied Garcia. 'She supported me and the rest of the team with the addiction retreats. She had an innate ability to disarm the clients and get under their skin, which in turn helped them understand the source of their inner pain and the reasons for their addiction. Once we knew that, we could help them come to terms with the pain and rewire their thinking around it. The ultimate goal is to remove their need to block it out with things like alcohol, drugs, sex or gambling.'

'And how often did she work here?' asked Jones.

'Twice a month, normally. We run twenty-four retreats each year and she was part of all of them. To be honest, I don't know what I'm going to do without her.'

Phillips cut back in. 'Your receptionist said you're delivering a retreat today.'

'That's right.'

'So was Juliet supposed to be part of that too?'

Garcia nodded sombrely. 'Yes. I've tried my best to step into her shoes with the clients this morning, but I have to say I feel as though I'm short-changing them.'

Phillips remained silent for a moment as she noted his body language. So far, he had been open and honest according to his silent cues, but she'd been doing this long enough to know not to trust those cues – in the right hands, they could easily be manipulated. 'Was AJ Lewis ever a client at this clinic?'

Garcia's posture tightened a fraction.

He'd tried to hide it, but Phillips had spotted it.

'I'm afraid I can't answer that; client confidentiality. You understand.'

'As I'm sure you're aware, AJ Lewis is dead, Mr Garcia,' Phillips shot back. 'The victim of a brutal murder, which means my questions around him supersede any confidentiality agreements you may have sanctioned when he was alive. So, I'll ask you again, was AJ Lewis a client here?'

Garcia stared at Phillips in silence.

She held his gaze, unflinching.

'Yes,' said Garcia finally.

'And when was that?'

'I can't recall the exact date but he came to one of the two-day retreats sometime late last year.'

'His wife told us he was a drinker,' said Phillips. 'Was that why he was here?'

'Yes.'

'And was Juliet working on his retreat?' Phillips asked.

'She was, yes. As I said, she worked on all of them.'

Jones made a note in his pad.

Phillips continued. 'Did they have much contact with each other during the retreat?'

Garcia chuckled. 'Of course. Like I said, Juliet was the reason those sessions were so successful. She was involved with all the clients intimately over the two days.'

'Were there any issues between them that you can recall?' said Phillips.

Garcia frowned. 'Not a bit. They got on great.'

'So everything went according to plan? Nothing out of the ordinary?'

'Not a thing. It was a total success.' Garcia sat back in his chair.

Phillips glanced at Jones, who was continuing to make notes, then locked eyes with Garcia once more. 'We're going to need a list of all clients and staff who attended that specific retreat or were in any way connected to it.'

Garcia folded his arms. 'You can have the staff list by all means, but the clients are protected by our cast-iron confidentiality agreements. If you want those, you will need a warrant, I'm afraid.'

'Which I'll have in my hand by Monday,' replied Phillips. 'So why not save yourself the trouble?'

Garcia flashed a thin smile. 'I'm not in the habit of getting sued, Chief Inspector. So I'd rather you follow due process. That way, the buck stops with you guys and *not* Mindset Mastery. We have a lot of high-profile clients, and they value their privacy. I'm sure you understand.'

Phillips glared at him in silence. 'If that's how you want to play it.'

'It is.' Garcia picked up the handset on the telephone in front of him and a moment later delivered his instructions to Henry to pull together the staff list, then replaced the receiver. 'It'll be waiting for you on your way out.'

Phillips detected an undercurrent of smugness in his tone. 'Right. Well, in that case, we'll be going.'

Garcia stood, a wide grin on his face. 'I'll show you out.'

A couple of minutes later, Phillips dropped into the passenger seat with the staff list in hand. 'Get onto the Saturday Magistrates' Court. I want those client details on my desk by Monday, ok?'

'It'll be my pleasure, Guv. Just to wipe that bloody grin off his face. Smug bastard!' Jones started the car. 'So where to now?'

Phillips glanced at the clock on the dash. It was coming up to midday. 'I don't know about you, but I'm starving. Let's grab a sandwich and get back to base. See what Whistler and Bov have managed to dig up.'

'Aye, aye, Captain,' said Jones with a smile, then reversed out of the space.

23

'H ere they are. The dynamic duo,' said Bovalino playfully as Phillips and Jones wandered into MCU.

'Er, it's DCI Phillips and DI Jones to *you,* Detective *Constable* Bovalino,' replied Phillips with a wink.

Bovalino's enormous frame shook as he chuckled in his seat.

'So how was Garcia?' asked Entwistle.

Jones removed his thick winter jacket and hung it in the coat rack behind his desk. 'Something special, that fella.'

Entwistle raised his eyebrows. 'In what way?'

Phillips, still wearing her coat, took up her usual position at the spare desk and placed the staff list on it, face down for the time being. 'He's about six-foot-seven and was wearing shorts and a flannel shirt.'

'In February?' said Bov.

'And no socks,' Jones shot back. 'Dickhead.'

Phillips continued. 'He's one of those all-American jock types, y'know, like you see on the TV. The way he talks makes him sound like he's from one of the southern states.'

'Reminded me a bit of Matthew McConaughey actually,' added Jones.

Phillips nodded. 'Yeah, totally. Anyway, he tried his best to fob us off, but after a wee bit of persuasion, he finally admitted that not only did Juliet work there twice a month as part of their addiction retreats, but she also worked directly with victim number one, AJ Lewis.'

'Bloody hell,' muttered Entwistle.

'Yep,' said Phillips. 'Not only are both victims linked by the Mindset Mastery Clinic, but AJ Lewis's van was also seen in the vicinity of the estate the night he was murdered. So as of now, Lyndon Garcia and anyone else who's passed through that building in the last three months is a person of interest.' She held up the staff list so the names were now visible. 'I want us to check out everyone on this list, and by Monday morning, Jones has promised me he'll have a warrant for all of their clients' details too.'

'He wouldn't give them up, then?' Bovalino asked.

Jones shook his head. 'Reckoned he'd get sued.'

'Typical American,' added the big Italian.

Phillips turned her focus to Entwistle. 'So, what else did you find on Garcia?'

'Surprisingly little so far, Guv. Just a couple of business articles online that were published in the States in 2009 by relatively unknown bloggers. They're sickeningly compli-mentary – *sycophantic* almost – talking about what a great business leader he is and how he changed the fortunes of a host of companies across the US. But when I looked for those same companies, I couldn't find any trace of them.'

'So what?' asked Phillips. 'Do you think the articles are fake?'

'Maybe.'

'Probably wrote them himself,' offered Bovalino. 'The web is full of fake news these days.'

'Sounds about right.' Jones's tone was sardonic.

Entwistle continued. 'The next time he shows up online is ten years later in the UK as the founder and CEO of the Mindset Mastery Clinic. One of the articles talks about the multi-million-pound renovation of the old stately home, which was derelict when he bought it.' He turned his laptop so Phillips could see the screen. 'The before and after pictures are pretty impressive.'

Phillips examined the images for a moment, then nodded. 'That place must have cost a fortune.'

'Looks like he's doing something right,' said Entwistle, "cos like I said earlier, they've got masses of cash in the bank, too. Oh, and I almost forgot, according to immigration he got his UK residency three years ago.'

Phillips placed her elbows on the desk and rested her index fingers under her nose. 'We really need to find out where this guy came from and how he made his money, because something's not right with this picture.'

'I'll keep looking,' said Entwistle.

'Great.' Phillips turned her attention to Bovalino. 'How'd you get on with the databases and any similarly posed bodies to our victims?'

Bovalino sighed. 'Nothing remotely like them in Manchester since we digitised all the records in the early nineties. There may be something in the paper logs, but we'll need more bodies on the ground if we're going to check those.' He passed across a couple of A4 printed images. 'But I did find these on the national database.'

Phillips stared down at the lifeless woman pictured on the page. A bunch of white flowers had been placed under her hands, which were crossed against her chest.

'Elaine Tomlinson. She was murdered as part of a pagan ritual in 1999 but as you can see, the only thing she has in common with our victims is the white flowers. She's holding lilies, whereas Lewis and Dobson were surrounded by roses.'

'Any mutilation to the body?'

'She'd been stabbed several times, Guv, but no organs had been removed. Her boyfriend, Nathan Hoster – a self-proclaimed Pagan high-priest – was found guilty of her murder in 2005. He's serving life in HMP Frankland, just outside Durham.'

Phillips studied the picture intently, looking for more similarities, but aside from the flowers there was little to connect this woman to their cases.

Bovalino handed her another A4 image, this time of a man wrapped in a white shawl. 'This is Emilio Gonzales, murdered in London in 2004 and found naked, wrapped in a shawl, in Hyde Park. He'd been strangled but aside from that, the PM notes show no other injuries.'

'And his killer?' asked Phillips.

'Steven Williams. According to the file, they'd been seeing each other for a few months when Gonzales tried to break it off. Williams couldn't stand the thought of him with anyone else, so lured hm to his flat on the pretence of wanting to remain friends and murdered him.'

Phillips felt her brow furrow. 'So what was the significance of the shawl?'

'It's actually a bedsheet. After he killed him, Williams stripped Gonzales and wrapped him in the sheet before dumping the body later that night, but he was spotted by a dog walker and the police picked him up a few hours later. He pleaded guilty and got life. He's in Wakefield nick currently.'

Phillips exhaled loudly as she passed back the printed images.

'That's as much as I've been able to find so far.'

'Keep looking. See if there's anything else on the system.'

'Will do, Guv.'

Phillips stood, collecting the staff list as she did. 'I'll divvy these names up and as soon as Bov gets back from the canteen with the coffees, we can start going through them.' She handed the big man a ten-pound note. 'Get a few sweet treats while you're at it. I think we could all do with a sugar boost.'

Bov flashed a cheeky grin. 'Thanks, Guv. You're so much better than our last gaffer.' He caught Jones's eye. 'He was a right tight bugger.'

'Piss off!' shot Jones, flashing the V-sign.

Phillips chuckled as she unbuttoned her coat and headed back to the office. They were in for another long day.

24

Saturday afternoon soon blurred into Sunday and the team found themselves hard at work in an otherwise quietened Ashton House – save for the usual uniformed comings and goings on the ground floor.

By 3 p.m. Phillips began to flag and decided it was time for the last update of the day before sending the guys home to grab the few remaining hours of the weekend for themselves. After heading out to the office to share the plan, she returned to sit at her desk as they filed in behind her.

'So, what have you found?'

Entwistle jumped in first. 'I've managed to speak to Interpol this afternoon—'

'Ooh, check you...' Bovalino cut him off in a high-pitched tone reminiscent of the school yard, '...with your international contacts.'

Jones chuckled at his mate.

'Ignore him.' Phillips smiled, knowing a bit of banter was good for morale after so many consecutive days on the job.

Entwistle continued undeterred. 'As I was saying, I've

spoken to Karim at Interpol, and he's sent over some interesting intel on Garcia.'

Phillips sat forward, her interest piqued. 'Like what?'

'Like the fact that he's actually called Lyndon-Paul Andrews.'

'So has he changed his name?' asked Jones.

'Yup. And for good reason – turns out he did time in the US for assault and aggravated burglary back in the nineties. Apparently, he developed a fixation for one of his neighbours and began stalking her. She subsequently reported him to the police on a number of different occasions and he was eventually given a restraining order. According to the case notes, that worked for a time, but it wasn't long before he was back to his old tricks, only this time he took it a step further and forced his way into her house one night. She attempted to flee but he pinned her down and tried to undress her. Anyway, she fought back and kicked him in the nuts, and while he was incapacitated, she ran out of the house and alerted another neighbour. Garcia legged it but was picked up the next morning by police. He got fifteen years and served ten after being let out on parole in 2008.'

Phillips caught Jones's eye. 'Well, that certainly doesn't match the image he painted yesterday, does it?'

'Not at all.' Jones snorted. 'So how the hell did he manage to get UK residency with a conviction like that?'

'Karim didn't have the details, so I checked with immigration and apparently he was given special dispensation from the Home Office. Someone high up vouched for him.'

'So, he basically bought it, then?' said Bovalino.

'There's no proof of that, sadly,' replied Entwistle.

Phillips said nothing for a moment as she digested the information. 'So, when did he change his name?'

'About five years ago, just before he entered the UK.'

'Covering his tracks, it would seem,' muttered Phillips. 'Anything else on him?'

'Just what I told you yesterday. He set up Mindset Mastery and he's well on his way to becoming a very wealthy man.'

Phillips nodded. 'What about the staff list? Any joy with that?'

Bovalino opened his notepad. 'Looks like Garcia isn't the only one with a conviction. The general manager, Jim Markham, did eighteen months for tax evasion in 2015, and one of the maintenance guys, Sammy Finch, has served a total of ten years for various burglary offences from 1991 through to 2008.'

'Well, well, well,' said Phillips. 'I wonder if Garcia knows about those two.'

'Their convictions are spent, so they wouldn't have to declare them when applying for jobs, but they'd still show up on any DBS checks,' replied Bovalino, referring to the Disclosure and Barring Service responsible for managing criminal records in the UK.

'Go and speak to Markham and Finch tomorrow, Bov. See what they have to say for themselves.'

'Sure thing, boss.'

'So do we have anything else?'

'Not from me,' said Jones.

Entwistle shook his head.

'That's everything so far,' added Bov.

Phillips reclined in the chair. 'In that case, you guys get yourselves off. I think we've all had enough this weekend.'

Each of the men nodded, before standing and filing back out to their desks.

Just then, Phillips's mobile began to ring on the desk next to her. It was Siobhan Harris. 'Siobhan. How's it going?'

'Good, Jane. How was your weekend?'

'Fox cancelled it for me and the team, so filled with work.'

'*Sorry to hear that.*'

'How about yours?'

'*Very interesting indeed. In fact, that's why I'm calling. I think I've found something on your posed bodies.*'

'Really?'

Jones appeared at Phillips's door wearing his coat and scarf. 'Everything ok?' he mouthed.

Phillips gave him the thumbs-up, then gestured for him to leave.

Jones nodded and headed for the exit.

'So, what have you got?'

'*I've been looking through those files you sent over and I've found a link that might explain the posing with the ring of flowers and the white shawls.*'

'Go on.'

'*Well. It took me a while to find it, but your victims' bodies have been posed in an identical way to ancient Polynesian tribes during their funeral rituals.*'

Phillips felt her nose wrinkle. What the hell did Polynesian tribes have to do with two dead bodies in Manchester?

Harris continued. '*A hundred and fifty years or so ago, when the ancient tribes buried their dead, they would first lay them out in a white shawl and surround them with white flowers, broken at the feet, as a mark of respect and to symbolise returning them to the earth.*'

'Ok, but how is that connected to our victims?'

Harris paused. '*Well, following that, they would then bury them in sand to preserve them.*'

'Er, right...' Phillips wondered where this was going.

'*Before eventually digging them up and feasting on their organs.*'

Phillips did a double take. 'They did what?'

'*They ate them, Jane. According to the ancient rituals, they*' would eat the heart, eyes, brain and tongue. I know this all sounds a bit weird but hear me out.'

'I'm listening.'

'These Polynesian tribes believed that by ingesting the critical organs of their elders and enemies alike – often killed in the field of battle – they were allowing their souls to live on within them, as well as taking on their strengths, knowledge and warrior spirit.'

'So what? You're saying our killer is doing the same?'

'I couldn't say with any certainty at this stage, but it might explain why the heart and brain have been taken.'

Phillips rubbed her left hand down her face and exhaled sharply. 'A real-life Hannibal Lecter, you mean?'

'Look, I know as a theory it's way out there—'

'You're not kidding,' scoffed Phillips.

'But the likenesses are uncanny. I've just this second sent some screen shots to your email.'

Phillips turned to her laptop as the email notification pinged. After clicking on the message from Harris, she opened the images attached and found herself staring at the screen in disbelief. There, before her, were artists' impressions of the ritual burial ceremonies, each containing a naked body wrapped in a white shawl and surrounded by white flowers broken at the feet. Each was an almost carbon copy of how Lewis and Dobson had been found. 'This is so fucked up,' she whispered into the handset.

'I know,' said Harris. 'They're virtually identical.'

Phillips stared at the images in silence.

'There's more, Jane.'

'God. Really? I'm not sure I want to hear this.'

'According to the ancient Polynesian tradition, they would preserve the bodies in sand until the next new moon. And as that new moon rose, they would harvest the organs and the feast would begin. Again, this is purely hypothetical at this stage, but if your *killer is following the same ritual, then chances are he may be working to a similar timetable.'*

'So, when's the next new moon?' Phillips feared the worst.

'This coming Friday.'

'Ah, shit!'

'I might be completely wrong here, of course,' said Harris. *'But if I'm even remotely close, you may well be looking at more deaths to come over the next five days as he collects the full set of critical organs, all in readiness for the feast on Friday. He has the heart and brain already; the eyes and tongue could well be next on his list.'*

Phillips shook her head in disbelief. 'Cannibalism, in Manchester? Surely that can't be what we're dealing with here, Siobhan.'

'I understand what you're saying, Jane,' said Harris, her tone grave. *'But as we both know – there's nothing quite as strange as reality at times.'*

25

As promised, Jones secured the warrant granting access to the patient records of Mindset Mastery at 10 a.m. Monday morning. By 10.15 he and Phillips were back in the car and heading towards Monk's Heath. They'd both been busy since they'd arrived at work that morning and not had a chance to catch up, so as yet she'd not shared Harris's theory on the link to the Polynesian tribes with him.

Now, as they sped around the M60, she hesitated as the sheer ridiculousness of what she was about to tell him hit her.

He'd obviously noticed something was bothering her. 'Everything all right, Guv? You seem a little distant.'

She nodded. 'That call I took as you were leaving last night...'

'Yeah. What about it?'

'It was Siobhan Harris.'

It seemed to take a moment for her name to register with him. 'The profiler from Newcastle?'

'Yeah, that's her.'

'What did she want?'

'I asked for her opinion on the Lewis and Dobson murders,' said Phillips.

'Really? You never mentioned she was working with us again.'

'She's not. Well, not officially. I just wanted to know what she thought of the way the bodies had been posed.'

'So what did she say?'

Phillips paused as she tried to find the right words. 'She's found a link to ancient Polynesian tribes and their funeral rituals.'

Jones glanced left, his face scrunched up. 'You what?'

'She found some information online which suggests the way they were laid out was identical to the way these tribes prepared their dead for the next life.'

'So, is that what she thinks happened to Lewis and Dobson?'

'It's certainly one theory, yes.'

Jones remained silent, clearly deep in thought.

'But that's not the worst of it.'

Jones glanced left again. 'Why do I suddenly *not* want to know what's coming next?'

'Apparently, these tribes would then go on to eat their dead in order to take on their spirits and strengths.'

Jones was incredulous. 'As in *cannibals*?'

'Yep.'

'But that's crazy. How can that have anything to do with our case? This is modern day Manchester, not ancient Polynesia!'

'That's what I said, but when I saw the images she was referring to, the likeness to our crime scenes was uncanny. I'm not kidding, Jonesy, *they were identical*.'

Jones fell silent again, his eyes fixed on the road ahead.

'I didn't sleep last night thinking about it.'

'I'm not surprised.'

Over the next ten minutes Phillips shared the remaining details of her conversation with Harris the previous evening, including the fact that the killer may well strike again in time for the new moon. When she was finished, neither said a word for a long time as they processed the strange ritual Harris was suggesting they may have inadvertently stumbled upon.

'Have you shared any of this with Carter?' asked Jones eventually.

'Not yet. I wasn't quite sure whether I should. I wanted to get your take on it.'

Jones shook his head. 'Well, at first it sounds like a load of ancient mumbo jumbo, but like Harris says, we've dealt with some equally weird shit in the past, haven't we? We know better than to think we've seen it all, that's for sure.' He indicated left as they approached the entrance to Mindset Mastery, then turned in through the gate posts.

'We've got Dobson's PM after this. I'd also like to get Tan's take on it before I tell Carter, but I can't help feeling Harris is actually onto something.'

Jones blew his lips. 'God help us if she is, because the eyes and tongue could be next.'

Phillips nodded sombrely.

Five minutes later, Jones strode towards reception and presented the warrant to Henry behind the front desk.

As the young man read it, his eyes widened. 'I need to speak to Mr Garcia.'

'So do we,' replied Phillips. 'As a matter of urgency.'

Affecting the appearance of a startled bunny, Henry disappeared once more through the door behind him, returning a few minutes later looking only slightly more composed. 'Mr Garcia will meet you in the Great Room where you spoke last time. Please, follow me.'

Henry led the way and, as had happened previously, deposited them in the large room off reception, only this time there was no offer of refreshments. Phillips and Jones took the same seats as before, ready for Garcia's arrival.

It was a full fifteen minutes before the door opened and the giant American walked through wearing the same outfit of shorts and flannel shirt as last time, albeit in different colours today. The broad smile had diminished somewhat, and his eyes betrayed the agitation he was evidently trying to hide. 'Back so soon?' He took a seat across from them.

'I told you we'd get a warrant for your client records, Mr Garcia,' said Phillips.

'And as I told you, you *needed* one. This is on *you* now, *not* Mindset Mastery. Henry said you needed to speak to me urgently.' He was clearly in no mood for small talk.

Phillips continued. 'We've been looking into your background.'

Garcia flinched slightly. 'Really? And why is that any of your business?'

Phillips ignored the question. 'I must say we were very surprised to discover you'd served ten years in an American prison for breaking into your neighbour's house and trying to rape her.'

Garcia's jaw clenched before he flashed a thin smile. 'It was assault and burglary. There was no rape, attempted or otherwise.'

'Sorry, my mistake,' said Phillips, returning his smile. 'Anyway, that had me wondering how you managed to get UK residency with such a conviction.'

'None of your business.'

'We heard someone from the Home Office did you a favour,' said Jones. 'You must be very well connected.'

'Look. I'm a busy man and I also know the law. I'm not

compelled to answer your questions unless you arrest me. Am I under arrest?'

'Not yet,' replied Phillips.

'Well in that case, unless you have anything of value to speak to me about, I think we're done.'

'Where were you on the nights of Sunday the 6th and Wednesday the 9th of February?' asked Phillips.

'Am I under suspicion, Chief Inspector?'

Phillips glared at him. 'Not if you can account for your movements on both those nights.'

Garcia shrugged. 'I was where I always am. Here. All night.'

'Can anyone vouch for you?'

'I'm afraid I was all alone. Unless, of course, you count my Siamese fighting fish?'

Phillips felt her brow furrow. 'I'm sorry. I'm not following you.'

'I have a tank full of them in my apartment on the top floor of the building.'

'So no one can confirm you were here on both nights?'

'No.'

Phillips changed tack. 'Are you aware that several of your employees have criminal records? Namely Jim Markham and Sammy Finch.'

'I am.'

'And are your clients aware?' asked Phillips.

Garcia sat back and folded his arms across his chest. 'We promote a culture of open dialogue at Mindset Mastery amongst all clients and staff. It's the only way to get to the root of our issues as flawed human beings. We also believe in the power of redemption. I made my mistake all those years ago and paid a heavy price – and rightly so for the pain I inflicted on Veronica. But I also discovered the power of the human spirit during those ten long years in prison. I walked out a changed man. The hate and judgment had gone, replaced by love and forgiveness, which are the very foundations Mindset Mastery was built on.'

'So let me get this straight,' said Phillips. 'People with addiction issues trust *you*, a convicted felon, along with your ex-con mates, to sort them out?'

Garcia let out a sardonic chuckle. 'That's a very blinkered view, Chief Inspector. I would have expected more from an intelligent woman such as you.'

Phillips held his gaze. 'Well. When you spend all day putting murderers and rapists away – like *we* do – it's kinda hard to believe they're all desperate to change their ways, if only someone would let them share their inner feelings.'

A slight snarl reached Garcia's top lip and he stood. 'I think we're done here. Henry will have your list waiting for you on your way out.' He turned on his heels and marched out of the room.

'I think you touched a nerve there, Guv,' said Jones playfully.

Phillips grinned. 'Yeah. I think I did.'

26

T hree hours later, Phillips and Jones cradled hot drinks in Chakrabortty's office in the pathology department of the Manchester Royal Infirmary, having just witnessed Juliet Dobson's post-mortem.

'So, we can be pretty confident the two murders were committed by the same killer?' Phillips took a swig of her coffee.

Chakrabortty folded her long slender arms across her chest as she leaned back into her chair. 'Considering the same animal anaesthetic was used and the way in which the brain was removed – carefully as opposed to surgically – I'd say so, yes. That said, chloroform was used this time as opposed to rohypnol.'

Phillips nodded. 'That could suggest the killer didn't have as much time to subdue Dobson in comparison to Lewis, and as you pointed out, the bruising on the face and chest was consistent with a road traffic collision. Based on the state of her car and where it was found, it appears as if he drove into the back of it and then abducted her. We can assume she was either unconscious due to the collision, or he knocked her out shortly after. Either way, we know he used chloroform at some point before she was killed by the anaesthetic.'

'That just about sums it up,' said Chakrabortty.

Phillips took another drink. 'Do you remember Dr Harris, who worked on the copycat killer case last year?'

'From Newcastle?'

'That's the one.'

'Why do you ask?'

Phillips placed her mug down on Chakrabortty's desk and took a long silent breath. 'She has a theory on why the killer may be taking the victims' organs.'

'Really? Is she working with you again?'

'Not officially, no. More of a favour at this stage.'

'And what does she think?'

Phillips glanced at Jones, who raised his eyebrows as he cleared his throat.

Chakrabortty's eyes darted between Phillips and Jones, a slight smirk on her face. 'What is it?'

'Well...' Phillips was struggling to try and find the right words. 'She thinks we could be dealing with a cannibal of some kind.'

Chakrabortty scoffed. 'You what?'

Phillips nodded sagely. 'I know. I know. It sounds ridiculous, but she makes a compelling argument.'

Chakrabortty sat forward now. 'I'd love to hear it.'

Phillips pulled her phone from her pocket, then took a moment to locate the email Harris had sent through on Sunday night before passing the handset across to the doctor. 'These are photographs of drawings that depict the funeral rituals of ancient Polynesian tribes.

Chakrabortty stared at the phone in her hand.

'If you pull up the crime scene photos Evans emailed over to us last week, you'll see the similarities between the two.'

Chakrabortty did as instructed and a moment later

images of Lewis and Dobson appeared on her laptop screen. For a moment she said nothing as she glanced between the two sets of photographs. 'They're identical,' she said finally.

'We know,' replied Phillips. 'Which is why it's impossible to dismiss Harris's theory. Based on the limited information we have on these tribes, we know they used to preserve the bodies of their own people as well as those of their enemies killed in battle. Then, on the turn of the new moon, they would eat their organs.'

Chakrabortty frowned as the words landed.

Phillips continued. 'The idea being they would take on the strengths and spirits of the dead.'

'I've heard it all now,' said Chakrabortty 'So are you taking this theory seriously?'

Phillips shrugged. 'Let's just say I'm keeping an open mind, but based on the likeness between those images, there's no way we can ignore it. Plus, I trust Siobhan's judgement. If she thinks there's something to explore, then we'll do it.'

Chakrabortty shook her head as she exhaled loudly. 'I wouldn't want to be the one to tell chief constable Fox about this.'

'Me neither, which is why I'll be briefing Carter as soon as we get back this afternoon.'

'So he doesn't know about the cannibalism theory, then?' asked Chakrabortty.

'Not yet. I wanted a bit more time to process it first and I thought it made sense to see how Dobson's PM went. Based on your findings, there's nothing to suggest Harris's theory couldn't be a possibility worth seriously considering.'

Chakrabortty handed Phillips's phone back. 'I'm not sure I know what to make of that, to be honest. I've got a cast iron stomach, as you know, but if it is true, that makes me feel sick. You must be wondering why you came back.'

Phillips chortled. 'The thought had crossed my mind.'

Chakrabortty glanced at her watch. 'Look, I'm really sorry, but I'm going to have to crack on. I have another two PMs to get through this afternoon. Is there anything else you need before I get washed up for the next one?'

'Not from me.' Phillips glanced at Jones.

'No.' He placed his mug on the desk. 'I think we've covered everything.'

Chakrabortty stood.

Phillips and Jones matched her before following her out.

Five minutes later they were making their way through the rain towards the multi-story car park when Phillips's phone began to vibrate. Fishing it out, she could see it was her senior CSI. 'Andy, what have you got for me?'

'It's the soil samples we found on the shawl wrapped around Juliet Dobson. They're a match for the mud we found in AJ Lewis's heels.'

'So they were both taken to the same location?'

'Exactly.'

'Any idea where?'

'Not yet, but I've spoken to the Pedology team and they're working on it.'

'Did they give you a timescale?'

'No. They're insanely busy and short staffed but I did stress the urgency. They said they'll try and get back to me within the week.'

'That's way too long, Andy. I need those results yesterday.'

'I hear what you're saying, Jane, but I'm not sure what else I can do.'

Phillips took a moment to think before answering. 'Leave it with me. I have an idea how we can speed things up.'

'Ok.'

'Anything else?'

'No. That's it for now.'

'Thanks, Andy.' Phillips ended the call, then shared the full details of her conversation with Jones.

'So what are you going to do?' he asked as they reached the staircase of the car park.

'Me? Nothing. Chief Superintendent Carter on the other hand? He's gonna kick someone's arse for us in Pedology. Then we'll see how quickly those results turn up.'

27

C arter stared in silence at Phillips, his expression blank.

'Told you you wouldn't believe it, sir.'

'I don't.' He shook his head. 'I mean, I do; I believe what you're saying – of course I do –but I can't quite believe *what* you're telling me.'

'I know, sir. I felt the exact same way when Siobhan shared it with me.'

Carter turned his attention back to Phillips's phone, which he held in his left hand. Prior to their meeting, she'd emailed him the crime scene photos of Lewis and Dobson to compare them to the ancient Polynesian examples on her phone. 'I mean the likeness between the two sets of images is ridiculous, Jane.'

Phillips exhaled sharply. 'How do you think Fox will take it?'

Carter closed his eyes momentarily as he let out a sardonic chuckle, then opened them again. 'Oh, I'm sure she'll be delighted with the fact we've got a potential cannibal praying on the good people of Manchester.' His tone oozed sarcasm. 'And I for one can't wait to tell her.'

Phillips couldn't think of anything to say.

Carter handed back Phillips's phone. 'So outside of this, is there anything positive I can share with Fox to try and soften the blow?'

'Like I said earlier, sir, we've managed to link both our victims to the Mindset Mastery Clinic in Monk's Heath. That's our focus at the moment.'

'And you say the guy who runs it... Garcia, was it?'

'Yes, sir.'

'He's got form?'

'In the States, yes. Nothing since he moved over here.'

'So what's your next play with him?' asked Carter.

'We secured a copy of the patient records this morning, and the guys have already been interrogating the staff list since yesterday. Bov and Entwistle were due to meet with a couple of the staff members who also have records, this morning: the managing director, a guy called Jim Markham, who served time for tax evasion, and one of the maintenance guys called Sammy Finch, who's done multiple stretches for burglary over the years. I'm expecting an update when I get back downstairs. I came straight up here as soon as I got back.'

Carter said nothing for a moment and appeared deep in thought. 'If I can swing it with her gaffer, how would you feel about Siobhan joining the team again for a few weeks to work out if there's anything in this ancient organ harvesting link?'

'I'd feel great, sir. Like you say, she knows her stuff and if we *are* dealing with potential cannibalism, it's way beyond me or the scope of my team.'

'In that case, I'll make the call as soon as we're done here.'

'Great.'

Carter nodded. 'Well, was there anything else?'

'There was one thing, actually.'

'Go on.'

'Evans has discovered that soil samples on Lewis's feet are a match for those found on Dobson's shawl.'

'Ok.'

'If we can narrow down where those samples came from, it could get us closer to the killer,' said Phillips.

'Makes sense.'

'Well, here's my issue. Pedology are dragging their feet and reckon it could take a week to get us the results, and that's just not quick enough when there's a chance he could kill again in the next five days.'

'So what can I do to help?'

'Well, I was hoping you could use your influence to speed things up for us.'

Carter nodded. 'I'll make it happen.'

Phillips smiled.

'Anything else?'

'Not from me.'

'In that case, I'd best let you get back to it.'

Phillips stood.

'In the meantime, I'm going to have to figure out a way to break this to Fox.'

'Good luck with that.' Phillips grinned. 'I feel like I've said this a lot this week, but rather you than me.'

Carter let out another sardonic chuckle. 'I knew today was going to be bad day. I could feel it in my bones when I was driving in.'

'You must be psychic,' replied Phillips.

'No.' Carter shook his head. 'I feel that way every day.'

BACK DOWNSTAIRS, Phillips strode into the main office and headed towards the team. By the looks on the faces of Bovalino and Entwistle, it was evident Jones had already brought them up to speed on Harris's theory.

'You've told them, then?' she asked.

Jones nodded.

'We knew this case was a weird one, boss,' said Bovalino. 'But this is on another level entirely.'

Phillips dropped into the chair at the spare desk.

'How did Carter take the news?' asked Jones.

'Like the rest of us: shock, horror, complete disbelief. The good news is he's trying to second Siobhan Harris to MCU to help us try and figure out who the hell is behind these murders.'

'Whistler will be pleased,' chimed Bovalino. 'Proper had the hots for her, didn't you, mate?'

'Piss off.' Entwistle blushed.

'Anyway. Hopefully he can make it happen, 'cos we need all the help we can get right now.' Phillips turned her attention to Entwistle and Bovalino. 'How did you guys get on with Markham and Finch this morning?'

Entwistle dropped his pen heavily on his pad. 'Both clearly as dodgy as they come, but both have cast iron alibis that have already checked out.'

'Unlike our friend Lyndon Garcia,' said Jones. 'There's something definitely not right with that guy.'

'True.' Phillips folded her arms. 'But is he our killer?'

Jones ran his bony fingers through his thinning hair. 'He was hiding something for sure, but murder? I just don't know.'

Phillips continued. 'Whoever it was, Chakrabortty reckons that when they removed Lewis's heart and Dobson's brain they were *careful,* as opposed to *skilful*.'

'So we're not necessarily looking for a surgeon,' Jones added.

'No,' said Phillips. 'He's more likely to have butchery or hunting skills.'

'Or maybe he could work for a funeral director?' Ventured Jones.

'It's another possibility, but whatever he does, our guy knows how to use a knife and enough about human anatomy to know exactly where to cut – but he's not precise. That said, he was skilled enough to be able to take what he wanted each time without messing with any of the surrounding organs.'

Bovalino shuddered. 'Gives me the creeps just thinking about it.'

'Me too,' added Entwistle.

'Right. Check the staff and client lists,' Phillips said. 'See if anyone has any history of working as a butcher or at an abattoir – or any connection to hunting or as Jonesy suggested, an undertaker.'

Bov and Entwistle nodded as they scribbled in their pads.

'Also, let's see if anyone has any links to Polynesia. It's a long shot, but right now, it seems as if anything's possible.'

A chorus of 'Yes, Guv's' filled the room as Phillips stepped up from the chair and headed into her office.

28

After buying himself a Diet Coke, he took a seat at a small table located in the corner of the old pub and waited for Carl Walsh to arrive. He'd been tracking Carl for weeks now and knew that by 6 p.m. he'd be occupying his usual spot, propping up the bar in the Red Lion in Finney Green. It was the same routine he followed every night on his way home from work at the dog food factory, which was located just a mile down the road. He checked his watch; 5.50 p.m. It wouldn't be long now. From his position seated at the table he could see the entrance to the pub and everyone who came and went. He'd recced the place a number of times before and had chosen this table for that exact reason.

A few minutes later and bang on time, the door opened and Carl Walsh stepped inside. He turned his head away so as not to be recognised, then waited for Carl to order his usual pint of strong cider, before daring to look back.

As ever, Carl dropped onto the high stool at the end of the bar and pulled out his newspaper before taking a few large mouthful of his drink. It was a routine as regular as clockwork.

For the next thirty minutes he remained seated at the table and watched on as Carl polished off three pints of cider, before ordering another one along with a whisky chaser.

It was time to make his move. Draining the remainder of his Diet Coke, he stepped up from the table and made his way to the bar where he ordered another one from the pocket-sized barmaid with her peroxide blond hair and tattooed wrists. The sickly-sweet smell of cannabis hung in the air. She had evidently smoked some recently.

Carl, it seemed, was yet to notice him.

When the barmaid returned with his drink, he paid cash and turned to face his quarry. 'All right, Carl?' he asked as he moved along the bar towards him.

Carl looked up from his newspaper and paused for a moment before a dawn of realisation spread across his face. 'What are *you* doing in here?' He took a swig from his cider.

'I was in the area and fancied a drink.'

Carl's eyes locked on his pint of Diet Coke and his brow furrowed.

'I'm driving,' he said by way of explanation.

Carl nodded but seemed eager to get back to his paper. He wasn't the chatty type at the best of times.

'Can I get you another?'

The change in Carl's demeanour was instant and notable. He nodded. 'Yeah. Pint of Strongbow, please.'

He turned to relay the instructions to the barmaid. She'd evidently been listening to their conversation and was already in the process of pouring his pint. A moment later she placed it on the bar and collected payment.

'Have you been working today?'

'I work every bloody day,' replied Carl before taking a slug of cider.

'Feels that way, does it?'

Carl didn't respond.

'What is it you do again?' He already knew the answer, of course, but he needed to keep him talking.

'Security, down the road.'

'It's the dog food factory, isn't it?'

'Yeah.'

'How long you been working there?'

'Too long.' Carl was already close to finishing his pint.

'You're ex-military, aren't you?'

'Twenty-two years in the Green Howards.'

'Wow. I bet you've seen some sights.'

Carl drained his glass. 'I need a piss.' He gestured towards the barmaid with his empty glass. 'Mindy, put another one in there, will you?'

He watched him head into the toilets, and as Mindy placed the fresh pint on the bar, he handed across a five-pound note. 'I'll get it,' he said with a warm smile.

Mindy took his money and as she turned to face the till, he slipped the small tablet into Carl's cider, watching it sink to the bottom and dissolve in an instant.

The barmaid returned with his change just as Carl made his way back to the bar.

'This one's on me, too,' he said warmly.

Carl shrugged as he retook his seat and got stuck into his drink.

'Actually, I have a bit of a confession to make.'

Carl eyed him cautiously.

'I wasn't just in the area. I'm here because I wanted to talk to you.'

'Oh yeah.' Carl took yet another mouthful. 'What about?'

'Your time in the army. I know a little bit about it, of course, but I'm fascinated by what you went through in Iraq and Afghanistan. I was hoping you might share some more of it with me.'

'There's nothing to say.'

'Now you're just being modest.'

'No. I'm not. I went to war because I believed we were fighting to protect the innocent people stuck in those god-forsaken hell-holes. Fighting for freedom and, ultimately, peace.'

'And you weren't?'

'Were we fuck!' Carl scoffed. 'We were there to ensure Britain and America got our share of the gold and oil. Our government didn't give a shit about the innocents – it was all about money. Pure and simple. The things I did, the atrocities I witnessed – they haunt me every day.'

'You seem quite bitter about it, Carl.'

'Wouldn't you be? Lied to every day. Ordered to kill people for our government's commercial gain. Damn right I'm bitter.'

He shook his head. 'Anger will eat you up.'

'I'm passed fucking caring, to be honest.'

'And is that why you drink like you do?'

Carl recoiled. 'Like what? I have a few pints on my way home to relax and that's it.'

He glanced at the near empty glass in Carl's hand. 'By my count that's your sixth pint.'

'What? You keeping score or something? And before you get all fucking preachy on me, let's remember *you* bought the last two.'

He raised his arms in defence. 'Look. I'm not here to start a fight. I just think it's a shame that someone like you, with all your experience and skills, who has more to offer the world than carrying all that anger and bitterness around, is drinking himself into a coma every night.'

'What else am I gonna do? There's nothing waiting for me at home, is there?'

'Ah, that's right. Your wife died last year, didn't she?'

Carl glared at him now, his mouth open, but no words would come out.

'Are you ok?'

Carl's eyes began to glaze over, and his face crumpled. 'I f-f-feel...a...bit...dishy...' He was beginning to slur his words. The rohypnol was kicking in.

Carl attempted to step off the stool but as he did he stumbled forward.

He stepped in to stop him tumbling to the ground. 'Maybe you've had enough for tonight.'

'Is he all right?' asked Mindy, a look of concern on her face.

He turned to face her. 'I think he's maybe had one too many.'

Mindy shrugged. 'Puts away twice as much most nights.'

He needed to move quickly now. 'I'll take him outside, see if that helps.'

Mindy nodded but her attention was soon drawn to a new customer who had just arrived at the bar.

With his shoulder propped under Carl's armpit and his arm around his back, he helped him through the front doors and out onto the car park. 'Can I give you a lift home?' he asked.

Carl mumbled his approval, and a moment later, the indicators on the car flashed as he disengaged the central locking. Opening the back door, he gently pushed Carl inside onto the back seat, where he lay in a motionless heap. Closing the car door once more, he scanned the area for any prying eyes but was pleased to see they were completely alone. Jumping into the driver's seat, he fired the engine, then glanced over his shoulder at Carl, who was now unconscious. He had to admit it was sad to see a real-life war hero so angry, with nothing to do but get drunk each night, but he took great comfort from the fact that he was about to change all that. Carl Walsh may not believe his life had purpose, but his death certainly would. *He* would make sure of that.

29

P hillips was sitting at the breakfast bar in her dressing
gown enjoying a freshly brewed coffee when Adam
walked in wearing nothing but a pair of sport shorts,
just before 7 a.m.

'Morning.' He rubbed his eyes.

'Morning, love.' It had been over nine months since he'd
been stabbed – an attack that had almost killed him – and the
cluster of scars on his torso was a stark reminder of the
horrific night she had discovered him, lying in their garden in
a pool of his own blood. She shuddered at the memory, then
found herself smiling as he yawned loudly and scratched his
muscular chest before pouring himself a coffee.

'What time did you get back last night?' He slipped onto
the stool next to her.

'About ten, I think.'

'I didn't hear you come to bed.'

She chuckled. 'I know. It's becoming a habit. You were
snoring like a trooper by the time I came up.'

Adam shook his head. 'Sorry, babe. It's these meds they've
got me on. They're like bloody horse tranquillisers.'

'Maybe I should try them. I've not had a decent night's sleep since I went back to work.'

He wrapped his arm around her shoulder. 'I'm worried about you. Are you sure this is what you want?'

Phillips took a mouthful of coffee. 'I've been asking myself that same question every single day and keep coming up with different answers. Sometimes I can't imagine doing anything else. Then other days I wonder what the hell I'm doing.'

'If you want to change your mind and walk away – *for good this time* – you know I'll support you, don't you?'

'I know, Adam, but I can't just walk away again. Not now. And besides, what would I do?'

'I dunno, but your skills must be very valuable in the private sector.'

Phillips wasn't convinced. She'd seen many a hardened detective lose their identity when they moved into civvy street.

'You don't owe them anything and I'm sure no one would blame you if you did. God knows they've had their pound of flesh over the years.'

Phillips nodded, but the truth was the job had sucked her in once again and all she could think about now was catching Lewis and Dobson's killer before he struck again.

'So what have you got planned today?' she asked.

Adam took a swig of coffee. 'Nothing this morning, so I thought I might head to the gym, but I've got a call with Raj at 2 this afternoon to firm up the plans for me going back to work.'

'That's great. Has he given you a timescale?'

'Next couple of weeks ideally. The HR director is away on leave, which will slow things down, but he's hoping to get all the paperwork signed off when she's back next week.'

'Brilliant,' said Phillips. 'I'm really pleased for you and I'm so proud of you for wanting to go back after everything you've been through.'

'I could say the same about you.' Adam leaned in and kissed her.

At that moment Phillips's phone – lying on the breakfast bar – began to ring. Glancing at the screen, she could see it was Jonesy. She frowned. 'He never rings this early unless it's bad news.' She answered it. 'What's up?'

'We've found another body, Guv.'

Phillips's heart sank. 'Shit. Where?'

Adam raised his eyebrows.

'Woodland near Alderley Park. An IC1 male, naked apart from the shawl and surrounded by white roses again, only this time he's cut the eyes out.'

'Jesus Christ,' Phillips whispered into the phone. She glanced at the clock on the wall. 'I'll be with you in an hour. Text me the location, will you?'

'I'll do it now.' Jones then rang off.

'Everything ok?' asked Adam.

'They've found another body. Same as the last two.'

'Oh God.'

Phillips slipped off the breakfast stool as her phone beeped indicating Jones's message had landed. 'I've got to go.'

'No rest for the wicked.'

THE SCENE WAS ALL TOO familiar. Phillips parked up the Mini Cooper next to an array of police vehicles that looked almost as if they'd been abandoned next to the large area of woodland. A uniformed officer stood guard at the entrance to the path that led down to the crime scene. After passing under the police tape, she made her way down the dirt track. Up ahead she could see a cluster of uniformed officers as well as a couple of paramedics in their green uniforms and high-vis jackets. Standing next to them she spotted Jones, suited and booted in a set of white forensics overalls.

He turned just as she reached him. 'Morning, Guv.'

'Is it? So where's the body?'

'Just through those trees.' He glanced at the paramedics who were packing up next to them. 'The medics declared life-extinct about thirty minutes ago. Evans and the team are setting up as we speak.'

'Right, well, let's get round there and take a look, shall we?'

Jones nodded and led the way.

'Who found him?' she asked over his shoulder.

'Dog walker, out with her two beagles. She walks them here every day and reckons this is a quiet spot and she rarely sees anyone most mornings.'

'Did she come this way yesterday?'

'Yeah. Said there was no sign of him then.'

'So we can assume he was killed in the last twenty-four hours.'

'Seems that way, yeah,' said Jones. 'Evans will no doubt give us a more accurate timescale.'

They continued walking across the uneven, frozen ground until they came to a clearing and the white CSI tent came into view. Bovalino was standing outside, and once again his massive physique appeared to be bursting out of his forensic suit.

'Prepare yourself,' said Jones as they reached the tent. 'This is the worst one yet.'

Bovalino handed her a set of white overalls.

'Thanks, Bov.'

A couple of minutes later Phillips stepped inside the tent. Evans and his team had already assumed their usual posi-tions over the body, photographing each area close up. As with the others, the victim was laid on the ground, his naked body wrapped in a white shawl, white roses placed in a ring around the body but once again broken at the feet. Moving closer, she could see the dark fleshy holes in his face where his eyes had once been. She felt her stomach turn. Jones was right: this *was* the worst one yet but, such was her experience in Major Crimes, nothing she hadn't seen before.

Evans turned to face them. 'As you can see, it's pretty much a carbon copy of the first two. Time of death roughly the same – killed elsewhere and moved here. No ID or any personal items that we've been able to find so far.'

Phillips nodded. 'Any soil samples on the body?'

'Too early at this stage, but I'll let you know if I find any. I'll be taking fingerprints shortly, so we'll get those on the system as soon as we can, too.'

'Thanks, Andy.' Phillips took a picture of the scene just before her phone began to ring in her hand. It was Carter. 'Morning, sir.'

He wasted no time with pleasantries. *'I heard we have another body.'*

Phillips wanted to ask who had told him but thought better of it as she stepped back outside the tent. 'Yes, sir. This time the eyes have been cut out.'

'Good God!'

'It's pretty gruesome. Like something out of a horror movie.'

'And has it been posed, like the others?'

'I'm afraid so,' replied Phillips.

Carter exhaled sharply on the end of the line. *'Any idea on who the victim is?'*

'No, sir, not yet. Like the others, there's no ID or personal effects.'

'I spoke to Fox last night about Lewis and Dobson.'

'And how did she react? Or do I even need to ask?'

'*No, you don't. As expected, she went off it and she's going to blow a gasket when I tell her about this.*'

Phillips remained silent, unsure how to respond to that.

'*Well, you'll be glad to hear we've had clearance to second Siobhan into the team. She'll be with you later today.*'

'Hopefully she can shed some light on what the hell is going on here.'

'*Yeah, let's hope so. For all our sakes,*' said Carter. '*As soon as you have anything, even the slightest breakthrough, you'll call me, won't you?*'

'Of course, sir.'

'*And I've had a word with the guys in Pedology. You should see movement on those samples very soon.*'

'Thank you, sir.'

'*Ok. Well, I'd better go and speak to Fox before the jungle drums start beating. I'll talk to you later.*' With that he ended the call.

A moment later her phone began to ring again. This time it was Entwistle.

'Whistler?'

'*Morning, boss. Jonesy told me we've got another victim.*'

'Yeah. Pretty much identical to the others, but this time the eyes are missing.'

'*That's totally fucked up.*'

'Yeah it is.'

'*On that, I thought you'd want to know. I've found someone on the staff list with a link to butchery.*'

'Really?'

'*A guy named Vasil Hoxha. He served eighteen months of a three-year sentence for GBH back in 2018, and when he was inside one of this work responsibilities is listed as butchery in the prison canteen. He's originally from Albania but now lives in Rusholme and works at Mindset Mastery in the kitchens.*'

'Oh, does he now?'

'*Yeah. I've sent his address to your email.*'

'Anything else you can tell me about him?'

'*Nothing yet but I'll keep looking.*'

'Do that and keep me across any updates as soon as you can get them.'

'*Will do. And one more thing. I think I've figured out who might have vouched for Lyndon Garcia on his residency application.*'

'Oh yeah? Who?'

'*The Home Secretary.*'

'You what? Seriously?'

'*Turns out his niece was a patient at the clinic last year. His sister's kid. Drugs and sex addiction, apparently.*'

'No wonder Garcia didn't want us to see that client list.'

'*That's what I thought.*'

'Great work, Whistler. Anything else?'

'*No, that's all I've got just now.*'

'Ok. Well, we'll head over to Hoxha's place and we'll see you in the office later.'

'*No worries. See you then.*'

Jones and Bovalino approached.

'Everything all right with Carter?' asked Jones.

'Yeah. Somehow, he already knew about the body.'

'How? I know he's our gaffer, but it should be down to *you* to tell him, not some fucking gossip at Ashton House.'

Phillips nodded. 'It pisses me off too, but that's the least of our worries right now. Anyway, the good news is Siobhan Harris's secondment has been approved.'

'So when is she coming down?' asked Jones.

'This afternoon. In the meantime, Whistler has come up with an ex-con who worked as a butcher in Hawk Green. An Albanian called Vasil Hoxha. Lives in Rusholme.' Phillips thumbed back in the direction of the cars. 'I think you and I should pay him a visit.'

'With pleasure, Guv.'

'We can head over in my Mini.' She turned to Bov now. 'You stay here and see if you can get Evans to sort those fingerprints ASAP.'

The big man nodded. 'I'll stand over him until it's done.'

30

Forty minutes later, Phillips and Jones found themselves stuck in stationary rush hour traffic on the Princess Parkway, one of the main arterial routes funnelling people from South Manchester into the city centre. As they crawled at a snail's pace past the large white Siemens building – which over the years had become an unlikely landmark for daily commuters – Phillips decided she'd had enough of the delay and turned right at the first available junction, then headed 'cross-country'. She knew the city well and spent the next twenty minutes zig-zagging her way through the suburbs of West Didsbury, Withington and Fallowfield before pushing on to their final destination in Rusholme.

Hoxha lived on Linden Road, in a typical Manchester row of terraced houses connected directly to the street. There were no gardens to speak of but each house did have its own small yard with access to a public alleyway to the rear. As they parked up in front of Hoxha's address, it was evident for all to see that his property was one of the less well maintained on the street. The green paint on the front door had blistered and begun to peel, and the front window to the left of it was half covered by a large piece of plywood, which looked to have been screwed roughly into place.

Phillips killed the engine.

A moment later, with Jones at her side, she rapped her knuckles on the front door and waited. Initially there was no response, so she tried a couple more times until eventually the door opened and a flabby man Phillips placed in his forties peered out.

He was wearing a grubby white sleeveless vest that exposed his thick, tattooed arms, and a pair of black Adidas tracksuit bottoms. 'Yes?' His eyes were narrow and bloodshot.

'Vasil Hoxha?' said Phillips.

'Who wants to know?'

She presented her ID. 'May we come in?'

Hoxha appeared reluctant at first as he stared out at them, his expression glazed. 'Am I under arrest?' His Albanian accent was thick.

Phillips was already running out of patience with him. 'No, but you will be if you don't let us in.'

A snarl formed on Hoxha's lip as he grunted and opened the door. 'Go through to the kitchen at the back.'

Phillips led Jones through and soon found herself in the tiny galley kitchen at the rear of the property. It reeked of stale cigarette smoke and, in keeping with the outside of the house, was in need of a major renovation, the peeling wallpaper yellow from the nicotine.

Hoxha seemed unwilling to offer them a seat and instead stood next to the cooker, his hands stuffed into the pockets of his tracksuit bottoms.

Phillips got straight to the point. 'Have you ever met a man named AJ Lewis?'

Hoxha shook his head but said nothing.

'What about a woman called Juliet Dobson?'

'No.' Hoxha pulled his hands out of his pockets and folded his thick arms across his chest exposing multiple, recent-looking scars on his forearms. 'Never heard of either of them.'

'Really?' pushed Phillips.

'Really.'

'Do you work at the Mindset Mastery clinic in Monk's Heath?'

'Yeah.' Hoxha was a man of few words.

'But you've never heard of either of the people I just mentioned?'

Hoxha shrugged. 'I don't think so, no.'

Phillips continued. 'Because Lewis was a client and Dobson worked at the clinic.'

'I work in the kitchens; I don't talk to anyone outside of that.'

'I see,' said Phillips.

'How long have you worked there?' asked Jones.

Hoxha paused before he answered. 'About three years.'

'And what did you do before that?'

Hoxha's eyes darted between Phillips and Jones, and he appeared reluctant to speak as he fumbled for a packet of cigarettes in his pocket.

'Cat got your tongue?' said Jones.

Hoxha placed a cigarette in between his lips, lit it and took a long drag before exhaling a large plume of smoke. 'I was in prison.'

'That's right, I remember now,' said Jones. 'You did time for GBH, didn't you? So what happened?'

'I was drunk and hit a man. He called the girl I was with a slut, and I lost my temper.'

'How long did you serve?' Phillips already knew the answer, but it was a simple way to gauge how truthful he was being with them.

'Eighteen months. I got out early for good behaviour.'

Phillips continued. 'Did you have a job at the prison?'

Hoxha exhaled more smoke. 'I worked in the kitchens.'

'Doing what exactly?'

'Preparing food, cutting up the meat and chickens mostly.'

'Like a butcher?' Phillips asked.

Hoxha shook his head as he took another long drag. 'Everything came pre-packed. I just cut it up into pieces to make it go further in the meals. Pretty boring work but it beat sitting in my cell all day.'

'So would you say you're pretty handy with a knife?' Jones jumped in.

Hoxha's eyes narrowed as he took one final drag before squashing the butt onto a dirty dinner plate on the worktop. 'What's this about?'

Phillips cut back in now. 'Where were you last night?'

'The pub.'

'Can you be more specific?'

'The Coach and Horses, just off the main road.'

'What time did you get there?' said Phillips.

'About two.' Hoxha lit another cigarette, much to Phillips's chagrin.

'Bit early for a Monday, isn't it?'

'I have a few days off this week, and I've got nothing else to do.'

'So, what time did you leave?' Jones asked.

Hoxha chuckled. 'I don't remember. I was pissed.'

'Roughly,' pushed Phillips.

'I dunno, about nine I guess.'

Phillips scanned the room. 'And can anyone vouch for you?'

'You can probably ask Sheila.'

'And who's she?' Jones asked.

'The landlady. She's always there.'

Phillips nodded. 'Can you tell us where you were on the night of Sunday the 6th of February between 8 p.m. and midnight?'

Hoxha exhaled. 'Probably in the pub.'

'And what about the same time Wednesday the 9th?' Phillips added.

'Are you gonna tell me what this is about or what?'

'Just answer the question,' said Jones, firmly.

Hoxha scowled as he locked eyes with Jones. 'The *pub*.'

Phillips studied his body language for any sign he was lying, but if he was, he was hiding it well.

'I know my rights,' growled Hoxha. 'Either you tell me what this is about, or you need to leave.'

'Very well. We're investigating the murders of AJ Lewis and Juliet Dobson.' Phillips studied his reaction. He didn't so much as flinch. 'AJ was a client at The Mindset Mastery Clinic and Juliet worked there as part of the addiction retreats.'

'So, what's this got to do with me?'

'We're talking to everyone on the staff list with a record,' said Phillips.

'Just because I made a mistake once,' Hoxha stubbed out his second cigarette with force, 'doesn't make me a killer.'

Jones cut back in now. 'What did you do in Albania, Vasil?'

'None of your business,' he growled.

'Got something to hide?'

'My life in Albania has got nothing to do with my life here. It is in the past and that is where it stays.'

Jones continued to push. 'Why? What's so bad that you won't talk about it?'

Hoxha remained stony-faced as he glared at Jones.

The room fell silent as remnants of cigarette smoke hung in the air.

'How did you get the scars on your arms?' asked Phillips.

'I don't have to tell you that.'

He was clearly unhappy at being questioned and was giving them nothing of value.

Phillips decided to cut their losses for the time being. 'Right, well, obviously we'll need to double-check your movements on the nights in question.' She pulled a business card from her pocket and passed it across.

Hoxha shoved his hands back into his pockets defiantly.

Phillips placed the card down on the worktop between them. 'If you think of anything we might need to know, my number is on there.'

Hoxha sniffed contemptuously but remained silent.

'We'll see ourselves out.'

Because the Mini was parked directly outside Hoxha's front door, Phillips waited until they were sitting safely back inside before she debriefed. 'He seemed pretty touchy when you asked him about his life in Albania.'

Jones nodded. 'Yeah. He really didn't like that, did he?'

'We need to know who he was and what he did over there. And I want full details of everything he did in prison. Work records, associates, psych analysis, the lot. Also, did he have any contact with Dobson while he was inside?'

'I'll get Bov straight onto it,' said Jones.

'We need to speak to this Sheila woman at the Coach and Horses, plus check any CCTV along the high street around the pub. See if we can find out what time he really left.'

'Whistler can organise that for us with the wider team.'

'So where did he get those scars on his arms?' Mused Phillips.

'None of the victims had any tissue under their nails so it's unlikely they're defensive wounds.'

Phillips fired the engine. 'No. They looked like they'd been done with a blade or a sharp edge.'

'So where to now, boss?' asked Jones.

'Back to the office. Let's see if we've managed to get this morning's fingerprints sorted.' She slipped the car in gear and pulled away from the kerb. 'And with a bit of luck, Dr Harris might even be there, waiting for us.'

few hours later, Phillips was sitting at her desk
when Entwistle knocked on the open door, causing
her to look up from her laptop.

'You got a minute, Guv?'

'Sure.' She leaned back in her chair. 'What's up?'

Entwistle took one of the seats opposite. 'We've managed
to ID this morning's victim.'

'That was quick.'

'Yeah. His fingerprints were in the system.'

Phillips raised an eyebrow. 'How so?'

'Ex-military. The name's Carl Walsh. He was a Colour
Sergeant in the Green Howards who served in Iraq and
Afghanistan: one tour of Iraq, two in Afghanistan. I haven't
had a chance to check his background in detail yet. As soon
as I'm done here I'll contact the MOD records office in Scot-
land and request his full file. They're usually pretty quick
when the request comes from us.'

'Do we have an address and next of kin?'

Entwistle glanced at his notes. 'His council tax records are
attached to an address in Finney Green, 14 Merion Street, but

he was registered for the single person discount, so he must have lived alone.'

'Any idea if he had a partner?'

'Not sure at this stage.'

'What about his work?'

'Nothing yet, but I'll be going through all of that this afternoon,' said Entwistle.

'Have you checked with MisPers to see if anyone reported him missing?'

'Just got off the phone with them but so far no one's been in touch.'

Phillips tapped her pen against her teeth for a moment. 'Maybe Mr Walsh was a bit of a loner.'

'Certainly appears that way, boss.'

'How long do you think it'll take to get his military records?' asked Phillips.

'If I call them now, we should have them by lunchtime tomorrow, with a bit of luck.'

'Ok, and what about the rest of his background?'

'I can get most of that today, I reckon. If he was married or has kids, they'll be on the government databases, which are easy to access.'

'Good,' said Phillips. 'As quick as you can, please, Whistler. We need to get a handle on who this guy was and why our killer may have targeted him.'

'Of course.'

'Oh. And check him against the client and staff lists at Mindset Mastery. See if he's got anything to do with them.'

'I'll get straight onto it.' He stood up and made to leave but stopped in his tracks.

'Knock, knock,' said Siobhan Harris from the doorway, a large suitcase positioned next to her. She looked as smart as ever, her petite frame dressed in a white blouse atop of a black pencil skirt that matched her dark shoulder-length bob. Her shapely legs ran into her trademark black stiletto heels. 'Room for a little one?'

'Here she is!' exclaimed Phillips, clapping her hands together.

Harris flashed a broad smile.

'You remember Siobhan, don't you, Whistler?'

Harris recoiled slightly. 'Whistler?' Her accent was soft north east.

'It's his nickname, now,' explained Phillips. 'Given to him by Bovalino. Must have been after the copycat case, which is why you've not heard us call him that before.'

'Hi,' said Entwistle coyly.

Phillips could see he was blushing slightly and smiled to herself. It seemed Bovalino had been right and Entwistle did have a thing for the good doctor. Not surprising, considering how attractive she was.

'Where can I put this?' Harris pointed to her case.

'Stick it in here for the time being,' replied Phillips.

Harris made to grab the handle, but Entwistle lurched forward and locked his hand onto it. 'I'll take care of that,' he said as he pulled it inside the office.

Harris flashed a smile. 'And they say chivalry's dead.'

'Whistler, close the door on the way out, will you?' said Phillips.

Entwistle nodded and headed for the door, stepping somewhat awkwardly past Harris, resembling a lovesick teenager in the presence of his high-school crush.

Phillips got up from the chair and drew Harris into a hug. 'If I didn't know better, I'd say someone has the hots for you.'

Harris's brow furrowed. 'Who?'

'Entwistle, of course,' whispered Phillips, remembering her office was not exactly soundproof.

'Give over.' Harris waved her away.

'Oh, come on. He turned pink as soon as he clapped eyes on you.'

'If you say so.' Harris chortled.

'And I thought *you* were the psychological profiler.' Phillips gestured for Harris to replace Entwistle in the seat opposite her as she sat back down at her desk. 'How was the journey?'

'Pretty good actually. Only took a couple of hours.'

'And where are you staying?'

'The Mal Maison.'

Phillips nodded. 'Nice. Carter's pulled out all the stops for you.'

'Diana sorted it, apparently.' Harris crossed her right leg over her left knee. 'So what's happening?'

'We've just this minute got an ID on the latest victim,' said Phillips. 'Ex-Iraq and Afghanistan combat veteran called Carl Walsh. Whistler is chasing down next of kin, but we believe he lived alone in Finney Green, which is within a five-mile radius of where he and the others were discovered.'

'And the body was posed in the same way as the previous two?'

Phillips nodded. 'I took a couple of pictures.' She located them on her phone then passed it across. 'As you can see, he cut out the eyes this time.'

Harris stared at the screen for a long moment. 'It's identical to the other two, isn't it?'

'We need the official PM results, of course, but there's no doubt in my mind we're looking at the same guy. And now we have three bodies, he's officially a serial killer.'

Just then, the door to Phillips's office opened and Carter stepped inside. 'I heard we had an interloper in the building,' he said with a broad smile.

Harris turned to face him, then stepped up out of the chair. 'Harry. Good to see you.'

'Hello, Siobhan.' Carter leaned in to kiss her lightly on the cheek. 'Thanks for coming down.'

'Glad to help and always up for a change of scenery.'

'Jane shared your theory about the Polynesian tribes.' Carter's eyes narrowed. 'Do you really think we're looking at cannibalism?'

Harris exhaled sharply as she shrugged her shoulders. 'Like I said to Jane, it's a possibility, but I couldn't say for sure. And considering some of the weird and wonderful cases you guys have investigated *before*, I certainly wouldn't rule it out completely.'

Entwistle appeared at the door now. 'Sorry to interrupt, boss, but I've found a next of kin. His daughter, Lily Dunn. Lives in Chester. Here's the address.' He handed over a yellow Post-it Note. 'He *was* married, but his wife died last year.'

'That explains the single person discount,' said Phillips.

Carter frowned and appeared confused.

'On his council tax bill, sir,' she explained. 'If he was a widower, he'd only pay for himself.'

'Ah. I see,' replied Carter.

Phillips turned to Entwistle. 'Thanks, Whistler.'

He nodded, then returned to his desk.

Carter turned back to Harris. 'Has Diana sorted you out with a decent hotel?'

'Yes, thank you. I'm at the Mal.'

'Excellent,' replied Carter. 'I'd certainly recommend their steak frites with a nice bottle of red.'

Harris smiled broadly. 'As long as it's not *Chianti*.'

Carter chuckled, catching the Hannibal Lecter reference. 'Quite.'

'Listen.' Phillips checked her watch. It was 4.30. 'I was thinking I could head over to Chester to see Lily Dunn. It's about an hour down the motorway and I can go home from there. Can I give you a lift to the hotel on the way through, Siobhan?'

'That would be great, thank you.'

'No need for that,' said Carter. 'I have a meeting in the city this evening, so I can take you if you like. It'll give is a chance to catch up.'

Harris smiled. 'Thank you, that would be lovely.'

Carter beamed back. 'Give me five minutes. I just need to get my things sorted.' He left the room with a spring in his step and set off back upstairs.

Phillips watched him go. It seemed the beautiful doctor had the same effect on men of all ages.

Harris turned back to Phillips. 'What time do we start in the morning?'

'Ideally 8 o'clock. We've got a team meeting and lots to bring you up to speed on.'

'That's fine with me.'

'And in the meantime, make sure you make the most of everything the Mal Maison has to offer, won't you? On MCU's tab, of course.'

'Ha!' scoffed Harris. 'I'm dreaming of a hot bath, room service and an early night.'

'Sounds like heaven.' Phillips grabbed her coat from the rack in the corner of the room. 'Am I ok to leave you here to wait for Carter? I want to try and beat some of the evening traffic if I can.'

'Of course.'

'Great. Just shut the door on your way out.' Phillips packed her bag and picked up her car keys. 'Right, I'll see you in the morning.'

32

T hanks to rush hour traffic on the M60, it was almost
6.30 p.m. by the time Phillips pulled up outside Lily
Dunn's address, a relatively modern detached
house on the outskirts of the historic city of Chester. A brand-
new Nissan X-Trail was parked on the double drive with its
boot open, displaying an array of shopping bags, some of
which a gangly teenager was attempting to carry into the
house. A moment later, a woman Phillips presumed was
Dunn appeared from the front door of the house and made
her way back to the car.

Phillips jumped out of the Mini and intercepted her as
she headed back inside with a heavy bag of shopping in each
hand. 'Lily Dunn?'

The woman stopped in her tracks and turned to face
Phillips, her brow furrowed. 'Yes?'

Phillips presented her ID. 'DCI Phillips from the Major
Crimes Unit in Manchester. Can I have a word? It's about
your father.'

Dunn did a double take. 'Dad? What's happened?'

Just then a different teenage boy appeared, evidently on his way to help empty the shopping.

Phillips glanced at him then back at Dunn. 'Can we talk in private?'

Dunn nodded as fear flashed in her eyes. 'This way.'

Phillips followed her into the hallway and waited as Dunn deposited her shopping bags in the kitchen.

She returned a moment later. 'We can go in the lounge.'

Phillips closed the door behind her as Dunn took a seat in a grey suede armchair, before dropping into the matching adjacent sofa.

'What's happened to him?' Dunn's voice was brimming with fear.

Phillips cleared her throat and sat forward slightly. 'I'm afraid to tell you we found a body this morning and we believe it's your father, Carl Walsh.'

Dunn stared at Phillips wide eyed and her mouth fell open.

'I'm so sorry,' added Phillips.

'So he's finally done it, then,' said Dunn, fighting tears.

Phillips's eyes narrowed. 'Sorry, done what?'

'Killed himself. He's finally gone through with it.'

Phillips shook her head. 'Your father didn't kill himself, Lily.'

A look of confusion spread across Dunn's face. 'I don't understand. If he didn't kill himself, then how did he die?'

Phillips's heart was racing in her chest. She hated this part of the job, but it had to be done. 'We believe he was murdered.'

'Murdered?' Dunn was incredulous. 'There must be some mistake.'

'I'm sorry, Lily, but there's no mistake. We've checked his fingerprints against the national database. It's your father.'

'How? *How* was he killed?'

Phillips paused. 'We need the pathologist to confirm the details, but we suspect he was probably given a lethal dose of anaesthetic.'

'Anaesthetic? What are you talking about?'

'We think your father was given a large dose of an animal anaesthetic.'

Dunn shook her head, her brow furrowed. 'By who? And why?'

'The honest answer is we don't know yet.'

'So where did it happen?'

'We don't know that either. His body was found in woodland, near Finney Green, but we believe he was killed elsewhere.'

The enormity of what was being said finally landed, causing Dunn to buckle and burst into tears, her sobs loud and guttural as she cradled her head in her hands.

Her crying prompted one of her boys to open the lounge door a moment later. 'Mum? What's the matter?'

Dunn suddenly checked herself and sat upright, sniffing loudly as she did. 'It's ok. I'm fine, Nate. DCI Phillips has just told me something I wasn't expecting to hear.' She wiped her nose with the heel of her palm. 'I'll tell you about it in a minute. Just leave us alone for now, will you?'

Nate appeared confused, but eventually nodded and closed the door behind him.

'The boys will be devastated, just like they were when Mum went last year. They loved their grandparents.'

Phillips had spotted a box of tissues sitting on top of a dresser on the other side of the room when she'd first sat down. Stepping up from the sofa, she quickly retrieved them and passed the box to Dunn.

'Thank you,' she said before blowing her nose loudly.

'I know this must have come as an awful shock,' said Phillips, 'but it would really help our investigation if I could

ask you a couple of questions about your dad. Would that
be ok?'

Dunn wiped her eyes with a second tissue and nodded.

'When did you last see him?'

She took a moment to think. 'Two Saturdays ago, I think.
He came down to see the boys for the day. Took them to the
rugby.'

'And how was he then?'

Dunn shrugged. 'His usual self: smiling when the boys
were looking, but really quite sad under the surface.'

'Why was that?' asked Phillips.

'He's been unhappy for a long time.' Dunn caught herself.
'Sorry, he'd been unhappy for a long time. I can't believe I'm
talking about him in the past tense.'

'I know,' said Phillips. 'I'm afraid these conversations are
never easy.'

Dunn pulled a fresh tissue from the box and sniffed
loudly as she rubbed her nose with it.

'Why was your dad so unhappy?'

'He's been like that for years. It started when he came
home from his last tour of Afghanistan. He couldn't reconcile
himself to what he'd done out there. Said they were sold a
pack of lies by the government and it wasn't about freedom. It
was about oil and money. He suffered with night terrors and
depression and was eventually diagnosed with PTSD. He'd
also been badly injured on his last tour and was medically
discharged after twenty years as a Green Howard. He didn't
want to leave but wasn't given a choice and he felt betrayed by
the army.'

'Sounds like he was very angry at the world,' Phillips
ventured.

'He was and it got a lot, lot worse after Mum died. He was
so low and he missed her so much, I was convinced he might

one day do something stupid. That's why when you turned up, I thought he'd killed himself.'

Phillips nodded gently. 'So was the visit a couple of weeks ago the last time you had contact?'

'No. We spoke a couple of times a week on the phone. Usually a Monday and a Friday. I tried calling him last night, actually, and he didn't answer.'

'Was that unusual?' asked Phillips.

'Not really. His mobile was as old as the hills and the battery was forever going, so it happened from time to time.'

'Did you try his landline?'

'No,' said Dunn. 'He fell out with his service provider a few years ago and got rid of it.'

'I see.'

'When did you say Dad was killed?' asked Dunn.

'We're not a hundred percent certain just yet – that will be confirmed in the next few days – but we believe it was late last night.'

Dunn's face wrinkled. 'What time?'

'Again, it's approximate, but about 10 p.m. Why do you ask?'

'Because I got a weird text message from him about 9.'

Phillips's pulse quickened. 'Can I see it?'

Dunn leapt up from the chair and left the room, returning a minute later with her phone in her hand. She passed it across.

Phillips narrated what she could see on the screen. '"My darling Lily. By sharing what I've seen, my soul can finally have peace."

'I couldn't make head nor tail of it. As soon as I read it, I called him, but it went straight to voicemail. I tried a few times last night, and again this morning, but couldn't get through. I was going to call again just now, once I'd put the shopping away.' Tears welled in Dunn's eyes again.

'And you say this came through at around nine o'clock?'

'Yes. It seemed especially odd, as he never called me darling. He wasn't affectionate like that.'

Phillips pulled out her own phone and took a picture of the message before handing Dunn's back. 'Did your father have any enemies?'

'I very much doubt it. He was a kind hearted soul underneath the gruff exterior. Even though he really struggled with his mental health, he always tried to make an effort with people. He said the army taught him to always put others first.'

'I see,' said Phillips. 'Was he close to anyone? Did he have any friends?'

Dunn shook her head. 'No. The only thing Dad was close to was the Red Lion. He practically lived in there.'

'I take it that's a pub?' asked Phillips.

'Yeah, about a mile away from his house on the main street in Finney Green.'

'And he went there a lot?'

'Every night on the way home from work, without fail. And all day Saturday and Sunday when he wasn't visiting down here.'

'You mentioned his job,' said Phillips. 'What was it?'

'He was a security guard at the dog food factory just outside Finney Green.'

'And how long had he worked there?'

Dunn paused. 'About five years, I think. He didn't particularly enjoy it but it was about as much as he could manage with his PTSD. The house was paid off when Mum passed, and with his war pensions, he didn't really need the money. It gave him something to do during the day and he spent his wages in the pub. In fact I was convinced he would end up drinking himself into an early grave one day...' Her words tailed off as tears streaked down her cheeks.

Phillips was acutely aware she was intruding on Dunn's grief, as well as the fact that her boys still had no idea why someone from the police had turned up and reduced their mum to tears. She wanted to leave them alone to try and process what had happened, but she still had a few more questions to ask. 'Do you know if your dad ever had any involvement with a place called the Mindset Mastery Clinic?'

Dunn nodded. 'For all the good it did him.'

'Really, how so?'

'I was worried about how much Dad was drinking so I offered to pay for him to attend a retreat there. I told him it was a kind of spa where he could relax and have a rest, but the truth was it was for people with addictions. He hated it and walked out at the end of the first day. Played hell with me for setting him up and wouldn't speak to me for a week.'

'When was that?' asked Phillips.

Dunn took a moment to think. 'Last October, I think. I remember paying the invoice in November, so it would have been October, I think.'

'I see,' said Phillips.

'Even though he left early, they still made me pay the full amount for the two-day program.'

'Do you remember how much it was?'

Dunn nodded vigorously. 'Two grand. Bloody extortionate, if you ask me, but I was desperate to get him off the drink.'

'I can imagine.' Phillips offered a faint smile. 'Look, Lily, there's something you need to know about what happened to your dad before it comes out in the press.'

Dunn's eyes widened.

Phillips took a deep breath and continued. 'We believe the person who killed him has also killed two other people.'

Dunn placed her fingers against her mouth.

'Have you seen the news in the last week; the deaths of the boxer AJ Lewis and the psychologist Juliet Dobson?'

'Yes.'

'We think the person that killed both of them also murdered your dad.'

'Oh my God.'

'Once Carl's name is released to the media, you should prepare for the fact that his death will make headline news over the next few days – not just locally, but nationally too.'

Dunn shook her head. 'I can't believe this is happening.'

'I understand and I'm so sorry to have to tell you that, but I wouldn't want you to be surprised when it comes out.'

Tears streaked down Dunn's cheeks. 'How am I going to tell the boys about this?'

'I know it's incredibly difficult, but in my experience, being honest with them is the best option.'

Dunn sniffed loudly.

'Look, I'm sure this is the last thing you want to do – and I'm sorry to ask – but there is one more thing I need from you.'

Dunn wiped her eyes. 'What is it?'

'Someone has to officially identify your dad.'

'I can do it.'

'Are you sure?'

'Yes,' said Dunn firmly. 'I'd like to see him.'

'In that case I should also warn you, your dad's face was mutilated when he was killed.'

Dunn stared back at her with wide eyes. 'In what way?'

Phillips took a long silent breath. 'The killer removed his eyes.'

'Oh my God.' Dunn's right hand flashed up to cover her mouth.

'I'm sorry to have to drop all of this on you without warning,' said Phillips. 'We can make arrangements for someone else to identify him if you'd prefer that.'

Dunn removed her hand from her mouth. 'No. No, I can do it.'

Phillips nodded softly. 'I'll arrange for one of our family liaison officers to make contact with you tomorrow. They'll be able to make the arrangements. Can I get your number?'

'Yeah, sure.'

Dunn reeled it off and Phillips made a note in her pad, then handed her business card across. 'The family liaison officer will support you throughout the investigation, but you have all my details on there. If you need anything, call me any time.'

Dunn stared down at the card in her hand. 'Thank you.'

Phillips stepped up from the chair and offered a sympathetic smile.

'Will you catch them? The person that did this to Dad?'

'I'll certainly do everything I can to, yes.'

Dunn nodded, but remained silent.

'I really am sorry for your loss.'

Dunn bit her bottom lip, then grabbed another tissue.

'I'll see myself out,' said Phillips, before turning and heading for the door.

As she walked back to the car, she felt her phone begin to vibrate in her pocket. Fishing it out, she could see it was Don Townsend calling. She suspected he was ringing for information on Carl Walsh's death, but she'd learnt her lesson with the MEN's chief crime reporter. 'No chance, mate,' she muttered as she rejected the call. A second later she opened the door to the Mini and jumped into the driver's seat. It was finally time to go home.

33

A t exactly 8 a.m. the following morning, the team – including Harris – gathered in the conference room. Entwistle's laptop was connected to the big display screen at the end of the room, showing CSI's photos of the three crime scenes and the bodies of Lewis, Dobson and Walsh.

In recognition of the early start, Phillips had bought each of them a hot drink and a round of bacon rolls. Bovalino was currently devouring his hunched over the large table they were sitting around.

'I spoke to Carl Walsh's daughter, Lily Dunn, last night. As you'd imagine, she was shocked to hear what had happened to him. She said he had no enemies that she could think of and that he was a decent man and a doting grandad to her two teenage boys. That said, she also described her dad as lonely and very angry at the world after so much time in active combat during his time in the army. She also suggested he was rather fond of a drink. He certainly spent a lot of his time in the local pub, The Red Lion in Finney Green.'

Entwistle nodded as he clicked through a number of

windows on his laptop and an excel sheet appeared on the big screen. He began typing and a moment later, Carl Walsh's name appeared. 'He was also a patient of Mindset Mastery. This is his file, which backs up what you're saying, Guv. He'd attended a retreat for an addiction issue, namely alcohol.'

'Her daughter confirmed as much to me last night,' said Phillips. 'So that's all three victims now connected to that place.'

'As well as our friend, Lyndon Garcia,' added Jones.

Harris's eyes narrowed. 'What's Mindset Mastery and who's Lyndon Garcia?'

'Garcia is a larger than life American,' said Phillips. 'Literally, he's about six foot six and owns this place called The Mindset Mastery Clinic. They're based in a renovated stately home out in Cheshire, and they claim to help people overcome their addictions. AJ Lewis and Carl Walsh were clients there. Juliet Dobson worked as part of their support team.'

'And do you think this guy, Garcia, is involved?' asked Harris.

'We're not sure, is the honest answer,' replied Phillips. 'When we spoke to him about Lewis's and Dobson's deaths, he had no alibi for the nights each of them was killed.'

'He's also got form for burglary and assault,' Jones cut in. 'Served ten years in the US in the nineties.'

Phillips nodded. 'Apparently, he had a history of stalking his neighbour. So much so, one night he broke into her house and tried and have sex with her. Thankfully she was able to fight him off and escaped.'

Harris made a note in her yellow legal pad. 'Sounds like a real charmer.'

'Actually, he is.' Phillips shot back. 'Almost too charming. If you know what I mean.'

'Like he's hiding something?' said Harris.

'Exactly.'

Harris continued making notes. 'It's not uncommon for violent men to adopt an overtly charming persona when connecting to others, in order to hide who they really are. Superficial charm is one of the key identifiers on both psychopathy and overt narcissism.'

'So do you think he could be our killer?' asked Jones.

Harris smiled. 'I'm a psychological profiler, Jonesy, not a psychic. I'd need to meet the guy and check him out properly before I can give you any kind of opinion on that.'

'That can be arranged,' said Phillips. 'In fact, now we know Carl Walsh was also a client at his clinic, we'll need to talk to him again. You can come along.'

'Great.'

Phillips focused back on Entwistle. 'How did you get on with Walsh's background?'

Entwistle tapped into his laptop and a second later a picture of Walsh in combat fatigues appeared. He was standing with another soldier in a desert somewhere, holding a rifle in his hands. 'Turns out Walsh was a war hero. He did three combat tours during his time in the Green Howards, one in Iraq and two in Afghanistan, where he was awarded the Military Cross – or MC. He was badly injured on his last tour when an IED was detonated near his patrol. He was medically discharged a few months later.'

'His daughter mentioned something about that, actually,' said Phillips.

'When he came out of the army, he had a couple of jobs in logistics before landing his final role as a security manager at the dog food factory in Finney Green. He was married to Michelle for thirty years, but she died last year from lung cancer. After she passed, he lived alone, and as far as we can tell had not been in a relationship with anyone else.'

'His daughter certainly never mentioned anyone being in his life.' Phillips turned to Jones. 'She also said he spent most of his evenings and weekends in the Red Lion pub. Check it out. See if any of the staff or regulars can tell us anything useful.'

Jones nodded. 'Bov and I can head over at lunchtime.'

'Did you say the Red Lion was on the main road in Finney Green, Guv?' asked Entwistle.

'Yeah.'

'In that case, I'll get onto the council and see if they've got any CCTV around the pub. We might be able to track his movements on the days before he died.'

'Good idea,' said Phillips.

'We can check with the local shops too,' Jones added. 'See if they've got any footage from their cameras.'

'Great. Anything else on Walsh we need to know, Whistler?'

'Just that Lily Dunn is his only child.'

Phillips picked up her phone. 'Like Bethany Lewis and Lee Dobson, Walsh's daughter also received a text from her dad's phone around the time Evans suggests he was killed.'

Jones sat forward. 'What did it say?'

Phillips read aloud from the screen. '"My darling Lily, by sharing what I've seen, my soul can finally have peace".'

Harris pursed her lips as she digested the message.

'Lily had absolutely no idea what he meant by it,' added Phillips. 'She says her dad never called her darling and that he wasn't affectionate in that way.'

'They were obviously sent by the killer.' Harris continued scribbling.

'Yeah.' Phillips nodded. 'That's what I was thinking.'

'But why?' asked Entwistle.

Harris shook her head. 'I'm not entirely sure. Do you have the other messages to hand?'

Entwistle pulled them up on the big screen.

Harris made a note of them. 'It may well be the killer is

trying to communicate to the families of the victims. Let me have a proper look at them.'

Phillips checked her watch. It was approaching 8.30 a.m. She locked eyes with Harris. 'In the meantime, do you fancy a trip out into the Cheshire countryside?'

Harris cracked a wry smile. 'Why, that would be lovely.'

'It'll be interesting to get your take on Mr Garcia.'

'I'm intrigued to meet him,' said Harris. 'He sounds like a very interesting specimen,'

'He's a specimen all right.' Jones chuckled. 'Like the kind you find in a fertility clinic.'

Phillips grinned. 'I think it's fair to say, Jonesy's not a fan.'

Jones flashed a playful grimace.

'Any questions before we crack on? asked Phillips.

Bovalino raised his hand from the table. 'I just wondered what the doc thought about the potential link to cannibalism. I mean, is it really likely?'

Harris's expression was suddenly serious. 'Chief Superintendent Carter asked me the same thing last night, actually. The similarities between your victims' posed bodies and the Polynesian funeral rituals is uncanny, and the missing body parts could be down to cannibalism, of course. We often think of cannibalism as being confined to the realms of ancient history and tribes such as the Polynesians, but you only have to go back a few decades and the case of Jeffrey Dahmer, who murdered and consumed seventeen young men between 1978 and 1991. He not only ate many of his victims, but also retained body parts as trophies.'

'I watched a documentary on him,' said Entwistle.

Harris continued. 'Then there was Armin Meiwes, known as the master butcher, who in 2001 posted an ad on a website called the Cannibal Café looking for an eighteen-to-twenty-five-year-old to be slaughtered and consumed. A guy called Bernd Brandes answered the advert and not long after – with

Brandes's consent – Meiwes amputated and cooked Brandes's penis, which they attempted to eat together.'

'That's sick,' muttered Bovalino.

'It gets worse,' replied Harris. 'Brandes was slowly bleeding to death – as you can imagine – so Meiwes decided to finish him off by stabbing him in the throat. He then dismembered the corpse and placed it in the freezer. Over the next ten months it's alleged Meiwes consumed over forty-four pounds of Brandes's flesh in various recipes he created.'

Jones shook his head. 'Just when you think you've heard it all.'

'And if that's not weird enough, nowadays a simple google search will bring up hundreds of websites where people can offer themselves up to be eaten by others purporting to be cannibals, all over the world.'

'But why would anyone want to be killed and eaten?' asked Entwistle.

Harris shrugged. 'To feel special.'

Entwistle frowned. 'But that doesn't make sense.'

'Not to you or me, but to some people with deep-rooted and chronic issues around self-esteem, it just might.'

'So, it looks like cannibalism is still alive and well, then,' said Phillips.

Harris nodded. 'As to whether it's in play here, I'm afraid there's still not enough evidence to say either way.'

'Well, whether it's cannibalism or not, what we do know is that our guy has murdered three people and taken three of the four so-called critical organs. Our only job now is to stop him getting that fourth organ. Ok?'

Each of the team nodded.

'Right,' said Phillips, getting up from the chair. 'Let's get out there and catch this psycho.'

As PHILLIPS and Harris approached the desk at Mindset Mastery, Phillips saw the male receptionist had been replaced by a young woman with a million-dollar smile and expensive-looking auburn hair. The badge on her chest declared she was called Lucinda.

After Phillips had presented her credentials and explained who they were here to see, Lucinda wasted no time in calling Garcia to alert him to their presence before ushering them into the same room as last time.

'It's a pretty impressive place,' said Harris as she took in the view of the gardens from the large window.

'That's why they charge a thousand pounds a day,' replied Phillips.

Harris flashed a wistful smile as she turned to face her. 'The joys of private practice.'

Phillips took a seat at the large table. 'You never fancied it yourself? From what I've heard, private shrinks can make some serious money.'

Harris dropped into the seat next to her. 'I think I'd be bored, to be honest. Listening to people's problems all day can't be much fun, can it?'

'No. I guess not.'

At that moment, the door opened and Garcia appeared, a broad smile fixed on his face. His cold black eyes, however, betrayed his obvious annoyance at the intrusion. 'Another visit, Chief Inspector? If I didn't know better, I'd say you've developed somewhat of a fixation for our little clinic.'

Phillips smiled back. 'Can I introduce Dr Siobhan Harris. She's part of our investigation team.'

Garcia eyed Harris for a moment. 'Really? In what capacity?'

'Dr Harris is one of the country's top psychological profilers.'

'In that case, I'm guessing I should be honoured.' He

offered his hand. 'Lyndon Garcia.' Taking a seat opposite them, he very deliberately looked at the chunky watch on his left wrist. 'I'm very busy with clients today. Is this going to take long?'

Phillips ignored the question and got straight to the point. 'What can you tell us about Carl Walsh?'

Garcia frowned slightly. 'I'm sorry, who?'

'Carl Walsh. He attended one of your addiction retreats late last year.'

'We have a lot of clients. I'm afraid I don't know them all.'

'Well, you might want to try and remember Carl.'

'Really?' Garcia flashed a patronising smile. 'And why is that?'

'Because he's dead. Murdered, like AJ and Juliet.'

'And what's that got to do with me?' replied Garcia without missing a beat.

'Well,' Phillips locked eyes with him, 'all three victims were connected to Mindset Mastery, weren't they?'

Garcia folded his arms across his chest. 'What *exactly* are you saying, Chief Inspector?'

Phillips sat forward. 'There's a running joke within my team, Mr Garcia. And that is that I do not – in any way, shape or form – believe in coincidences.'

'*And?*'

'*And* – the fact that three murder victims were either clients of or employed by Mindset Mastery is no coincidence. Someone connected to this place is behind these murders. I'm sure of that.'

Garcia shook his head. 'Do you have any proof to back that up?'

'Not yet.' Phillips folded her arms. 'But it's only a matter of time.'

Garcia's jaw clenched. 'Well, until you do, I've got nothing more to say to you.'

Phillips was in no mood to let him off the hook. 'Where were you on Monday night between 8 o'clock and midnight?'

'Did you not hear what I just said?'

'It's a simple enough question.'

Garcia glared at Phillips, barely able to hide his anger. 'In my apartment, and before you ask, I was alone. *All night*.'

'Is there any way you can prove that?' asked Phillips.

'CCTV,' replied Garcia, his gaze unflinching.

Phillips felt her brow furrow. 'What do you mean, CCTV?'

'We have cameras fitted all over the building, including the hallway outside my apartment. The footage will show me going in around seven on Monday night and leaving again on Tuesday morning at around 6 a.m., when I went for a swim in the spa.'

'We're going to need copies of those tapes.'

A slight snarl touched Garcia's top lip. 'It'll take time to find the footage.'

'We can wait,' said Phillips.

Garcia waved her away. 'No need. Lucinda will dig it out and send it over later today.'

'Just make sure she does,' said Phillips firmly.

Garcia looked at his watch again, his irritation plain to see. 'Now, is there anything else?'

Phillips glanced at Harris, who shook her head.

'Well, in that case,' said Garcia, 'I need to get back to my clients.'

'Don't let us keep you,' Phillips replied, standing.

Garcia headed for the door. As he pulled it open, he turned back to the room. 'And if you want to talk to me again, Chief Inspector, call ahead next time. That way I can make sure my lawyer joins us.'

'Of course, Mr Garcia,' said Phillips with forced deference. 'I'd be happy to.'

34

'He's a piece of work, isn't he?' said Harris once they were safely back in the Mini, heading back down the long gravel drive.

Phillips slowed as she approached the gates adjacent to the main road. 'So, what did you make of him?'

'Well, he's an arrogant arse for one, and he definitely has issues with women.'

Phillips nudged the car out into traffic. 'Yep. He doesn't like being challenged by me, that's for sure.'

'Not at all. I was watching him throughout, and as much as he attempted to hide it, he was seething from the moment he walked in. I mean, all that shit about you having a fixation on his "little clinic", as he put it.' Harris made air quotes with her fingers. 'That was totally passive aggressive.'

'Yeah, he's such a dick.'

Harris chuckled.

'Look, I know you've only just met him, but do you think he *could* be involved?'

Harris exhaled sharply as she gazed out the window.

'Potentially, but the truth is, it's too early for me to say. I'd need more time to properly assess him.'

'Which, based on the comments about his lawyer, he's not going to volunteer any time soon.'

'Doesn't look that way, no.'

The car fell silent for a time before Phillips spoke again. 'It's interesting what you say about him not liking women, though. He was definitely different today with two of us in there. The last couple of times, it's been me and Jonesy, and as much as he's never been happy to see us, he was far more charming during those visits. He was downright hostile today.'

'It could be down to him having issues with us both being women. Or... it could be that he's used to getting his own way; you know, people buying into his charm pretty easily. If you keep coming back and challenging him, it's going to wear thin very quickly for a man like Garcia. Throw in the fact that he displays narcissistic tendencies and you've got yourself a very complex individual indeed.'

'I could really see the stalker in him today,' Phillips mused. 'The underlying menace that's clearly hiding behind the facade.'

'Without a doubt,' Harris agreed. 'I certainly wouldn't want to get on the wrong side of him.'

'Me neither,' replied Phillips as she accelerated onto the dual carriageway and back towards Ashton House.

'So WHAT DID you think of our American friend?' asked Jones as Phillips and Harris made their way into MCU's conference room.

'An arrogant, passive aggressive misogynist who displays narcissistic tendencies,' replied Harris as she took her seat.

Jones produced a wide grin. 'That just about sums him up.'

Harris pulled her yellow legal pad from her bag and placed it on the conference table.

'Would you go so far as to say a potential serial killer?' asked Jones.

'Too early to tell, Jonesy, but he's definitely someone I'd be keeping a close eye on.'

'Speaking of which.' Phillips turned to Entwistle. 'One of Garcia's assistants was supposed to be sending you some CCTV footage from the clinic that he claims will prove he was at home the night Carl Walsh was murdered. Has it come through?'

Entwistle shook his head. 'Nothing as yet.'

'Well, as soon as we're done here, I want you to chase that up, and if they try to be clever or you think they're messing you about, let me know. I'll be only too happy to get a warrant and send Bovalino to pick it up personally – with a van load of uniform to boot.'

Bovalino reclined in his seat and linked his thick hands behind his head. 'I quite like the sound of that.'

'I'll make it a priority, Guv.' Entwistle scribbled in his pad.

Phillips addressed Jones again. 'So how did you get on at the Red Lion?'

He picked up his pad. 'The landlady, Mindy Hepworth, remembers seeing Walsh on Monday evening. He came in just after six on his way home from work. Sat at the bar and read his paper, by all accounts. But then he got talking to a guy he seemed to know, and this fella bought him a couple of pints. They left together about an hour later.'

'Could she describe him to you?'

Jones exhaled. 'Nothing of any real value. Average height, average build. Wore a baseball cap.'

Entwistle keyed into his laptop and a moment later a

CCTV video appeared on the big screen. It was black and white and low quality. 'Looks like she's talking about this fella.'

Each of the team stared at the screen as the video played.

Entwistle narrated what they were watching. 'This is from the council CCTV camera located down the street from the Red Lion. As you can see from the timestamp in the corner of the screen, it was just after 7.15 p.m. when Walsh left, propped up, it seems, by the man in the baseball cap.'

Phillips gazed at the video. 'Did the landlady say he was drunk when he left?'

'She didn't mention it, no. But I can't say that surprises me.' Jones locked eyes with Bovalino. 'She didn't come across as someone who paid much attention to anything, did she, Bov?'

The big Italian shook his head. 'I think it's fair to say she might like a few spliffs of an evening.'

'Play it again, Whistler,' said Phillips.

Entwistle obliged.

'Pause it there.' Phillips stared at the screen and the still image of Walsh and the man helping him along the pavement.

'He's wearing glasses as well as the cap, and he's keeping his head down so we can't see his face,' said Entwistle.

'He knows where the camera is,' Phillips said. 'Did the landlady not mention the glasses to you?'

Jones shook his head. 'Nope. Like we said, she had all the awareness of a house brick.'

Phillips focused on Entwistle again. 'Did these two show up on any other council cameras around there?'

'No, Guv. But I did get a partial plate number on a large Mercedes van from a camera located behind the pub.'

Phillips sat forward. 'And have you run it through the system?'

'Yeah. As it's only a partial plate, it's flagged up about fifty possible vehicles in the Greater Manchester area, and because the footage is in black and white, we know it was dark in colour, but not the actual colour; could be blue, green, brown, grey, etc. It's gonna take time to go through them all.'

'How long?' Phillips was trying hard to mask her growing impatience.

'If I can draft in PC Lawford and a couple of the other support team, a day maybe.'

'Do it.' Phillips pointed to the man on the screen. 'And I want printed copies of this image distributed to everyone in Ashton House. See if anyone recognises this guy.'

'I'll do it straight after this.'

Phillips turned back to Jones. 'Any CCTV from the pub?'

'No, Guv. It's an old man's boozer.'

'Proper spit and sawdust,' added Bovalino. 'It didn't even have TVs on the wall.'

'And what about the surrounding shops?' asked Phillips.

'We got a few tapes. I'll be going through them as soon as we're done here,' said Bovalino.

Phillips turned her gaze back to the big screen. 'Whoever this guy is, he was one of the last people to see Carl Walsh alive. Finding him is our number one priority. Ok?'

Each of the team nodded.

'I'll order some pizzas.' Phillips stood up from the chair. 'And you'd better call home and make your excuses. I think it's gonna be another long night.'

35

The final preparations were starting to take shape. He only had a few days left before he could make the ultimate journey towards everlasting life. Staring down at the two eyeballs contained within the icy cold plastic box, he tried to imagine what sights they had seen; the battles they had witnessed, the victories etched in every sinew of their wondrous form. They really were breathtaking. To ensure they had retained the spirit and strength of their previous host, he had frozen them in liquid nitrogen within minutes of harvesting them from Carl Walsh – just as he had with AJ's heart and Juliet's brain. If truth be told, he should not have removed them from the freezer this evening, but he simply could not help himself. The urge to gaze at them, to study their form and to connect to their power was too great to ignore. The battle between his human desires and his reverence for the ancient rituals had been intense and lasted for most of the evening. Finally though, after much push and pull, he had relented, but only after he had promised himself and the elders that his study of the eyes would be brief; undertaken in the hope of further connecting to the life they had once witnessed.

With a heavy heart and growing impatience, he took one last look at the eyeballs before closing the lid and returning the plastic container to the freezer, where it nestled between the boxes that contained the heart and the brain.

After closing and locking the freezer door, he wandered over to the opposite wall where he cast his gaze across the patchwork of photos of the person who was to be the final piece of the puzzle. Staring at the images attached to the cork board, he felt his heart skip a beat as he revelled in the aura of the young woman smiling back at him: stunningly beautiful, talented beyond compare and as courageous as a battle-hardened warrior. In fact she had spent most of her adult life fighting for the rights of animals, those helpless creatures trapped in science labs and unable to fight back against their captors. Sarah Norman was perfect in every way, and he could think of no finer way to fulfil his destiny than through her ultimate sacrifice.

Glancing at the large wall-calendar pinned up next to her photographs, he allowed himself a smile. The end was now tantalizingly close.

Soon he would transcend this life and become an all-powerful entity, *finally* worthy of the ancient teachings, and complete his journey to spiritual immortality.

36

E arly next morning Phillips was sitting at her desk checking back through her decision logs when her phone beeped on the desk next to her. Glancing at the home screen, she spotted a notification from the Manchester Evening News. Her heart sank when she saw the click-bait-worthy headline:

FLOWER KILLER MURDERS WAR HERO!

Clicking through to the newspaper's app, she found her worst fears confirmed; Don Townsend had been at it again. Reading through the article, it was evident his source had relayed an annoyingly accurate description of the crime scene and the way Carl Walsh had been found surrounded by flowers just like Lewis and Dobson. Plus, a detailed background on the man himself – which focused on his time in the military and in particular his heroics in Afghanistan. As with the previous story, it was balanced and fair, but Phillips knew that wouldn't matter to Fox. The chief constable would once more be furious that her beloved Greater Manchester

Police – but more importantly *her name* – was being dragged through the mud in the press. With a sinking feeling swirling around her guts, she placed the phone back on the desk and waited for the inevitable call. She didn't have to wait long; a moment later her desk phone erupted into life. Taking a long deep breath, she picked it up. 'This is Phillips.' She waited for the fireworks.

'Jane. Have you seen the MEN online?' It was Carter. He sounded panicked.

'I have, sir. In fact, I thought you were Fox calling.'

'I've already had that pleasure a few minutes ago.'

'Ouch,' replied Phillips. 'How was it?'

'Well, I think it's fair to say she's not happy.'

'Even though we've been working flat out for almost two weeks without a break?'

'Makes no difference, Jane.' said Carter. *'You know that. As soon as a case makes headlines, the only thing she cares about is her precious reputation.'*

'God, I despise that woman.' The words spilled from Phillips's lips before she could stop them.

Carter didn't react. *'Anyway, you'll be pleased to know only I've been summoned for the obligatory dressing down.'*

'Really? That's a result.'

'For you, maybe.' Carter chuckled.

'Oh, yeah. Sorry. Didn't mean to gloat.'

'It's fine. I'm sure I'd be the same if it was the other way round. Look, I'm meeting her at ten. Before I go in, have you got any good news I can share with her on the case?'

'Nothing at the minute, but I'm just about to do the morning briefing with the guys.' She checked her watch. It was approaching 8.30 a.m. 'I'll call you back in half an hour with an update.'

'Great. I'll be in a meeting with the finance team, but I'll let Di

know to put the call through. Anything you come up with is far more important than a bunch of spreadsheets.'

'Ok. I'll be as quick as I can.'

'Thanks, Jane. Speak then.'

Five minutes later, Phillips gathered the core MCU team – including Harris – in the conference room. As usual, Entwistle's laptop was being mirrored on the big screen as each of them cradled steaming hot drinks collected from the canteen by Bovalino.

After briefing the team on the contents of her call with Carter, she waited expectantly for any information that might offer their boss a slightly easier ride in his pending show-down with the chief constable.

Bovalino was first to respond. 'I've connected to the Albanian embassy in London, who've sent me a load of infor-mation on the kitchen porter's background over there. Turns out Vasil Hoxha's ex-military.'

Phillips's interest was piqued. 'Really?'

'Yeah. He served ten years with what they call their Land Forces as a Commando, which is kind of a mix of our Paras and Marines. He completed two tours of Iraq in 2007 – 2008 as part of the coalition forces' Iraqi Freedom campaign.'

'That could be a possible connection to Walsh,' said Jones.

Phillips nodded. 'Carry on.'

'He was medically discharged in 2010 after being diag-nosed with borderline personality disorder brought on by PTSD.'

Phillips locked eyes with Harris. 'What does that mean in English?'

Harris sat forward. 'Well. People with borderline person-ality disorder – or BPD – present with a range of symptoms such as anger issues, rapid mood changes and seeing the world in extremes. Things tend to be either great, or very bad. Many patients have major issues and distorted views of their own self-image and can self-harm as a way of regulating their emotions.'

'That might explain the scars on his arms,' said Phillips. 'They looked like they could have been self-inflicted.'

Jones nodded. 'Are people born with it?'

'No,' replied Harris. 'It's normally triggered by extreme trauma, usually in childhood, but most patients only present with it in later life. Usually after experiencing more trauma as an adult.'

'Such as going to war?' said Phillips.

'Exactly. By the sounds of Mr Hoxha, he may have experienced trauma as a child which he managed to bury – as a lot of kids do – which was then triggered in combat and the subsequent post-traumatic stress. BPD is very common in veterans who served in war zones like Iraq and Afghanistan, and in men in particular.'

'If Hoxha does suffer with borderline personality disorder, would that make him violent?' Phillips asked.

'Not necessarily, but his PTSD might.' Harris hooked her hair behind her right ear. 'A lot of veterans – particularly those connected to the so-called oil wars of Iraq and Afghanistan – have issues with anger management. They feel like they were sold a pack of lies by their leaders. They went into battle and risked their lives for freedom, but soon realised it was all about money and oil. Every soldier in those wars lost friends, many of them right in front of them. That's hard to take, especially when they perceive their comrades died for nothing but profit.'

Phillips pursed her lips for a moment. 'Could Hoxha's PTSD have caused him to become a killer?'

'Possibly,' replied Harris, 'but I'd need to know more about him and what he went through to be able to say with any real degree of certainty. But for argument's sake, let's say it did. PTSD is trauma based. People who have been trauma-tised tend to lash out, to kill in the heat of the moment. You see, when someone is traumatised, the amygdala goes into hyperdrive.'

Bovalino frowned. 'Amygdala?'

'It's the part of the brain that produces creative, survival and emotional thoughts. Increased activity in the amygdala can cause the brain to make someone relive the trauma at a later date – but as if it is happening to them for the very first time. The enhanced sensory overload can overwhelm them, causing a slew of negative thoughts and difficulty controlling emotions. This is how many patients suffering with PTSD describe how they feel when stressed. Often, they will lash out – almost as a last resort – to try and escape from those feelings.'

'Whereas our killer is very considered,' said Phillips.

'Exactly,' Harris replied. 'Hoxha *could* be your killer, but if he is, I doubt it's down to post-traumatic stress. From what I've seen so far – killing with anaesthetic, posing the bodies, then carefully, almost deferentially, removing the organs – I'd say we're dealing with someone thoughtful. Our killer is careful and detailed. He plans his abductions with precision and carries them out with stealth. It seems nothing is left to chance, and I think there is a very good reason he took the specific organs from the different victims.'

'Which is what?' said Jones.

'My guess would be that each of the organs has meaning based on the person it was harvested from.' Harris flicked through to the relevant page on her pad. 'He took the heart from a boxer, arguably the most valuable part of a fighter. As Sugar Ray Robinson said, "Rhythm is everything in boxing. Every move you make starts with your heart. Without heart, a boxer will rarely win".'

Phillips nodded.

Harris continued. 'Similarly, a psychologist relies on the power of their brain and the information it can process to help understand the issues of their patients.'

Jones's brow wrinkled. 'I get those two, but why take a soldier's eyes?'

'I must admit I was puzzled by that one too, initially, but then it struck me: maybe he wants them for what the eyes have seen and witnessed? Compare these murders with the ancient Polynesian rituals. They consumed the organs of their dead in the belief they would ingest their powers. Maybe your man really is planning on consuming their organs in the hope of being imbued of their unique strengths.'

'It's really starting to look that way,' said Phillips.

Harris cut back in. 'And if it *is* cannibalism, and he *is* following the ancient Polynesian rituals, then there's something else we need to factor in.'

'The new moon.' said Phillips.

'Yes.'

Bovalino frowned.

'Have I missed a meeting or something?' asked Entwistle.

Phillips nodded towards Harris. 'I haven't shared this part of your theory with Bov and Whistler yet, so you may as well explain.'

Harris linked her fingers together on the desk. 'The ancient Polynesians used to bury their dead soldiers and enemies alike in sand to preserve them. They'd then dig them up in readiness for a tribal feast which would take place on the eve of the next new moon.'

'What?' replied Entwistle. 'And you think that's what he might be doing here?'

'It's possible, yes,' said Harris.

Phillips rubbed her face with her hands, forcing it to

redden. 'And the *really* good news is that the next new moon happens at 3 a.m. tomorrow morning.'

'It's possible our killer could be planning his own feast or some kind of ritual for the same time,' added Harris.

'Jesus,' muttered Bovalino.

'Now there's an update Carter can take to Fox. She'll be over the moon,' Jones cut in, his tone sarcastic.

Phillips took a moment to digest the information. 'If that is a possibility, we should bring Hoxha in for questioning. Keep him locked up and out of the way just in case.'

'But based on what?' asked Jones. 'His alibis checked out.'

'True, but people lie for their mates all the time. Get him in and stress test them. Hopefully he'll let something slip and give us a reason to search his house.'

Jones cast his gaze to Bovalino. 'Let's saddle up.'

The big man nodded.

'Right.' Phillips stood up from the chair. 'Let me know once he's in custody. I need to brief Carter.' With that she left the room.

A COUPLE OF HOURS LATER, Jones appeared at her office door. 'Hoxha's downstairs and being processed.'

'How did he take being asked to come in for questioning?'

'Not too well,' replied Jones. 'But the fact he has extreme anger issues worked in our favour in the end.'

'How so?'

'Well,' Jones grinned. 'It meant we were able to arrest him for *assault*.'

Phillips recoiled. 'He assaulted someone. Who?'

'Bov.'

'And is he ok?'

Jones chuckled. 'Yeah. Hoxha literally bounced off him. I wish I'd had a body-cam on. It was hilarious.'

Phillips rolled her chair back and stood. 'So, we can now officially hold him for twenty-four hours.'

'Yup. Played right into our hands,' said Jones. 'The only thing *he'll* be feasting on tonight will be a stale sandwich from the vending machine.'

Phillips felt a sudden surge of much-needed energy. 'Right. Well, let's see what he has to say for himself.'

Just then Entwistle rushed in carrying his laptop. 'Guv. You're gonna wanna see this.' He placed the machine down on Phillips's desk and pressed play.

Jones moved to her shoulder so he could see the screen.

Entwistle explained what they were looking at. 'This is a still taken from an ANPR camera within half a mile of the Red Lion pub. It's a dark-coloured van matching the one we saw on CCTV, passing the camera just a few minutes after Carl Walsh walked out with our mystery man. The registration is a match for the partial plate we saw the other day. Guess who it's registered to.'

'Vasil Hoxha?' said Phillips hopefully.

'Not quite. But almost as good. It's registered with Mindset Mastery.'

'Bingo!' said Jones.

'And it gets better.' Entwistle clicked on another image on the screen. 'This was taken from a parking camera at the shopping precinct in Monk's Heath. They use the images to capture registration plates going in and out for parking fines.'

'That's where the vet was burgled and the anaesthetic was taken, wasn't it?' said Jones.

'Yep,' replied Entwistle. 'This photo was taken on the day of the break-in.'

Phillips stared at the screen and the image of a man at the wheel of a van entering the car park. 'That looks like Hoxha.'

Entwistle flashed a satisfactory grin.

Phillips moved closer to get a better look, then slammed her hand down on the desk. '*It is Hoxha!*'

'Let's see him talk his way out of this one,' said Jones.

'Yeah, let's! Right, first things first. We need to impound that van and get forensics all over it.'

'I'll get Bov to organise a warrant and head over there with a uniformed team straight away,' replied Jones.

Phillips turned back to Entwistle. 'Can you email me those pictures?'

Entwistle bent over the laptop and typed at a furious speed. 'Done.'

'And just so you know, Guv, Hoxha's asked for a lawyer,' said Jones.

Phillips felt her jaw clench. She should have expected it, of course, but she was desperate to start interrogating him now. 'Who's on the roster for today?'

'Sonia Lofthouse,' Jones replied.

'She's pretty smart,' said Phillips. 'She won't make it easy for us.'

'No, but at least she's local, which should speed things up.'

Phillips nodded as she dropped back into her chair. 'Ok, shout as soon as she arrives.'

'Will do,' said Jones before leading Entwistle out of the office.

37

Hoxha was sitting on one of the plastic chairs behind a white veneered table when Phillips and Jones walked into Interview Room Three just over an hour later. Next to him, his court-appointed lawyer, Sonia Lofthouse, was making notes in her pad. Phillips suspected Lofthouse was likely in her mid-fifties. A slight woman with dyed red hair, bony features and the wrinkled skin of an ex-smoker, she was well known to Phillips and Jones as she regularly represented the criminals that passed through MCU. In fact, thanks to the sheer volume of work she had picked up from Ashton House over the years, her firm had recently opened a second office just a couple of streets away from where she now sat.

As Phillips and Jones took their seats, Lofthouse looked up from her pad and forced a smile.

Phillips remained silent as she opened up her laptop and placed it on the desk to her left.

Next to her, Jones pulled out his notepad and pen.

After explaining the protocols of the interview – that

everything would be filmed on CCTV as well as recorded on the digital interview recorder – Phillips got stuck in. 'Vasil. Where were you on Monday night at around 7 p.m.?'

Lofthouse's brow furrowed. 'I'm sorry, Chief Inspector, but what does this have to do with my client being charged with assaulting a police officer earlier today?'

Phillips moved her gaze from Hoxha to Lofthouse. 'It goes to motive for attacking my officer.'

'How so?'

'We believe Vasil was involved in the abduction and murder of Carl Walsh, which is why he assaulted DC Bovalino and tried to make his escape.'

Lofthouse appeared incredulous. 'I'm sorry, but I was not made aware of any of this when I was briefed by the custody team.'

'It must have slipped their minds,' replied Phillips coolly.

'I'm going to need to meet with my client in private.' Lofthouse closed her pad then lifted her bag onto the small table, before slipping the pad inside.

Phillips's frustration was palpable. They really didn't have time for any further delays, but Lofthouse was well within her rights to ask for time with Hoxha. 'Very well,' she sighed. 'DI Jones will escort you to a private room. DCI Phillips suspending this interview at 2.22 p.m.'

A moment later, Jones led them out.

Phillips made her way to the observation suite at the end of the corridor, where she found Harris and Entwistle huddled around the large screens which carried the feed from Interview Room Three.

Just then, Jones pushed the door open, stepped inside and sighed. 'We said she wouldn't make it easy for us.'

Phillips nodded.

'So, what happens now?' asked Harris.

Phillips took a seat. 'Now we wait.'

Thirty minutes passed before one of the custody team alerted them to the fact that Lofthouse and Hoxha were ready to resume the interview.

Five minutes later, Phillips and Jones resumed their positions opposite the pair. Phillips once again reminded everyone of the protocols before restarting the DIR. When the long beep finished, signalling the recording had begun, she repeated her earlier question. 'So, Vasil. Where were you on Monday night at approximately 7 p.m.?'

Hoxha stared across at Phillips with black eyes. 'In the pub.'

'Which pub?'

'Same as always.'

Phillips was in no mood for games. '*Which is?*'

'The Coach and Horses, down the road from my house.'

'And can anyone vouch for you?' asked Phillips.

'Sheila. She served me the whole time I was there.'

'I see. Have you ever met a man called AJ Lewis?'

Hoxha shrugged. 'Don't know him.'

'What about a man named Carl Walsh?'

'No,' replied Hoxha.

'Are you sure? They were both clients at the Mindset Mastery Clinic.'

'I never meet the clients. I work in the back.'

'What about Juliet Dobson? Did you ever meet her?'

'No.'

'So, you've never met any of the names I just mentioned?'

Hoxha glanced at his lawyer briefly, then shook his head. 'No.'

Phillips eyed him for a long moment, then turned her laptop so Hoxha and Lofthouse could see the screen. 'This is a still from a CCTV camera positioned outside the Red Lion pub in Finney Green. The image was captured at just after seven on Monday night.' Using her pen, she pointed to the black and white image. 'This man is Carl Walsh and later that night he was murdered.'

Hoxha swallowed hard.

Phillips pointed to the second man on the screen. 'And we believe this is you, Vasil.'

'That could be anybody,' scoffed Lofthouse. 'The image is way too grainy to stand up in court.'

Phillips ignored her and clicked on another picture on the laptop. 'This photo was captured at the Monk's Heath shopping precinct. It comes from one of the parking cameras they use to track number plates as vehicles drive in and out. As you can see, these are HD digital cameras, and the quality is very high. Do you recognise that van?'

Hoxha stared at the screen without speaking.

'You should do.' Phillips tapped the screen with her pen once more. 'Because that's you behind the wheel.'

'What has this got to do with why we're here today?' said Lofthouse.

'Later that day, a veterinary practice located in this same shopping precinct was burgled and a large quantity of animal anaesthetic was stolen.'

'And what's that got to do with my client, exactly?'

'We believe Vasil stole the anaesthetic and used it to kill AJ Lewis and Juliet Dobson.'

'What? Lofthouse spat back. 'Based on what evidence?'

Phillips continued unabated. 'We're also confident that when Carl Walsh's post-mortem is complete, the results will show that the same anaesthetic was used to kill him too.'

Lofthouse shook her head. 'This is preposterous. Hundreds of people no doubt use that car park every day. Are you talking to each of them too, Chief Inspector?'

Phillips glared at Lofthouse. 'That's true, but that same

van was also captured on an ANPR camera less than half a mile from where Carl Walsh was abducted the night he died.'

'But everybody uses that van, not just me.'

'We're well aware of that,' Jones piped in. 'And in the next few hours we'll know for sure who was driving it on Monday night.'

'So why not save us all a lot of time and just tell us the truth, Vasil,' said Phillips.

'It wasn't me. The last time I used the van was on Friday to pick up the fruit for the clients' smoothies. I've been off work since then.'

Phillips stared at him in silence before leaning forward on the table. 'Are you sure about that, Vasil?'

Hoxha nodded furiously. 'Yes.'

'If you're lying to us, we'll find out, because as we speak, we have a team of officers heading to the clinic to impound that van. Then our forensic experts will work through the night checking every inch of it. If you've left anything behind, they'll find it.'

Hoxha scratched at his scarred bare wrists.

'So I'll ask you again, Vasil, did you abduct and murder Carl Walsh on Monday night?'

Before Hoxha could respond, Lofthouse placed her hand on his wrist, leaning in to whisper in his ear.

A few seconds later, he straightened and locked eyes with Phillips.

'No comment.'

For the next thirty minutes, Phillips and Jones attempted to break Hoxha's newly adopted "no comment" stance but to no avail, and with all their preliminary questions asked, Phillips drew the interview to a close.

With Lofthouse insisting on her client being fed and allowed a period of rest, Jones escorted Hoxha back to the custody suite and his cell for the night.

As Phillips made her way back along the corridor to the observation suite, she checked her watch. It was approaching 4 p.m., which meant they had just under twenty-one hours to question Hoxha before they had to either charge him for murder or settle for the far lesser offence of assaulting a police officer. Pulling her phone from her pocket, she stopped just outside the door to the observation suite and called Bovalino.

'Hey, Guv,' he answered promptly.

'Where are we at with the van?'

'I just received the warrant on email and I'm heading to the clinic now with uniform.'

'Has Evans been briefed?'

'Yes, boss. He's drafted in some extra hands for the night shift but needs you to approve the overtime.'

'Ok. I'll speak to Carter to sort that out,' replied Phillips. 'We need it back here ASAP.'

'Understood.'

'Call me as soon as it's locked down, won't you?'

'Of course, Guv.'

Phillips ended the call and stared down at the handset for a long moment before pulling up Adam's number. Despite her promises that the job would no longer get in the way of their relationship, that was *exactly* what it was doing once again.

She knew the right thing to do would be to call him and explain, but she was running on empty. So instead, she opened a new SMS message and began typing.

Sorry, love.
Something urgent has just come in.
Gonna be home late.
Don't wait up. Love you. J xx

She hit send and waited for the swish noise to signal it had been sent, then placed the phone back in her pocket.

Taking a deep breath and with a heavy heart, she pushed open the door to the observation suite and stepped inside. They were in for another long night.

38

Half an hour later Phillips was back in her office debriefing on the Hoxha interview with Harris and Jones when her phone beeped, indicating an SMS had landed. Picking up the handset, she could see it was from Adam:

Hi, Janey
That's a bit of a shitter for you. I was about to start
cooking dinner.
Looks like a microwave meal for one, then.
Be safe. Axx

Staring at the message, she felt an overwhelming sense of guilt wash over her.

'Everything all right, Guv?' Jones asked.

Phillips sighed. 'Yeah. Just Adam reminding me what a crap girlfriend I am.'

'One of the perks of the job,' said Jones with a sardonic chuckle.

At that moment, Bovalino called back. Phillips switched the phone to speaker so everyone could hear him.

'Well that was fun, Guv.' His tone oozed sarcasm.

'Why? What happened?'

'Garcia wasn't happy. Proper kicked off when we told him we were taking the van. Said it was harassment and a witch hunt and that we were trying to ruin his business. Lots of talk about lawsuits and all that shite.'

'Was he physically aggressive in any way?' asked Harris.

'He did get a bit lairy with PC Lawford, actually.'

'One of our female officers,' Phillips explained.

'Doesn't surprise me given his past,' said Harris. 'As we've seen before, he has massive issues with women in authority.'

'Yeah, but he backed down pretty quickly when I offered to nick him for obstruction.'

'So where are you now?'

'Just leaving the clinic. We're following the low-loader that's carrying the van.'

'Which means you should be back within the hour.'

'Yep. We'll blue light it so traffic won't be an issue.'

'Ok. See you when you get back.' Phillips ended the call and turned her attention back to Jones and Harris. 'Not an unexpected reaction from Garcia.'

'There's something not right about that guy,' said Jones.

Harris nodded. 'He's hiding something; that's for sure. I certainly wouldn't want to be left on my own with him.'

'Me neither,' added Phillips. 'But *is* he involved in the murders?'

Jones folded his arms across his chest. 'It's certainly possible. I mean, as Lofthouse was at pains to point out in there, the guy pictured in the CCTV with Carl Walsh could be anybody, really. The quality of the footage is so grainy and the camera angle makes it hard to distinguish the height of the man supporting Walsh.'

Phillips didn't respond.

'And the van *is* registered to *his* business,' Jones continued. 'There's every possibility he could have been driving it on Monday night as opposed to Hoxha. Again, like Lofthouse said, just 'cos Hoxha was pictured in the car park the day the vet was burgled, it doesn't mean he was the one who broke in. It's a busy shopping precinct, after all.'

Phillips remained silent as she digested what he was saying. The weaknesses in their case against Hoxha were evident for all to see. If truth be told, all they had him on was assaulting Bovalino, which in a perverted way had been somewhat of a lucky break. Without that indiscretion Lofthouse would have walked him out the doors of Ashton House hours ago.

'What you thinking, Guv?' asked Jones.

'Just how little evidence we have on Hoxha.' She locked eyes with Harris. 'What did you make of him?'

'Not a lot, I'm afraid, as he didn't really share much of himself. I'd need to ask him a lot more questions if I was to try and get inside his head.'

'And with Lofthouse in tow, that would no doubt result in just another round of "No comment" answers,' said Jones.

Phillips leaned back in her chair and drummed the fingers of her right hand on the desk. Having initially been so confident Hoxha was involved in the murders, she was now beginning to have serious doubts. And if *she* didn't believe it, then there was absolutely no way a jury of twelve people would either. 'We really need a warrant to search his house.'

'Which, based on the evidence we have currently, we won't get,' said Jones.

'So what are our options?' Harris asked.

Phillips pursed her lips and sat forward. 'We wait for the CSIs to take the van apart and pray to God they find something that links either Hoxha or Garcia – or anyone else for that matter – to Carl Walsh.'

'Otherwise, we're back to square one,' said Jones.

'And if that's the case,' Phillips added, 'it means our killer is still out there – and God only knows what he plans to do next.'

'Jesus,' muttered Jones. 'This is not good.'

Just then Phillips's mobile began to vibrate in her pocket. As she pulled it out, she could see it was senior CSI. 'Andy.'

'I've think we've caught a break.'

'What? On the van? That was quick.'

'No, I'm still waiting for that to arrive. I'm talking about the vehicle that rammed Juliet Dobson.'

Phillips's pulse quickened. 'Really?'

'Based on the height of the impact point to the rear of Dobson's car, it looks like it was a large four-by-four. We tested the paint samples it left behind and we've found a match within the Land Rover family. It's Byron Blue and looking at their range of vehicles, I'd say it was either one of the large Land Rovers, like the Discovery or Defender, or the biggest Range Rover, the Vogue.'

'And you're sure of that?'

'Positive. I'm emailing you a couple of images of the three vehicles now in case you're not a petrol head.'

Jones and Harris looked at her with wide, expectant eyes.

Phillips's laptop pinged, indicating the email had landed, and she greedily clicked it open.

'Anyway,' added Evans. *'I'd better go; the van's here.'* He ended the call.

'What did he say?' asked Jones.

'He's found a vehicle match for the car that hit Dobson the night she was killed.' She spun the laptop so Jones and Harris could see the screen. 'One of the large Land Rovers like these.'

Jones's eyes narrowed. 'Didn't we see one like that at Mindset Mastery the first time we visited?'

'I think we did, yeah.' Phillips jumped up from the chair and headed out into the main office.

Jones and Harris followed her out.

'Whistler,' she said as she approached his desk. 'Can you find out if Lyndon Garcia owns a Land Rover or Range Rover for me?'

'Of course,' said Entwistle, and a second later he began typing into the laptop.

Phillips stood at his shoulder, her nerves jangling as she stared at the screen anticipating the results of the search. She didn't have to wait long.

'Here we go. Lyndon Garcia, registered keeper of a Land Rover Defender.'

'What colour?' asked Phillips, praying for the answer she was looking for.

'Er... says here, Byron Blue.'

'Fucking get in!' growled Phillips, unable to hide her excitement.

Entwistle turned to face them all, a puzzled look on his face. 'What have I missed?'

'Evans just called,' explained Jones. 'The car that hit Dobson on the night she was killed was a large Land Rover and it left behind traces of blue paint.'

'Byron Blue?' said Entwistle.

Jones nodded.

Phillips clapped her hands together. 'Jonesy, let's go and see our friend, Mr Garcia, shall we? See if we can locate his car.'

'Shouldn't be too hard,' said Jones. 'The bloody thing's enormous.'

Phillips turned to Entwistle. 'I want a uniformed team there with us, and a custody van.

He's a big man and if we end up nicking him, we're going to need the muscle.'

'I'll call through now.'

'And have a low-loader on standby,' Phillips added. 'If we need to impound his vehicle, I want everyone ready.'

Entwistle nodded as he picked up the phone.

'Is there anything I can do?' asked Harris.

Phillips shook her head. 'For the time being, no, but if we do end up bringing Garcia in for questioning, it'd be great to have you in the observation suite.'

Harris smiled. 'I'll be ready and waiting.'

39

T he uniformed team were already on scene by the time Phillips and Jones strode across the gravel drive towards the main door of the Mindset Mastery clinic.

'No sign of the Defender.' Jones nodded in the direction of the CEO's now empty parking space as they made their way up the steps in front of the building. 'Maybe he's stashed it.'

'Yeah, but where?' replied Phillips.

Sergeant Hope, a tall, muscular copper with thick arms that matched his neck, greeted them as they stepped inside the entrance hall. 'We've made the night porter aware you need to speak to Mr Garcia urgently. Apparently, he's on his way down from his residence as we speak.'

Based on her earlier conversation with Bovalino after he'd impounded the van, Phillips was not expecting a warm welcome from Garcia, and she was proven right as he stormed into the large reception area of the clinic wearing his usual attire of shorts and a linen shirt, but this time with bare feet.

'What the hell do you want now?' he growled.

'Where's your car, Mr Garcia?' Phillips asked coolly, thumbing back towards the door.

Garcia recoiled. 'My car? What the fuck's that gotta do with you?'

Jones took a step forward. 'Hey. There's no need for bad language, sir.'

Garcia looked him up and down and then cast his gaze back to Phillips, his jaw clenched.

'It's a simple question, Mr Garcia,' said Phillips. 'Your Land Rover Defender – where is it?'

'Why do you want to know?'

Phillips locked eyes with him. 'Because we believe it was used to abduct Juliet Dobson.'

'This is harassment,' scoffed Garcia. 'Plain and simple.' He pulled his phone from the pocket of his shorts. 'I'm calling my lawyer.'

Phillips held his gaze. 'Your car, Mr Garcia. Where is it?'

Garcia's nostrils flared as he stared back, his black eyes betraying his anger. 'It's in the shop.'

'What do you mean it's in the shop?' said Jones. '*What shop?*'

'It's being repaired,' replied Garcia flatly.

'It's in the *garage*, you mean?' Phillips cut back in.

Garcia nodded. 'Shop, garage; it's all the same to me.'

Phillips knew full well that if the car had already been repaired, they'd almost certainly have lost all forensic evidence. 'When did it go in there?' she asked, attempting to hide the panic in her voice.

'I dunno.' Garcia shrugged. 'Last week sometime. Henry sorted it.'

'Henry?' asked Phillips.

'My assistant.'

The image of the smiling male receptionist flashed across Phillips's mind's eye. She glanced at Jones, whose concerned expression matched her own.

'He looks after all our vehicles,' Garcia added.

'In what way?'

'On a day-to-day basis, he books them in and out when the team need them, and in a wider context, he manages the leases, maintenance, insurances, etc.'

'Including the van we impounded today?'

Garcia's eyes narrowed. 'Yes. Like I said, he manages all our vehicles. Why is any of this important?'

Phillips ignored the question. 'How would we find out who used the van on Monday night?'

Garcia shrugged. 'It'll be on the vehicle logs.'

'And where are they?'

'On Henry's laptop.'

'Show us,' said Phillips.

Reluctantly, Garcia marched across the reception area and stepped behind the desk. 'That's odd,' he said, his face wrinkling.

'What is?' asked Phillips.

'His laptop's gone.'

'And why is that odd?'

'Because we have a strict policy on anyone working outside of business hours. I'm totally against it as it's bad for mental health, so all laptops must remain fixed in their cradles at the clinic, at all times.'

'Has Henry ever taken his laptop home before?' said Jones.

Garcia shook his head. 'Not that I'm aware of.'

'Did he ever borrow the van we've just impounded?'

'I have no idea.'

Phillips continued. 'But he could have if he wanted to?'

'Well, yes,' replied Garcia. 'But I can't think why Henry

would want to. It's a clunky old thing and we have a bunch of other vehicles he could use.'

'Like the Defender?' asked Phillips.

'Yes.'

'So why *was* the Defender taken into the garage?'

'One of the team pranged it when they were out buying groceries, apparently.'

'Did you see the damage?' Jones jumped back in.

'No. Like I say, Henry told me about it and was sorting the repair. To be honest, living in-house, I hardly ever use it.'

'What's Henry's last name?' asked Phillips.

'Parker.'

'And when did you last see him?'

Garcia took a moment to answer as he rubbed his stubbly chin with thick fingers. 'Tuesday morning, I think. He was in early to tidy up some paperwork, then headed off. He had quite a lot of vacation time to take so he's been away this week. Lucinda has been standing in for him.'

A spike of adrenaline surged through Phillips's body. 'Did Henry ever have contact with AJ Lewis or Juliet Dobson?'

'Of course,' said Garcia. 'Henry is our main man in front of house. He's the first and last point of contact for all our guests and staff.'

Phillips locked eyes with Jones, and she instinctively knew what he was thinking. Without saying a word, she set off back towards the car park with her second in command hot on her heels.

'Hey?' Garcia shouted after them. 'Is someone going to tell me what the hell's going on?'

Sergeant Hope had maintained his position at the front entrance to the clinic.

Phillips broke stride for a moment as she reached him. 'Keep Garcia down here in reception until you hear from me.'

'Yes, ma'am.'

'Do not let him out of your sight. Even if he goes for a shit, you stay with him. Understood?'

Hope nodded.

'No phones of any kind, and if he gives you the slightest bit of grief, *nick him*.'

'Yes, ma'am.'

A second later Phillips's feet crunched against the gravel drive once more as she and Jones raced towards the car, and she dialled Entwistle.

'*Guv?*'

'I need an address from the staff list for Henry Parker.'

'*Give me a second.*'

Phillips could hear Entwistle typing as she tried to keep up with Jones ahead of her.

'*It says here it's called The Maltings and it's just off Stubby Lane, not far from where you are now and about half a mile from the A34.*'

'Can you text me the postcode?'

'*Doing it now.*'

Phillips heard the audible beep of the message landing.

'*Who is this guy, Guv?*' asked Entwistle.

'I'll explain later,' said Phillips as she reached the car, 'but I want a tactical team put on immediate standby in the area, ok?'

'*You got it,*' replied Entwistle.

Phillips hung up then jumped in the passenger seat, pulling the door shut just as Jones fired the ignition.

40

Parker's house sat some fifty metres back from the main road. His closest neighbour was probably three hundred metres away on either side. As they pulled onto the long, bumpy drive at the front of the property, it appeared to be cast in total darkness.

Drawing closer, Phillips guessed the single-story building had likely been built in or around the 1960's. Even in the shadows of the night, it was obviously in need of a large amount of repair.

After stepping out of the car, Phillips and Jones headed for the boot and collected a large flashlight each.

Phillips's heart pounded and her mouth felt dry as a bone. 'You ready for this?'

Jones grinned. 'Always.'

During her twenty-year career in the police, Phillips had suffered a number of ferocious beatings and countless injuries whilst searching through properties looking for suspects on her own. She carried the scars to this day – both mentally and physically – and after promising Adam on her return to work she would never again allow herself to be put in harm's way like that, she was adamant they should search the house and land together. No more solo heroics for either of them.

They moved in tandem towards the front door. It soon became evident it had been fitted with an industrial style roller shutter which was padlocked closed at the base. When they cast their torches over the windows along the front of the house, it was clear they too carried the same protective covering.

'Bit extreme, isn't it?' said Jones. 'This level of security for a battered old gaff like this?'

'Just a bit. Makes you wonder what the hell he's got inside.' Phillips ran the torchlight along the underside of the roof. 'Doesn't look like there's any CCTV, though.'

For the next few minutes, they made their way carefully around the outside of the entire building and discovered that every window and door was fitted and locked up with the same impenetrable metal shutters.

'What's that over there?' asked Phillips as she caught sight of another structure sitting a further thirty metres from the rear of the property.

'Looks like a garage of some kind,' said Jones as he set off towards it.

Phillips tucked in behind him as they made their way through the long, uncut grass that surrounded the property. It had been raining most of the day, which meant it wasn't long before Phillips's suit trousers were soaked up to the knees.

Jones's flashlight illuminated the front of the outbuilding. It contained a large double garage door, which again appeared to be padlocked to the ground.

'We need to find out what he's keeping behind all this security,' said Phillips.

Jones turned to face her. 'Have we got enough for a warrant?'

Phillips remained silent for a moment, then swung her flashlight back towards the house. 'Did you hear that?'

'Hear what?'

'Sounded like someone cried out.'

'Really?' Jones pointed his flashlight onto the house alongside Phillips's beam. 'I didn't hear anything.'

Phillips placed the torch under her chin, illuminating her face, and winked at Jones. 'I think you'll find you did.'

'Aahh! Right.' A wide grin spread across his face. 'Now you mention it, I think I did hear someone crying for help.'

Phillips pulled her phone out and called Entwistle.

'Everything ok, Guv?'

'We're at Parker's house and it's all locked up with security shutters. We can't find any sign of him. We need to get inside and find out what the hell he's hiding.'

'And what's Parker got to do with all this?'

'Garcia claims he had regular access to the Defender and the van registered to the clinic.'

'So do you think he's involved?'

'At this stage we don't know, but he was the last person to drive the Defender and Garcia's not seen him since Tuesday morning. Plus, he's gone to a lot of trouble to keep prying eyes out of his home.'

'Do you want me to try and get an emergency warrant?'

'No. Based on imminent threat to life, I want you to send me that tactical team to help break in.'

'Is there another victim?'

'Off the record, no, but for the purpose of this exercise, yes there is. We think we've heard them shouting for help from inside. Ok?'

'Understood. I'll call it through now. They shouldn't be long.'

'Thanks.' As Phillips ended the call she checked the time on the screen: 9.09 p.m. Time was well and truly ticking.

THE TACTICAL TEAM arrived ten minutes later, and Phillips was relieved to see it being led by Sergeant Louise Andrews. Andrews was a tall, athletic woman who had been kicking down doors on behalf of the Greater Manchester Police for over ten years. She was a master of getting into buildings criminals wanted to keep her out of and she was just what they needed right now.

'We'll open the front door first, ma'am,' said Andrews. 'Then get that garage door up. If there's someone inside, we'll find them.'

'Great,' replied Phillips. 'I'll take the house with you and one more of your team. DI Jones will take the garage with the rest of your guys.'

'Spot on,' Andrews said with a firm nod, before ordering her team to get to work.

A moment later there was an ungodly roar as the diamond-coated circular saw burst into life, and within a minute, the lock on the front door had been obliterated and the shutter released.

'On me,' said Andrews as she led them into the dark hallway.

Phillips watched as Jones, along with a couple of the tactical team, peeled away in the direction of the garage, before following Andrews into the building.

The inside was identical to the outside – unkempt, unloved, and damp. Oddly, each light bulb had been removed from the light fittings that hung from the ceiling.

As it was a single-story house, it took no time to complete

the search, and much to Phillips's enormous disappointment, it produced nothing.

'It appears clear, ma'am. No sign of anyone.'

'Damn it!' Phillips replied. 'We should check the floor-boards and walls. We're looking for signs of a hidden opening or hatch.'

Phillips, Andrews and the second tactical officer spent the next five minutes pressing their feet against the floor and rubbing their hands along the walls, but to no avail.

Jones appeared. 'You find anything, Guv?'

'No.' Phillips sighed. 'You?'

Jones flashed a wide grin as he nodded. 'The Defender. It's in the garage under a tarp and the front end is all smashed up.'

A cold chill ran down Phillips's spine. 'Show me.'

Jones led them back through the wet grass to the garage.

As Phillips drew closer she could see the unmistakeable rear end of the massive 4x4. The tarp had been pulled clear and the tactical team stood at a safe distance examining it under torchlight.

Jones moved down the side of the vehicle and beckoned for Phillips to join him. 'Take a look at this.' He shone his torch along the line of the front bumper.

Phillips could see it was buckled and bent. Leaning in to get a closer look, she also noticed large silver coloured dents across the paintwork. 'What colour was Dobson's car?'

'Silver,' said Jones.

Phillips straightened. 'I want forensics down here ASAP. I know they're working on the van, but tell Evans to draft in more bodies. I don't care what it costs in overtime; he just needs to make it happen.'

'I'll call him now.'

'And call Sergeant Hope at the clinic. Tell him to arrest Garcia on suspicion of conspiracy to murder. Let's get him into Ashton House and see just how much he knows about Parker's activity in this thing.'

Jones nodded as he pulled his phone from his pocket and walked out of the garage.

Phillips returned to the house with a renewed vigour. There was no doubt in her mind Parker was either the killer or working alongside the killer. Now all they had to do was find him.

Jones joined her in the main lounge a few minutes later. 'That's all sorted. I've briefed the guys back at base too. Told them to expect Garcia to arrive in the next hour or so.'

'Good. He'll need to stew in his cell overnight until we can get back there and question him. But for now, I just want him locked up and out of the way.'

Jones's eyes narrowed suddenly as he stared at something behind Phillips's head. 'What's that?'

Phillips spun on her heels and followed the beam from his flashlight.

'Do you see it? Up there in the corner of the room?'

Phillips's eyes narrowed. 'What am I looking at?'

'That section there; it looks a slightly different colour to the rest of the ceiling.'

'Oh, yeah.' Phillips moved to stand underneath it, then shouted to Andrews.

She strode into the room a moment later. 'Yes, ma'am?'

'Have you got a step ladder?'

'Of course.'

Phillips pointed to the spot on the roof with her flashlight. 'I want you to check this section of the ceiling.'

'I'll be right back,' said Andrews before rushing out of the room.

Andrews soon returned with a step ladder along with the rest of her team. Positioning it in the corner of the room and with a torch in her left hand, she climbed up a few steps of the ladder and pressed the fingers of her right hand carefully against the ceiling. 'Looks like a separate panel.' She rapped it with her knuckles next. 'And it's hollow.'

'Open it up,' said Phillips.

Andrews followed the instruction and, with the slightest of effort, was able to push a small square up and away from the rest of the ceiling.

Phillips's heart was pounding in her chest. 'Be careful, Louise.'

With all three members of her tactical team standing around the base of the ladder, Andrews climbed further up the steps. With her flashlight leading the way, she poked her head up through the hole. 'Jesus Christ!'

'What is it?' shouted Phillips.

'You really need to see this, Guv!'

WITH JONES AT HER SIDE, Phillips surveyed the hidden room that had been built into the roof space and ran the length of the property. The floor had been carefully boarded out. It also had its own electricity supply with heavy-duty bulbs secured in the fittings, which lit up the space like a football stadium. A large desk and chair were positioned against the gable end wall at the opposite end of the room, next to a tall filing cabinet locked with a thick padlock.

'This case is getting weirder by the minute, Guv,' ventured Jones as he slipped on a pair of latex gloves.

'Yeah,' said Phillips absentmindedly as she did the same, then made her way towards the desk, stopping just a few feet in front of it.

'What the hell?' he muttered as he appeared at her side.

Phillips stared wide-eyed at the overlapping images pinned to the large cork board on the wall above the desk: a mixture of colour and black and white photographs that pictured all three murder victims. They'd clearly been shot from a distance through a zoom lens. 'He's been spying on them.'

'And for quite a while judging by the number of photos,' Jones added.

Positioned on the far right of the cork board was a grouping of photographs of an attractive young woman. Phillips stepped forward to get a closer look. 'Jesus,' she muttered as she spotted the distinctive tattoo on the woman's neck. 'It's the receptionist at the vets, Sarah...what was her last name?

'Norman.'

'That's the one.'

'Looks like she could be the final victim,' said Jones.

Phillips stared at the photos for a long moment, then turned to Sergeant Andrews. 'We need to get inside that filing cabinet.'

Andrews nodded and shouted for one of her team to join them from the floor below.

While they waited, Phillips inspected a large chart on the wall. '"Patterns of the new moon".' She tapped it with her gloved finger. 'Tomorrow's date is circled.'

Just then one of Andrews' men joined them and, with the aid of an enormous set of bolt cutters, sliced open the padlock.

Phillips greedily pulled open the top drawer and removed a stack of manilla folders. She passed a couple to Jones, then opened the first one in her pile, labelled *Dr Dobson*, and began scanning through the contents.

Jones did the same with his files.

'It's got Juliet's entire life history in here,' said Phillips. 'Where she went to school, photos from university, lecture notes, photos of her house and car, the works.'

Jones glanced across at her. 'Same in here with AJ.'

'We have to find Sarah before it's too late.'

Jones laid the documents down on the desk then pulled out his phone. 'I'll get Bov to call Dr Fisher and get her address.'

Phillips moved her search of the cabinet to the second drawer down as Jones gave instructions to the team behind her. 'Look at these,' she said when he was finished.

'What are they?'

'Recipe cards.'

Jones's eyes widened. 'Don't tell me...'

Phillips nodded. 'Recipes for cooking brains, heart, eyes and tongue. Albeit, these are meant for sheep organs.'

'What the fuck is this guy doing?'

'Exactly what Harris had warned us about all along. He's cooking a feast. *Tonight,* in readiness for the new moon.' Phillips glanced at her watch. 'Which is in less than five hours.'

'Bov's calling Dr Fisher as we speak.'

Phillips went back to the same drawer and retrieved a file containing photocopies of articles that appeared to feature ancient texts and had been printed from the internet.

Jones stood at her shoulder.

She read the title on the first page, '"A complete history of Polynesian funeral rituals, by JP Hartness. First published in 1934 by Oxford Publishing".'

'It would appear Harris called it right,' said Jones.

Phillips reached back into the bottom drawer and pulled out a metal box. Inside she found an Australian passport. Flicking through the pages, she came face to face with Henry Parker, only with a different name. 'Makai Homasi.' She passed it to Jones, then went back to the box.

'He changed his name.'

'Looks like it.' Phillips unfolded a battered old piece of

paper. 'Here's his birth certificate. Makai Homasi. Born 18th March 1987 in Tuvalu.' She pulled out her phone and began taking pictures of everything they'd discovered in the filing cabinet.

Just then, Bovalino called Jones back. He flicked it to speaker phone.

'*We've found an address for her.*'

'Where?'

'*Chelford Village. Thirty-four Oak Lane,*' replied Bov. '*I'll text you the postcode.*'

'We'll need a firearms unit,' added Phillips.

'*I'll call in one of the airport teams now. Also, Fisher said she received a text message from Sarah first thing this morning telling her she was quitting, and she'd not been in today.*'

'Did Fisher tell you what the message said?'

'"*Consider this my final notice to quit*",' said Bovalino. "*I'm tired of being small and insignificant. It's time for me to soar and for my voice to finally be heard'.*"

'What the hell does that mean?'

'*Fisher didn't have a clue. She reckons Norman has always been a bit odd. Fond of poems and riddles, so just put it down to that. She tried calling her to see what was going on, but it went straight to voicemail.*'

'It's the same kind of message that was sent from the other three victims' phones, which suggests he's already got her.'

'*Yeah, that's what the doc thought too. One last thing, boss. I've checked, and as far as I can tell, she's not and never has been in any way connected to the Mindset Mastery clinic.*'

'Ok,' said Phillips. 'Can you put Entwistle on?'

Bovalino did as instructed.

'*Guv?*'

I'm about to email over some images of Parker's passport and birth certificate.'

'*What do you want me to do with them?*'

'It looks like he changed his name a few years back and his real name is Makai Homasi. I want everything you can find on Homasi as well as anything on Tuvalu.'

'*Tuvalu? Where's that?*'

'That's what I need you to find out.

'*No worries.*'

Phillips set off towards the roof hatch. 'Can you put the doc on?'

'*Sure.*' Entwistle passed over the phone.

'*Hi, Jane,*' said Harris.

'Looks like you were right. We've found a load of articles on Polynesian funeral rituals locked away in Parker's house. I've taken some pictures, which I'm sending your way. See what you make of them.'

'*I'll get onto it as soon as they land.*'

'Thanks, Siobhan.' Phillips hung up, then climbed back down the ladder and into the main house.

41

The satnav in the patrol car suggested they'd be at Sarah Norman's house in fifteen minutes, but at the speed Jones was driving under blues and twos, it would likely be closer to ten.

As they wound their way along the country road towards Chelford Village, the in-car hands-free system suddenly burst into life.

Phillips could see on the dashboard screen Harris was calling. 'Siobhan?'

'Hi Jane. I've just googled the full texts you sent and, based on the various articles, coupled with where he was born and the lunar charts, I'm now totally convinced he's trying to emulate the warriors of his ancestors. Everything is pointing to him taking part in a new moon feast, just like they did.'

'Which is happening tomorrow,' Jones cut in.

'Its is. I've double checked that online as well, and the next new moon appears at 3 a.m. tomorrow.'

Phillips glanced at the clock on the dash. 'That's four hours away, which means there's a chance Norman may still be alive.'

'*Maybe,*' said Harris. '*But based on his actions so far, he seems to be following a strict plan and pattern with each of his kills. If that is the case, with Norman's boss receiving that message this morning, I fear she may already be dead.*'

Phillips's heart sank. 'Well, until we find a body, I'm not giving up hope.'

Just then, the car's radio crackled into life. '*Mike-Charlie-one, this is Tango-Foxtrot-two. We are six minutes out.*'

'Sorry, Siobhan. We've gotta go.'

Jones grabbed the radio. 'Tango-Foxtrot-two. This is Mike-Charlie-one. Our ETA is two minutes.'

TEN MINUTES LATER, Phillips pulled on her stab vest as she briefed Sergeant Matthews and his three-strong team on the goal of the operation: to locate Sarah Norman alive within the house or grounds of the property.

The building itself was a small cottage located down an alleyway that fed off the main road just outside the village. As had been the case at Parker's, the house was shrouded in darkness and there appeared to be nobody home.

Following the plan, Matthews approached the door and rang the bell. With no response forthcoming, he took a knee and shouted through the letterbox. 'Armed police. Please open the door or we'll break it down.'

The night air was filled with an eerie silence.

Matthews tried again. 'I repeat. Armed police. Open the door or we'll break it down.'

With no signs of life from inside the house, Matthews gave the order and a second later one of his team smashed into the door with a handheld battering ram. The frame splintered on impact and the door swung open on its hinges.

With his Heckler and Koch G36 submachine gun pulled

hard into his shoulder, Matthews led his team inside. Shouts of 'Armed Police' echoed round the small house.

A few minutes later, he reappeared at the front door and switched on the entrance hall light. 'The place is empty, ma'am.'

'Have you checked the roof space?' asked Jones.

'Yes, sir. There's no hatches or obvious entrance points.'

'It's worth checking again after what we found at the last place,' said Phillips.

Matthews nodded and headed back up the steep stairs to the first floor.

With the lights switched on, Phillips and Jones moved freely through the ground floor of the small cottage. It appeared unremarkable, with few clues as to the person who lived there. Based on Norman's age, Phillips guessed the house had been decorated by an older person, most likely the landlord, and someone unwilling to spend money on quality furnishings. Surprisingly, there was no TV in the lounge but a small turntable was sitting on a table between two modest stereo speakers. A pile of vinyl records was neatly stacked on the floor next to it.

'This place hardly screams out political poet or activist, does it?' said Jones.

'No. Quite the opposite, in fact.' Phillips cast her eyes around the room. 'Whoever lives here is used to conforming. It seems oppressively tidy.'

'Which is strange, given her age. She can't be that much older than my eldest, and *she* doesn't know the meaning of the word tidy.'

Phillips moved through to the tiny kitchen beyond the lounge. Switching on the light, she was faced with a similar scene: simple furnishings and military clean surfaces. Her eye was suddenly drawn to something stuck on the side of the fridge. As she stepped closer, she realised it was a picture calendar, the kind you would order online, with a personal photograph downloaded and attached to each month. Looking at the dates, she could see today and tomorrow had been circled in a thick red pen. Then she noticed the picture sitting above the days. 'Jonesy!'

He was at her side in a flash. 'What is it?'

She tapped her index finger on the photo containing a couple, pictured cuddling in the sunshine. 'Recognise these two lovebirds?'

'You've got to be kidding me!'

Phillips shook her head. 'Sarah Norman is Parker's girlfriend.'

42

P hillips had just finished sending a photo of the calendar to the team when the phone began to ring in her hand. It was Andy Evans.

She flicked it onto speaker so Jones could hear what was being said. 'Andy. Please tell me you've got good news.'

'*I have,*' he replied. '*Pedology have finally come back to me on the soil samples.*'

'And?'

'*You remember I said they contained high traces of arsenic and chromium?*'

'Yes.'

'*Well, since Carter organised the overtime for Pedology, Luke has been working flat out to try and narrow down the samples.*'

'And?'

'*Well, he's discovered elements within the samples that suggest they were taken from earth that not only contains high levels of arsenic and chromium but is also near – or adjacent to – a large area of oak trees that is likely connected to an area that contains gravel.*'

'Which means *what* in English?' Phillips glared at Jones.

Her senior CSI's fixation with every single detail was not what she needed at this exact moment.

'He's managed to narrow down the origins of the soil to two different locations, one on the outskirts of Ashton towards the Pennines, and the other, in a place called Whisterfield. Both were formally the sights of industrial tanning works and have since been abandoned.'

'Andy, I could kiss you,' said Phillips, grinning from ear to ear.

'We do our best,' said Evans bashfully.

'Can you send me the exact locations of both sites?'

'Emailing them as we speak.'

'Have you found anything on the van yet?' asked Jones.

'We're working through the interior now, but I did take a sample of mud from the tyres and it also contains high quantities of arsenic and chromium. I'm ninety-nine percent certain it's the same soil as the previous cases.'

'Great. Keep at it,' said Phillips then hung up.

'What do you wanna do?' Jones asked.

'Whisterfield is the closest to us, so we can take that with Matthews and his team.' Phillips opened the favourites folder in her phone. 'I'll call Bov. He can take the other site with another TFU.'

———

JONES PULLED the squad car off the road under the branches of a large row of trees and parked out of sight of the old industrial building, which was located about a hundred feet from the main road up a broken concrete track. Matthews and his team slipped in next to them in their BMW X5.

Phillips nudged forward in her seat and looked up through the windscreen. 'Oak trees, just like Evans suggested.'

Jones turned off the engine.

As they stepped out of the car, she noted the gravelly ground under her boots.

A moment later, with each of the team out of their respective vehicles, she drew them into a huddle and spoke in a low voice. 'Forensics say we're looking for a place near oak trees and gravel. Both of which we can see around us.'

Matthews and his officers nodded.

Phillips continued. 'If our guy is in there, he's already killed three people so far, maybe even four. He's likely armed and very dangerous.'

'So how do you want to play it?' Matthews asked.

'There's an imminent threat to life so we need to get in there as quickly as possible and eliminate that. However, we also need to factor in that we could still have a live victim inside the building. As much as I'd love to use maximum force on this creep, we cannot risk Sarah Norman getting caught by a stray bullet. So we'll be going in with tasers first. You'll have your pistols if you need them, but no machine guns, understood?'

'Understood,' said Matthews.

Phillips nodded. 'Let's do it.'

With taser in hand, Matthews led them in single file along the edge of the track to the dilapidated old building. The oak trees running adjacent to the path cast long shadows that provided plenty of cover as they moved closer inch by inch. A few minutes later they arrived at a point parallel with the front of the old tanning works and stopped. Standing there in the silence of the darkness, Phillips could hear the faint sound of music in the distance. It appeared to be coming from inside.

Matthews moved left first, then one by one and again taking advantage of the shadows, they made their way along the front of the building until they reached the double wooden doors of the main entrance. The music was louder now.

Phillips watched as Matthews tested the doors' movement with his hand. They opened a fraction but suddenly stopped.

'It's locked on the inside. Looks like a padlock across the latch.' He turned to the officer behind him. 'Paddy, do the honours.'

PC Patrick Connelly – aka Paddy – stepped forward and inserted a pair of heavy-duty bolt cutters into the gap in the doors. He slammed them together with all his might. There was a thick crunch and a thud as the padlock dropped to the floor on the other side.

Paddy stepped back and Matthews replaced him at the front, pushing the door open silently.

As Phillips followed the firearms team inside, the volume of the music increased tenfold – a low rhythmic beat, a woman singing somewhere in the distance – and she was struck by what could only be described as a delicious aroma.

'Is that garlic?' whispered Jones behind her.

Phillips nodded. 'Yeah, and onion, I think.'

They now found themselves in a long corridor that ran from the front to the back of the building, connecting what looked like the offices of the old tanning works.

With his taser trained and ready, Matthews opened the door to the first office, then signalled the room was clear.

As he moved towards the next room, Phillips followed along and peered through the first door. A large metal table was positioned next to the wall and contained what appeared to be boxes of vials and hypodermic needles. She pointed towards it. 'Alfaxalone?'

Jones nodded.

Phillips continued along the corridor after Matthews and his crew, who had just secured the adjacent room. Stepping to the doorway, she scanned the next space, which contained a camp bed covered in a sleeping bag and a large bucket in the corner next to the wall.

The contents of the following room made her blood run cold. In the middle was a small table, set for dinner, with just one place setting. Beyond, on a large portable gas stove, sat two large pans, their contents simmering, the smell of garlic suddenly pervasive and nauseating.

'This is sick,' whispered Jones next to her.

Back in the corridor, Matthews had stopped just outside the final room.

Phillips moved to his side and pressed her finger to her lips as she moved her ear closer to the door. She could hear voices mixed in with the music.

'Are you ready?'

She recognised the accent; it was Parker.

The voice that replied came from a young woman. 'I am.'

'I promise you won't feel a thing, Sarah. And I'll take good care of you. I love you.'

The woman was crying now. 'I love you too, Mak.'

'It's time. See you on the other side, sweetheart.'

'Go! Go! Go!' shouted Phillips.

Matthews and his men burst through the door to shouts of 'Armed Police.'

Phillips, a beat behind them, rushed inside but was stopped in her tracks by what she saw: Henry Parker, semi-naked and wearing some form of native dress, standing over a medical table, holding a syringe. Lying on her back below him, unrestrained, was a fully naked Sarah Norman, her body heavily tattooed.

'Drop the syringe and put your hands in the air!' barked Matthews, his laser sight locked on Parker's chest.

Parker didn't flinch.

'Do it! Do it now!' Matthews repeated.

Suddenly, Norman lifted herself up and jumped off the

table, taking up a protective stance in front of Parker. 'Leave us alone. He's done nothing wrong.'

'He was about to inject you with a lethal dose of anaesthetic, Sarah,' said Phillips.

Norman shook her head.

'He was, Sarah. Henry's not who you think he is. He's killed three people already with anaesthetic and he was about to do the same to you.'

'No. No. You don't understand.'

Phillips took a step forward. 'What don't we understand? Tell us.'

'Why he's doing this. *I want to die.* I've had enough.'

'Enough of what? said Phillips.

Tears streaked down Norman's cheeks. 'This miserable place. A shitty world and all the horrific people polluting it. I want to die. I want to be the next sacrifice.'

'I don't believe that, Sarah.'

Norman swatted away the tears. 'It's my destiny.'

Phillips took a step forward. 'You know we're not going to let that happen.'

'It's not up to you.' Norman glanced back at Parker and nodded. 'Do it.'

Parker rammed the needle into her neck.

A split-second later Matthews fired his taser, fizzing loudly as it connected.

Parker's body went rigid before dropping to the floor like a stone, taking Norman down with him.

Rushing across the room Phillips dropped to her knees.

Norman was lying face down on the floor, a motionless Parker on his back next to her. Phillips yanked the syringe from her neck and realised it was still half full. 'He didn't get it all in.' Feeling for a pulse, she turned to Jones. 'She's still breathing. Call an ambulance!'

43

Phillips stood staring at the large TV screens attached to the wall of the observation suite and watched Henry Parker as he sat in silence behind the desk in the middle of Interview Room Two. With his Polynesian ceremonial garb now bagged and tagged and on its way to the forensic lab, he cut a dejected figure dressed in the disposable blue overalls he'd been issued with when they'd arrested him at the tanning works just under two hours ago.

'He's refused any legal representation,' said Bovalino from over her shoulder. 'Claims he has God on his side.'

Phillips turned to her left to face Harris, who was sitting next to Entwistle in front of the monitors. 'Is that what this has all been about? Is he some kind of religious nut?'

'You'll soon find out,' said Harris. 'If he *is* on a mission from God, he'll be keen to share it with you. I'm certain of that.'

Phillips sighed. 'We found all the missing organs in a small fridge when we arrested him. Looks like they'd been frozen and then defrosted ready for the pot.'

'That's sick,' said Bovalino.

'Isn't it just?' Phillips replied. 'Any news from the hospital?'

Bovalino nodded. 'Norman's just been moved to intensive care. Jonesy says she's still unconscious, but stable.'

'As soon as she wakes up, I want to know about it.'

'Of course.'

Entwistle stood up and passed Phillips a manilla folder. 'This is everything I managed to get from the Australian immigration records on Parker.'

Phillips opened it up and began leafing through the pages.

Entwistle continued. 'Because of the time difference, I managed to speak to one of the immigration officers, who gave me what they had on file. As you suspected, his real name is Makai Homasi. He was born in Tuvalu but moved to Melbourne as a refugee at the age of eleven after the floods of 1998. I've printed off a few newspaper articles from that time, which are also in there. Anyway, he was given Australian citizenship in 2000 and left the country in 2009. He's not been back since.'

'Where did he go?' asked Phillips.

'Not sure at this stage, but he first showed up in the UK two years later, in 2011.'

'Anything else I need to know?'

'Just that his record's clean and, according to his National Insurance file, he's been in various employment since he arrived here.'

Phillips closed the folder and exhaled loudly as she locked eyes with Bovalino. 'Right then, we'd better get in there.'

A few minutes later, Phillips took her seat opposite Parker and placed a number of folders and files on the desk to her left. Bovalino sat down next to her.

Parker shifted in his seat and appeared agitated.

'How are you, Henry?' Phillips asked. 'Can I get you anything. A cup of tea? A sandwich?'

'You've got to let me go,' Parker shot back. 'Please, before it's too late.'

Phillips remained silent as she started the DIR. The loud beep sounded for a few seconds and when it had finished, she began. 'Detective Chief Inspector Phillips commencing the interview with Henry Parker at 1.37 a.m.' She locked eyes with Parker. 'Could you repeat what you just said to me before the tape started, please?'

Parker glared back. 'I said you've got to let me go. Before it's too late.'

'Too late for what?'

'*Their souls.* They need safe passage to the next realm as the new moon rises. If they don't get it, they'll stay in purgatory for eternity.'

'And which souls are you referring to?' asked Phillips.

'AJ's, Juliet's, Carl's and Sarah's.'

'Ah, right.' Phillips folded her arms and sat back in the chair. 'Bit of a problem there, I'm afraid. You see, Sarah's not dead.'

Parker's shoulders sagged and he closed his eyes as he dropped his chin to his chest.

Phillips continued. 'Thankfully we were able to taser you before you managed to give her the full dose of anaesthetic. She's in intensive care, but stable. Hopefully she'll make a full recovery.'

Parker looked up now and a tear rolled down his cheek. 'You shouldn't have done that. Sarah *wanted* to die.'

'But why? Why would your girlfriend want *you* to kill her?'

'So we could be together for eternity.'

Phillips felt her brow furrow. 'Tell me about your plans,

Henry. How were you going to give these souls safe passage to the next realm?'

'By carrying them within me.' Parker swallowed hard. '*I am the vessel that will deliver them to eternal life.*'

'I see,' said Phillips flatly. 'And how does that work? How do you get them to the eternal life?'

'By consuming their souls through the sacred feast.'

'Eating their organs, you mean?'

Parker nodded.

'For the tape, Henry Parker nodded his agreement.' Phillips opened the top folder on the pile and pulled out several photographs that had been blown up to the size of A4 sheets. She laid them down on the desk in front of Parker so they were facing him. She tapped the first image. 'This is a picture of AJ Lewis's body when we found him in the churchyard. His heart had been cut from his chest. Did you do that?'

Parker stared down at the photo. 'Please, we're wasting time. You must let me go so I can finish what I started.'

Phillips ignored his plea. 'Answer the question, Henry. Did you murder AJ Lewis and cut his heart out?'

'You need to let me go now!'

Phillips held his gaze for a long moment. 'Tell me what I want to know and maybe we can talk about that.' Ordinarily a suspect would see through such a blatant lie, but Parker was clearly not in his right mind. 'Quid pro quo, Henry. You give me what *I* want, and *maybe* you get what you want.'

Parker folded his arms across his chest and began rocking slightly in the chair.

'So. Did you give AJ Lewis a lethal dose of alfaxalone before cutting his heart out?'

Parker nodded as he continued to rock.

'One again for the tape, Henry Parker just nodded.' Phillips tapped her finger on the next image. 'This is the body of Dr Juliet Harris as we found it in Warford cemetery. She'd been murdered, the top of her head had been removed and her brain cut out.'

Parker continued to rock back and forth.

'Did you kill her, Henry? Did you cut out her brain?'

'We're wasting time,' growled Parker.

'Remember, Henry. Quid pro quo.'

Parker stared at the table.

'I'll ask you again. Did you kill Juliet Dobson and cut out her brain?'

'Yes.'

'See? Now we're getting somewhere.' Phillips tapped the final image on the table. 'And did you do this to Carl Walsh?'

Parker suddenly sat still and locked eyes with Phillips. 'Yes. I killed him and I cut his eyes out! Now, please, let me go before it's too late.'

Phillips gathered the images together into one pile and placed them back into the folder. 'I'm intrigued. What made you pick the different organs from each of the victims. For example, why specifically did you choose AJ's heart and Juliet's brain? Why not the other way around?'

'Isn't it obvious?' he scoffed.

'Not to me, no.'

Parker shook his head. 'Are you really that stupid?'

'It would appear so.'

Parker snorted with frustration. 'Because AJ had the heart of a lion, and Juliet's mind was extraordinary.'

'And were you aware she'd been diagnosed with breast cancer?'

'Did I *know*? Why do you think I chose her?'

'What? Are you saying you chose her *because* she had cancer?'

'Of course I did. Thanks to me, that disease never had a chance to destroy her. I stopped it spreading. I saved her from a horrific death.'

Phillips took a breath. 'What about AJ? What were you saving him from?'

'Himself.'

'How so?'

Parker sneered. 'All that talent, all that ability – being lost to alcohol. I couldn't sit by and let him fade away to nothing.'

'But his wife said he'd quit the drink and was getting his life back together,' said Phillips. 'After one of Mindset Mastery's clinics, no less.'

'But for how long?' Parker shot back. 'He was an addict. Addicts don't change. They can't. It was only a matter of time before he succumbed again. So I delivered my own form of intervention.'

Phillips studied his face for a moment. 'And Carl? Why kill him – why take his eyes?'

Parker's face lit up. 'Carl had witnessed epic battles. He'd seen and survived the most horrific encounters of unlawful wars. And while the rest of him may have been slowly poisoned by his anger and loneliness, the power of those encounters remained locked in his eyes, undiminished by this mortal realm.'

'So you saved him too, did you?'

Parker nodded.

'For the tape, Henry Parker nodded,' said Phillips. 'So, you think you have the right to choose who lives and who dies, do you?'

'Not at all. I take who God sends me.'

'And how do you know who God has sent you?'

Parker placed his right hand on his chest. 'I feel it in here.'

'Explain what you mean.'

Parker tapped his sternum. 'When God sends me a sacrifice, I come alive in here. It's like a surge of electricity rushing through my chest. I can feel their energy as if it's my own.'

'And you felt that when you first met AJ, Juliet and Carl,

did you?'

'Yes.'

'So *where* did you first meet them?' asked Phillips. 'Was it at the clinic?'

'Yes. When they shared their pain.'

'During the retreats?'

'Yes.'

Phillips shifted in her seat. 'So what about Sarah? Where did you two meet?'

Parker slammed his hands down flat on the table. 'Look. I've done what you asked. I've admitted to killing them. There's nothing else to say. Please, you need to let me go so I can complete the feast and help them pass over.'

'All in good time.'

'No! Time is running out.' Parker appeared desperate now. 'Look, you don't understand. In just over an hour the new moon will rise and if the feast does not take place, AJ's, Juliet's and Carl's souls will be trapped in limbo forever. That cannot be allowed to happen!'

Phillips didn't flinch. 'We had a deal, Henry. You tell me what I want to know, and *then* we can talk about letting you get back to the feast.'

Parker's nostrils flared in anger, his breathing heavy.

'And like you say, the clock is ticking, which means it's in your interests to tell me what I want to know quickly. So once again, how did you and Sarah meet?'

Parker exhaled sharply. 'We met online. A dating app.'

'And how long have you been together?'

'A couple of years.'

'That sounds quite serious,' said Phillips.

'It is.'

'So why did you try to kill her?'

'Because she *wanted* to die.'

'Why? A young woman in her prime?'

'So we could be together.'

Phillips tilted her head to one side. 'You said that before and I have to be honest, I'm a little confused. If she's *dead* – and you're sticking around to eat her, along with the rest of your victims – how were you going to be together?'

'Because I'll die too.'

'Really? How?'

'Starvation.'

Phillips scoffed and glanced at Bovalino. 'A little ironic, don't you think? The man who eats other people's organs starves himself to death.'

'You *really* don't get it, do you?'

'Enlighten me.'

Parker shook his head. 'After consuming the feast, I would never need food or water again. I would simply lie down on my bed and allow the power of their souls to fill my mortal body and then carry them to the next life with me.'

Phillips's mind flashed back to the tanning works. 'Was that what the camp bed was for? You were going to starve yourself to death there?'

'Yes.'

'But that could take weeks.'

'I know.'

'And would be incredibly painful.'

Parker nodded solemnly. 'That is to be *my* sacrifice. The price of eternal life.'

Phillips glanced at Bovalino, whose expression suggested he was thinking the same as her: Parker was insane.

'Were you responsible for the text messages sent from the victims' phones the nights they died? asked Phillips. 'And remember, Henry, quid pro quo.'

Parker glared at her in silence for a few seconds before nodding. 'Yes.'

'So, what was the point of those?'

'I wanted their families to know their sacrifice was for the greater good.'

Phillips recoiled. 'What? By sending a cryptic clue not one of them could make head nor tail of?'

Parker ran his hand through his hair. 'In time they would have figured it all out. It was my way of letting them say good-bye. Letting them know they would live on for eternity.'

Phillips didn't respond as anger clawed at her gut.

'Can I go now?' asked Parker abruptly.

'Tell us about Makai Homasi,' said Phillips, changing tack.

Parker flinched.

'Why did you change your name?'

A snarl formed on Parker's lip. 'It was a mistake.'

'Why was it?' asked Phillips.

'Because I tried to fit in.'

'Where?'

'*Everywhere.* Growing up in Melbourne I was always the poor little brown-skinned boy from Tuvalu. A refugee and an outcast. I had no friends. I was a different colour to my adoptive family – always on my own. So, when I left Australia, I decided to change it. To be more *normal,* whatever that really means.'

Phillips opened another file and pulled out copies of old newspaper articles Entwistle had found during his search into Tuvalu. She pointed to a headline that read *Thousands die in flash floods*. 'You said you were adopted as a kid. Is this what happened to your family?'

Parker stared down at the articles for a long moment. 'Yes,' he said finally, his voice barely audible.

'Tell us about it.'

Parker's eyes remained locked on the newspaper. 'The heavy rains burst the riverbanks and the floods hit our village when we were asleep. By the time we realised what was going on, it was too late. Dad pushed me onto the roof of our house and was trying to get my mum up too, but he slipped and fell into the water. I had hold of mum's hand and was trying to drag her to safety, but I wasn't strong enough and I let go. She went into the water and never came back up.'

'That must have been hard for you,' said Phillips softly.

Tears welled in Parker's eyes. 'I should have saved her. I should have been stronger.'

Just then the door opened behind them.

Phillips turned. 'For the tape, DC Entwistle has entered the room.'

'Sorry to interrupt, Guv. DI Jones needs to speak to you urgently.'

Phillips turned back to the DIR. 'DCI Phillips suspending this interview at 1.56 a.m.'

'Where are you going?' asked Parker, clearly agitated.

'I won't be long.' Phillips patted Bov on the shoulder as she stood. 'DC Bovalino will stay and keep you company.'

'*But I have to go.* I've told you everything you want to know. I need to get back to the feast.'

Phillips ignored his pleas as she strode out of the room.

Outside, Entwistle handed her his phone, then headed off in the direction of the observation suite.

'What have you got, Jonesy?'

'*Norman's awake, Guv.*'

'And what's she saying?'

'*That it was all part of some grand plan to be together. She's not at all happy we stopped it. She's sticking to the fact that she wanted to die, and she wanted him to kill her. It's all very Romeo and Juliet, to be honest. She confirms he planned to eat her tongue—*'

'Did she say why?'

'*Apparently it was her sacred gift from God.*'

Phillips felt herself nodding. 'He's said more or less the

same thing about the reasons why he killed Lewis, Dobson and Walsh.'

'*So he's admitted to killing them?*'

'Oh yeah. I said if he told me everything about what he's done, I'd think about letting him get back for the feast.'

'*And he bought that?*'

'Hook, line and sinker. He's singing like a canary in there.'

'*Well, he's clearly no criminal mastermind.*'

'No. Quite the opposite,' said Phillips. 'This guy's insane – thinks he's doing God's work, somehow.'

'*And how does he make that out?*'

'It's a long story, and right now I need to get back in there with him.'

'*Understood,*' said Jones. '*So, what do you want me to do with Norman?*'

'Arrest her for conspiracy to murder and get a couple of uniform to stay with her until she's fit to be discharged. Once she is, we can bring her in for questioning.'

'*Got it.*'

'Anything else?' asked Phillips.

'*Not at the minute.*'

'Ok. Once you're finished there you may as well go home and get some kip. We can debrief in the morning.'

'*Are you sure you don't need me?*'

'Certain. We're going to need to break soon anyway; we've all been awake way too long.'

Phillips ended the call and made her way back into the observation suite, where Entwistle and Harris remained seated in front of the monitors. Harris's pad was filled with notes. 'So, what's your take on him, Doc?'

Harris picked up her pad and began reading. 'Borderline insanity, potentially schizophrenic, likely suffering survivor's guilt and complex PTSD, displays symptoms of borderline personality disorder as well... The list goes on.'

'So he's mad, but is he *bad*?'

'If you mean, does he know what he did was wrong? From what I've seen so far, I'd say yes, but it's wrapped up in high levels of delusional justification.'

Phillips glanced at the screen where she could see Parker and Bovalino sitting in silence opposite each other. 'Which means I can charge him on three counts of abduction and homicide and potentially one attempted murder.'

'That's your area of expertise,' said Harris. 'But you should be aware the court-appointed psychiatric team may well decide he's unfit to stand trial due to diminished responsibility given his obvious mental health issues. If I was trying to get him off, that's what I'd go for.'

'Well, that's for the lawyers to fight about,' said Phillips. 'As far as I'm concerned, he's a stone-cold killer. Whatever his so-called justification, he stole the lives of three innocent people with a lot to live for. Their families will spend the rest of *their* lives in pain, grieving for people that mattered the most to them. Which is why...' She pointed to the screen now. '...I'm going to make sure *that* animal spends the rest of his life in prison.'

AFTER TAKING a much-needed break to freshen up, Phillips returned to Interview Room Two and retook her seat next to Bovalino. She clicked on the DIR. 'DCI Phillips, resuming interview with Henry Parker at 2.14 a.m.'

Parker stared at her with wide, expectant eyes. 'So, can I go now?'

Phillips offered a thin smile. 'I'm afraid not, Henry. You see, you've just admitted to murdering three people and the attempted murder of a fourth. Based on your confession, I'll be calling the Crown Prosecution team in the morning to request they charge you on those counts as well as three further counts of abduction.'

Parker's whole body appeared to shake and his eyes danced in his head.

Phillips continued. 'The only place you're going, mate, is back to your cell, which I'd suggest you get used to. Based on what you did to your victims, you're looking at three life sentences served concurrently. And that means the only way you're ever getting out of prison is in a box.'

'You fucking bitch!' Parker leapt up from the chair and lurched forwards, his arms outstretched across the desk, and grabbed Phillips by the throat. His hands instantly began crushing her windpipe as she attempted to fight him off.

A split-second later Bovalino pushed her back and out of reach, then slammed his thick fist into the side of Parker's head knocking him against the wall. The big man followed with huge left hook which landed with a sickening crack on the bridge of Parker's nose, causing him to slump onto the table like a rag doll, before sliding sideways onto the floor with a satisfying thud.

'Jesus! He almost strangled me.' Phillips was panting as she surveyed the scene.

Bovalino stared down at the crumpled, bloodied figure on the floor. 'Let's see how *he* likes being knocked out for a change.'

She turned to face the big Italian. '*Thank God* you were here.'

Bovalino grinned. 'Well. I think it's fair to say, when it comes to lunatics like him,' he pointed to Parker, 'that the big man's on *our* side.'

Phillips smiled softly as she was reminded of their journey to catch Parker over the last two weeks. She patted his thick forearm as she steadied herself. 'Do you know what, Bov? Maybe you're right.'

44

MONDAY, 14 MARCH - ONE WEEK LATER

I t was just after 7 a.m. Phillips was sitting at the breakfast bar in the kitchen nursing a strong coffee and staring at her phone when Adam walked in, fresh from the shower, with a towel wrapped around his waist.

'Have you seen my backpack?' he asked.

'Your work one?'

'Yeah.'

'Under-stairs cupboard. I hung it up on the back of the door last week.'

Adam disappeared into the hallway and returned a moment later carrying his black rucksack. 'What you looking at?' he asked as he poured himself a coffee.

'The MEN app. Townsend's done another piece on the "Flower Murders" as they're now calling them.'

'You're a glutton for punishment, reading that tripe.'

'I need to keep on top of what's being said in case I get pulled in by Fox for another bollocking.'

Adam took a sip of his drink. 'She can't still be pissed off, surely. I mean, you caught the guy.'

Phillips nodded. 'Yes, but Fox likes her cake and eats it

too. She wants us to catch these psychos but without anyone ever knowing they existed in the first place. She hates this stuff getting into the press.'

'That Townsend must have some serious sources,' said Adam. 'He always seems to be one step ahead.'

Phillips could feel the resentment simmering in her gut. 'It's someone on the inside; it has to be.'

'That must really piss you off.'

'Like you wouldn't believe. But I'll find them, and when I do, they'll wish they'd never laid eyes on Don-bloody-Townsend.'

Adam nodded towards her phone. 'So, what does it actually say?'

'Well,' said Phillips. 'In all honesty, aside from the click-bait headline, it's quite balanced, actually – well, as balanced as a story about a modern-day Hannibal Lecter can be.'

'So.' Adam took another mouthful of coffee. 'Are you honestly glad you went back?'

Phillips nodded. 'D'y'know, I really am. There were a few hairy moments in the last few weeks where I thought I'd made a mistake. But when I was listening to Parker preach to me about killing those people because it was his purpose in life, I realised that this was my purpose: to stop people like him from living out their sick, delusional fantasies.'

'You certainly look happy to be back now.'

'I am. It's funny; I'm not religious in the slightest, but Bov said something that really made me think. That when it comes to lunatics like Parker,' Phillips pointed upwards, 'the big man's on *our* side. For the first time in my life, I really feel like this is what I was put here to do. Does that make sense?'

'Yeah, it does.'

'Anyway,' said Phillips. 'Today's not about me. It's about you. So how are you feeling to be going back to work?'

Adam placed his mug down on the countertop. 'I'm shitting myself if I'm honest. I feel like I did on my first day as a junior doctor: nervous excitement coupled with abject terror!'

Phillips opened her arms and drew him into a hug. 'That's totally how I felt going back, too. You'll be amazing. I know you will.'

'Thanks, babe,' he whispered in her ear.

Pulling out of the clinch, she patted him on his bare chest. 'Right, well, you'd better get dressed. You don't want to be late for your first day, do you?'

Adam smiled. 'No. I don't.'

Just then, Phillips's mobile began to vibrate on the breakfast bar. Glancing at the screen, she could see it was Jones.

'Duty calls,' said Adam as he kissed her on her forehead before heading back upstairs.

Phillips answered it. 'Morning, Jonesy. What's up?'

Jones waited a moment before answering. *'Guv. You're gonna want to see this...'*

ACKNOWLEDGMENTS

As ever, a host of amazing people helped make this book possible.

My wife, Kim, who never falters in her support for me.

My gorgeous boy, Vaughan, who constantly encourages me to keep writing so I can take him to Disney Land when he's old enough.

Carole Lawford, ex-CPS Prosecutor, Bryn Jones and Lambo; your guidance on British Law was invaluable in navigating this complex story.

Lionel Etheridge who offered hands-on expert knowledge of pedology. And thanks Mike E for the introduction.

My coaches, Donna Elliot and Cheryl Lee, from 'Now Is Your Time'. Your belief in me inspires me every day.

Thanks to my publishing team of Brian, Jan, Garret, Claire, Alice and Ella. I couldn't do this without you.

And finally, thank you to my readers for reading *Deadly Craving*. If you could spend a moment to write an honest review on Amazon, no matter how short, I would be extremely grateful. They really do help readers discover my books.

Best wishes,

Owen

ALSO BY OMJ RYAN

DEADLY SECRETS

(A crime thriller introducing DCI Jane Phillips)

DEADLY SILENCE

(Book 1 in the DCI Jane Phillips series)

DEADLY WATERS

(Book 2 in the DCI Jane Phillips series)

DEADLY VENGEANCE

(Book 3 in the DCI Jane Phillips series)

DEADLY BETRAYAL

(Book 4 in the DCI Jane Phillips series)

DEADLY OBSESSION

(Book 5 in the DCI Jane Phillips series)

DEADLY CALLER

(Book 6 in the DCI Jane Phillips series)

DEADLY NIGHT

(Book 7 in the DCI Jane Phillips series)

DEADLY CRAVING

(Book 8 in the DCI Jane Phillips series)

DEADLY JUSTICE

(Book 9 in the DCI Jane Phillips series)

Printed in Great Britain
by Amazon